THE
HOLLYWOOD
MURDER MYSTERIES

PRAY for US SINNERS

The Hollywood Murder Mysteries

PETER S. FISCHER

GROVE POINT PRESS

Pacific Grove California

BOOKS BY PETER S. FISCHER

The Blood of Tyrants
The Terror of Tyrants

The Hollywood Murder Mystery Series

Jezebel in Blue Satin
We Don't Need No Stinking Badges
Love Has Nothing to Do With It
Everybody Wants An Oscar
The Unkindness of Strangers
Nice Guys Finish Dead
Pray For Us Sinners
Has Anybody Here Seen Wyckham?
Eyewitness to Murder
A Deadly Shoot in Texas

To my son, Chris
...the brains behind the business

CHAPTER ONE

War is being waged at Notre-Dame-des-Victoires.
This is not a battleground like Omaha Beach or Bosworth Field, this is a church in the center of Quebec City, Canada. The weapons are not M1 rifles or sabers or Sherman tanks but words. Some are multi-syllabic, others consist of four letters and are direct and to the point. They are often accompanied by glares, shrugs, looks of condescension or contempt or at times, both. The two sides are not separated by deep well-fortified trenches but by years. A patina of civility cloaks the proceedings but there is no doubt that this clash of wills is becoming more and more destructive. At stake is not life, liberty and the pursuit of happiness but the well being of a motion picture into which many millions of dollars have been invested with more to come.

On one side we have Montgomery Clift, at age 33 an exciting young actor who in five short years has elevated himself into the top echelon of Hollywood's bankable talent. His roots are in New York City and the Broadway stage where he learned his craft, specifically the "method", a technique already being used to great effect by Marlon Brando. Often moody, at times insecure, always introspective, Clift has been labeled "trouble" by some of those with whom he has worked. It's more likely that he is a perfectionist who demands the same commitment to the work that he himself invests and will tolerate nothing less.

On the other side, we have Alfred Hitchcock, England's gift to the art of motion pictures, a man of unquestioned taste and talent, whose track record as a director of profitable films is unequaled by his peers. At age 54 Hitchcock comes from a different school of film making. Often dictatorial in his methods, some say he regards actors as a necessary evil to be tolerated in the making of a motion picture. Prior to filming, Hitchcock storyboards the entire film, every long shot, every close up and every transition. When the camera finally begins to roll on Day One, in Hitchcock's opinion, the film is already complete. Actual production is merely going through the motions. In Hitchcock's world, actors hit their marks, say their lines and cause no trouble. Clift is disturbing Hitchcock's well-ordered way of doing things.

Hence, the time-consuming, wearying war of words that has been going on since the first day of shooting last week back at the studio in Burbank. The move to Canada has apparently only exacerbated the situation. This is Day One in Canada. Will it be like this for the rest of the month? I dread the thought.

The film is entitled "I Confess". It stars not only Clift but Anne Baxter, Karl Malden and Brian Aherne. It is slated for release in early spring of 1953. Most of the picture will be filmed in Quebec City with a few scenes already shot on the sound stages at the Warner Brothers studio back in Burbank. Additional scenes may or may not be shot on stages when we return from Canada. A lot will depend on the weather. It's early September. We have no reason to expect weather delays but in the movie business, you plan for everything and hope that your worst fears do not materialize. Hitchcock is known for finishing on time and on budget but this is the first film he has made with Clift (and probably his last) so we shall see. Sherry Shourds, the production supervisor, says we are already falling behind and now she starts off each day with a call to the national weather service. Quebec City is not Miami Beach. Snow is always a possibility.

The cast and members of the production staff are staying at the Chateau Frontenac, the massively luxurious hotel that dominates the Quebec City skyline. The crew is being housed at the nearby Citadel. The only cast member to eschew the luxury of the Frontenac is Clift who has opted to move in with some priests at one of the local churches, the better to get an in-depth feeling for Fr. Michael Logan, the priest he is portraying in the movie.

My name is Joe Bernardi and I am a feather merchant. Put more politely, I work in the Press and Publicity Department of Warner Brothers Studios. My job is to weave fanciful stories that make our stars seem better than they are and to promote each and every one of our movies as distinguished quality entertainment. It's also my job to run interference when something pops up that casts a negative light on a star or the studio. Given the voracious nature of Hollywood's gossip columnists for salacious news, this is by far the more difficult assignment.

I have been assigned a small room at the far end of the farthest wing of the hotel. I have no complaints. It is comfortable and has its own bath and affords a magnificent view of the city which nestles up against the St Lawrence River. The city dates back to the early 1600's and parts of it have yet to succumb to the Twentieth Century (or even the Nineteenth, for that matter). Church spires abound and an agnostic in search of God couldn't find a better place to look for Him.

Today I awakened at seven a.m., dressed quickly and grabbed a quick breakfast in the dining room. Now I am sitting at my desk in the Production Office which is located on the first floor down a long corridor from the lavish well appointed lobby. We have taken over a modest sized meeting room which will be Ground Zero for the duration of the shoot. We are the nerve center of the operation overseen by Sherry and her assistant, Barbara Keon. Along with a dozen desks and our own private phone system, we have tables, dozens of chairs, bookcases, mimeograph machines, postage meters, as well as cartons of paper and envelopes and office supplies.

I am on the phone to my boss, Charlie Berger, and filling him in on what I know of the slow down in production at the church this morning. On paper it's a relatively simple scene. Otto Keller, the handyman played by O.E. Hasse, confesses to Father Logan that he has killed a man. Two actors, one on one dialogue, a limited number of setups. It should have been going quickly. It hasn't. I suspect that Clift, who to the best of my knowledge is not Catholic, is having trouble dealing with the concept of the Seal of the Confessional. Having heard Keller's confession, Father Logan may not reveal by word or deed, commission or omission, anything that he has been told to him under the Seal. In Clift's mind he probably feels he must become that priest in order to convey the "truth" of the scene. This is a far cry from Hitchcock's "hit your marks and say your lines."

I can hear the annoyance in Charlie's voice. I know that he's glad it's me and not him on location and having to deal with this situation. Nonetheless he will be hearing from Jack Warner, if he hasn't already, and whatever ass-kicking Charlie gets, he will pass it on to me. Of course the one who really needs the ass kicking is Hitchcock himself who as producer and director hired Clift in the first place. Did he not know what he was getting into? I don't know but I do know you don't administer any ass kicking to Alfred Hitchcock.

I look up as Father Paul LaCouline comes in the room. LaCouline is our technical advisor and was instrumental in getting the picture back on track just when it looked as if it were headed for the trash pile. He is carrying the latest script changes in his hand.

"Good morning, Joe," he says.

"Good morning, Father," I reply. Even though I am a non-believer, I am always respectful to members of the clergy and especially to those like Fr. LaCouline who are easy going and leave the proselytizing to missionaries in far off lands. "I didn't expect you back here so early," I say to him.

He shrugs. "They finally got through the master and Monty was superb. I'd swear he graduated first at the seminary if I didn't know better." The master is the all encompassing take that sets the geography of the scene. It is followed up by close-ups and other specific angles that the director is going to want to use in the completed film. These angles are called "coverage" and the performances by the actors are identical to the way each played the scene in the master.

Fr. LaCouline is always on the set whenever a scene is shot that involves Catholic traditions or dogma. If something isn't right, he's there to correct it on the spot. If we film something wrong, it's a sure bet that thousands of Catholics will write in castigating us for being sloppy or, worse, anti-Catholic. These are letters we don't wish to receive and more to the point, don't want to answer.

"How does Hitch feel?" I ask.

"He seems happy about what he's getting but the price he's paying to get it is driving him mad."

I smile. "I won't quote you on that."

"Merci, mon ami," he says returning the smile.

He sits at a desk and starts to read over the revised pages.

9

The second writer on the script, William Archibald, has accompanied us to Canada and is available to incorporate revisions requested by Hitchcock or in some cases by the actors and in other cases by production personnel. The original writer of the script, George Tabori, is no longer involved in the production.

Hitchcock had sewed up a number of the local churches for filming but when the key prelates of the diocese read the original script, they rescinded their cooperation. In Tabori's script Father Logan is tried and found guilty of murder and executed. When Tabori refused to rewrite the script to Hitchcock's specifications, he was fired and Archibald signed to replace him. In the Archibald version Father Logan is found not guilty but with the stigma of an unpopular verdict hanging over him. At this point, Keller thinks he is being betrayed both by his wife and by Father Logan and he blurts out his admission of guilt within earshot of the authorities. He murders his wife and is about to kill Logan when the police shoot him dead in the grand ballroom of the Chateau Frontenac. With Fr. Couline interceding, the diocese agreed to reconsider their objections and made the churches once again available.

I sip my coffee and lean back in my chair. My approach to this film demands a modicum of decorum so outlandish attention-getting stunts are out of the question. I've already planned an interview with Karl Malden on what it's like to work with Hitch. Malden and I worked together on "Streetcar" and we get along well. He'll give me what I need. I also have the names and phone numbers of the entertainment writers and editors for all of the major newspapers in Ontario and Quebec Province. I'll start making my get-acquainted calls after lunch and perhaps some time early next week I'll stage a fancy press dinner here at the Frontenac where they can ask questions of Hitch and the cast members. As far as I can tell the only possible resistance will come from Clift, a notorious loner, but I won't know that until I ask him.

My phone rings. I pick up. Connie Lederer, our assistant assistant production assistant whose main job is to filter out crank calls is on the line.

"For you on One, Mr. Bernardi. A Mr. Cockburn. He said you'd know what it was about."

"I'll take it," I say and indeed I do know what it's about. Wiley Cockburn is a private detective, one of the best in Los Angeles and came highly recommended to me by my friend Mick Clausen, a successful bail bondsman who just happens to be married to my ex-wife. Several months ago I hired Wiley to track down my former live-in, Bunny Lesher, who I had every intention of making my wife number two. Through an unfortunate set of circumstances Bunny left me to take a career-making job in New York City. We had hoped to keep our romance alive with bicoastal visits but it didn't work out. Neither did her job and now she is out there somewhere in the company of a man who is using her and will surely discard her at the first sign she is becoming tiresome. I know that she's drinking too much. She may be into other things, equally as destructive. I knew immediately when I last talked to her six months ago that I could not sit by and let this happen to her. Hence, Wiley Cockburn. I may be on a fool's errand. Even if Wiley finds her, Bunny may want no part of me. But that's a risk I've been willing to take. If there is one chance in a million that I can get her back, I'm taking it.

"Wiley?" I say.

"Joe, good to hear your voice," he says.

"Where are you?"

"L.A. Running the office."

"Any news?" I ask.

"Nothing good," he says. "My guys tracked her to Lincoln, Nebraska, but got there too late. The guy she was traveling with, a man named Jacob Fryman, is in jail. Drunk, disorderly, assault, wanton destruction of property. I think it was a bar fight that got out of hand. He hasn't got two nickels to rub together so I think he's looking at six months minimum at county expense."

"And Bunny?"

"Near as my guy could figure four days ago she hopped a ride with a fella driving a big rig. So far, nobody knows what the truck looked like or even what direction it was headed."

"Damn," I mutter.

"Joe, this one's rough. Very rough. The only way we got as close as we did was because Fryman got sloppy. Bunny is sharp. Very sharp. She doesn't use credit cards, doesn't write to anyone and at the bar where the fight broke out, Fryman had introduced her as Diana so she's not even using her real name."

"Are you quitting on me, Wiley?"

"Hell, no," he says. "I'm on this as long as you want but we are really nowhere and I feel as if I'm stealing your money."

"That's my worry, Wiley."

"You do know, Joe, that even if we find her, we have no way to force her to return to you."

"Yes, I realize that. What's your next step?" I ask.

"We keep asking about the big rig, about the driver if anyone knows him, the rig itself, whether it's independent or owned by a big shipper. We canvass all the major truck stops in every direction and show Bunny's picture. We have a very slim chance of success and we're using a lot of expensive manpower."

"Do it," I say. "I'll be here at this number for the next two weeks minimum, maybe as many as three."

"You're the boss," he says and hangs up.

I lean back in my chair and think about my dwindling savings account. Five steady years at Warners has allowed me to put aside some decent money but it's fast disappearing. I don't care. If it goes, I'll borrow but I won't quit on Bunny, not as long as I think there's a chance that she needs me and wants me. Sure, maybe I'm being a fool. It wouldn't be the first time. Why is she running and hiding? I have no idea but I'm determined to find out. There is one thing I am certain of and that is that she loves me. I quit only when we stand face to face and she tells me she doesn't. Until then, I search.

For a moment I think about Jillian Marx with whom I've been having a casual affair for the past several months. It's mostly about sex and not much else but it's been convenient for both of us. We accompany one another to social events, we enjoy our occasional theater dates, and we are compatible dinner companions. There's no great depth of feeling on either of our parts and that's the way we both like it. Jillian knows of my past ties to Bunny. She does not know about Wiley Cockburn and our nationwide search. To tell her would only complicate matters and right now, my life can do without complications.

I hear a commotion at the far end of the room and look up. A man I don't know is in a heated conversation with Connie Lederer and he is plainly angry about something. He turns and his eyes scan the room.

"Bernardi!" he calls out. "Is Bernardi here?"

All eyes turn toward him as I rise up from my chair. He sees me and ignoring Connie starts toward me with a forceful stride.

"Are you Bernardi?" he asks when he reaches my desk.

"I am," I say.

He whips out a small leather folder containing his business

cards and hands me one. I look at it. His name is Mackenzie Starr and he is a reporter for the Quebec City Chronicle-Telegraph.

"I arrived at your church this morning to get an interview with Hitchcock and was turned away by your security guard who obviously had no idea who I am."

Neither do I, but I know the type and he is not indigenous to Canada alone. The USA is full of them. Arrogant and self-important with egos the size of Saskatchewan, editors and reporters like Starr believe that rules are made for others but not for them. On his tombstone a fitting epitaph would be: "Let me through the Gates. Passes are for the other guys."

I smile politely. This is the number one job requirement for someone in my profession. No matter the provocation, smile and then smile some more.

"Is it possible, Mr. Starr, that you didn't receive our memo about the restrictions on contacts with company personnel, particularly Mr. Hitchcock and members of the cast?"

"I got it," he snarls,"'but I am the Entertainment Editor of the biggest newspaper in the province outside of Montreal."

"Yes, I'm sure," I say continuing to smile, "but we can't allow distractions during working hours which is why requests for interviews have to come through me."

"Well, I don't work that way," he says.

"But I do," I say, still smiling.

Starr is a little man, no taller than five-six with a ferret-like face. I put him in his early thirties but he could be older. His brownish hair is sparse and he's already employing a combover to feed his vanity. I've known guys like him all my life, loud and obnoxious until you stare them down and then they run off and hide in the nearest corner, tail between their legs.

"Look, Bernardi---"

"That's Mister Bernardi, Starr," I say, not backing off.

"Don't antagonize me. I can do you a lot of good. I can also tear you and your little film to shreds should I so choose."

"When's your deadline?" I ask. "Ten p.m.?"

"Eleven," he says.

I nod. "I'll try to set something up for this evening."

Starr shakes his head. "I have plans for this evening."

I shrug. "Then I can't help you," I say.

He glowers. "I don't think you quite heard me, Mister Bernardi," he says, chewing off both syllables of 'mister' like he was biting into a Snickers bar.

"Mac!"

We both hear a loud female voice and both turn to see a feisty redhead approach with flames shooting from her grey-green eyes. She's no taller than five-four but her body is picture perfect from top to bottom and her form fitting cashmere sweater and tight cotton skirt do nothing to hide her attributes.

"What the hell do you think you're up to?" she demands, stopping an inch away from Starr and facing him with a glacial stare. In the process she seems to have grown a couple of inches. He appears to have shrunk.

"Now don't get in my face, Jeanne," he says, almost whining.

"Then don't you start jerking me around. You know the rules, Mac. Either go with them or go back to your office."

"I was just trying---"

"I don't want to hear about it," she says. "If you can't play by the rules, I'll pull your credentials."

He glares at her. She glares back.

"De foutre le camp d'ici, vous merde," she snarls loudly.

"Fine. Have it your way," he says. He looks over at me. "I'll call you later about that interview with Hitchcock."

He turns on his heel and marches off in a huff.

The woman he called Jeanne watches him go and then turns to me.

"Joe Bernardi?"

I nod. "That's me."

She sticks out her hand with a broad grin. I take it.

"I'm Jeanne d'Arcy with the Quebec Province Film Commission and you're my new assistant."

CHAPTER TWO

"Excuse me?" I say.

"Excuse you for what?"

"I thought I heard you say that I was your new assistant."

"That is correct, Mr. Bernardi," Jeanne d'Arcy says.

"Well, Miss d'Arcy, it doesn't quite work that way. I am in charge of all press activities on this picture. It's what I do and what I have been doing for several years now without interference by local police, politicians and certainly not by employees of any film commission."

She smiles sweetly and extracts a box of Gitanes cigarettes from her purse. She lights up and takes a deep drag and then blows the smoke toward the ceiling. Still I get the smell of it full blast. I make a note not to take up French cigarettes.

"First of all I am not just an employee, I am the director. I get to read your script and say yea or nay on what's in its pages. I have the power to withhold permits for filming, prohibit the use of private security forces on our streets, and enforce noise abatement laws which go into effect every evening at nine p.m. If you wish to hire local citizens as extras, I can speed up the paperwork to as little as a week if sorely pressed. Otherwise it will take longer, if at all. And by the way, do you speak French?"

"I do not," I admit.

"And that is why," she nods sweetly, "you are my assistant."

She looks into my face with a quirky smile as if daring me to say something. I decide not to which is when she breaks into laughter.

"Please, Mr. Bernardi, spare me the little boy frown. I have such powers but I have never used them. I think if you do your job well and I do mine, we will make a very formidable duo, n'est pas?"

She offers her hand and I take it. We shake. She has a grip like a longshoreman.

"I will call you Joe," she says, "and you will call me Jeanne."

"Jeanne," I say. "Jeannie."

"That, too, is acceptable. So Joe, did you hire a French speaking stenographer as was requested?"

I turn and point out a substantial looking woman in blue sitting at a typewriter at a far desk.

Jeanne smiles. She lights up another cigarette.

"Ah, Claudette. The very best. You chose wisely. You will write your releases, Claudette will prepare a version for the many French-language newspapers in the province. She will also prove invaluable in translating for you should the occasion arise."

I nod. I'm beginning to like this gal. She's all business but I can see she has a sense of humor. This might turn out to be a fun couple of weeks.

"Now, as to dinner this evening. If you have plans, cancel them. We are dining together at Clarisse. I have made a reservation for eight o'clock. Wear a tie. They are fussy about such things."

I raise my hands defensively.

"I'm not sure I can----"

"But of course you can and you will. The food is superb, Joe, and they have the best wine cellar on the city. We will chat, we will drink, we will get to know each other. That way the next two or three weeks will be a delight."

I smile. I had no plans for the evening and it sounds like fun but on the other hand a man doesn't like to be treated like just a pretty bauble. I do have my pride. But before I can voice another objection, she continues.

"Now as to ground rules, I never sleep with my dates until I have gotten to know them well. This process ordinarily takes a month but since you are going to be here only a short time, I think we can reasonably shorten up that time frame to a matter of days. So, assuming we like each other, I should think we'd be looking at Friday or Saturday. Any problems with that?"

At a near total loss for words, I shake my head and mumble something. She smiles, pleased.

"Excellent," she says. She takes another cigarette from the box.

"They say those things will kill you," I say as she lights it.

"So will falling in the bathtub. Do you suggest I not bathe?"

I smile. "That would be criminal."

"Indeed," she says. "Now tell me what we have planned on the publicity front."

We spend the next hour batting around ideas. She's sharp and she has some excellent thoughts. I take copious notes. By the time she is ready to leave I have plenty of material to deal with. We shake hands once again but this time I am ready for her and give as good as I get. She promises to pick me up just outside the main entrance at 7:30 and once again reminds me about the tie. I assure her I won't forget.

I glance at my watch. Time to make a run over to the church. I know what Hitch is going to say about the one-on-one with

Mackenzie Starr but I have to go through the motions. Hitch is something of a hambone and he thrives in a group situation. Individual interviews mainly bore him.

I stop by Connie Lederer's desk and have her order a company car which will pick me up at the front entrance. As I'm leaving the production office, Karl Malden is just coming in. He smiles when he sees me and we hug each other in greeting like two old frat brothers. He plays Inspector LaRue, the tough cop who suspects Fr. Nolan right from the start. It's a good part and he's perfect for it. I haven't seen him in almost two years when we worked together on "A Streetcar Named Desire". I ask him if he's taking good care of the Oscar he won for Best Supporting Actor. He laughs.

"Do you mean am I using it for a doorstop in our downstairs bathroom? Not a chance," he says.

We both know the actress who does just that to our mutual dismay. These babes try so hard to get nominated and spend a fortune in ads and p.r. to win and then when they do, they feel they have to act blase about it. Actresses. With the exception of a few delightful souls who always cheer up my day, you can have the rest of them.

"How's Mona?" I ask, inquiring about his wife.

"Fine. Just fine," he says. "She wanted badly to come at least for a few days but the girls are getting ready to go back to school so it doesn't work out."

"Well, the time will fly," I say. "Hitch will keep you busy."

He grins.

"I expect he will."

"What do you think of Clift?" I ask.

The smile on his face freezes for a moment.

"He's good," Malden says almost noncommittally.

"As good as Brando?" I ask.

"Apples and oranges, Joe. Both brilliant. Both dedicated. And as different as night and day. You remember Brando. Outgoing, loved a joke, part of the gang. Clift's quiet, introspective. I almost want to say tortured. Maybe it's the part he's playing."

"And what about Clift and Hitch?"

He smiles, shaking his head.

"Sorry. You're not getting me in the middle of that."

"How serious is it?"

"Serious enough," Malden says.

"It's cost us time," I say.

"It'll cost you more." Malden says and by this time he's not smiling. He puts out his hand. I take it. "Nice to be working with you again, Joe. You take care now," he says and he walks off.

I walk out of the main entrance and look for my ride. The studio's contracted with a local limousine service to provide transportation for cast and crew during our stay. Not everybody gets a limo. Some have to make do with a Lincoln town car or one of the brand new Peugeot 404 saloons imported from France and loaned to us courtesy of a local dealer. Speaking of which, one of the Peugeots pulls up on front of me and I get a quick beep-beep from the driver. I hop in and after a quick "bonjour" he tears away from curbside headed for the street.

His name is Nate McIver and he is loquacious and good natured with just a whisper of the old country in his speech. He came to Canada at the age of 14 and has never regretted it. He loves his family, his country and his job in that order, and even though he is approaching 50, he considers himself a young man in the prime of life. A lapsed Catholic who is twice divorced he lives with his 83 year old mother and three spinster sisters, all of whom he adores. He says he is ex-military and a holds a black belt in karate. I believe him. There isn't an ounce of fat on his compact frame. This is the kind of guy you want watching your back in a barroom brawl.

Before I know it, we pull up in front of Notre-Dame-des-Victoires. The front of the church is more or less clear of traffic but the side streets are jammed with vans and trucks carrying equipment and trailers for hair and make up. Hitch has his own trailer-dressing room as does Clift who is the only star working this location today. Police from Le Service police de la ville de Quebec (i.e. the local cops) are handling the streets, keeping away gawkers, but they readily accommodate Nate who drives right up to the front entrance. Proof that it pays to hire locals.

"You want me to wait, boss?" he asks.

"If you can," I say.

"No problem," he grins. "I'll be sitting right here."

I hurry up the wide stone steps. The church itself is under the control of private security hired by the studio. At the doorway I flash my credentials and go inside.

It is quiet and dim. Nothing is happening. I spot the camera and see Hitchcock sitting on his folding chair next to it. He is leafing through the script, page by page. Robert Burks, the cinematographer, is sitting in a nearby pew chatting in low tones with his cameraman. Other members of the crew are clustered here and there, whispering and waiting. O.E. Hasse, the other actor in this morning's scene, is down front near the altar reading a newspaper. I don't see Clift.

"Good morning, Mr. Hitchcock," I say as I approach him.

He looks up and smiles.

"Good morning, Mr. Bernardi," he says.

I look around at the inactivity.

"Equipment breakdown?" I ask, knowing that it isn't.

A pixie-ish smile crosses Hitchcock's face.

"Indeed, you might gather as much. The malfunctioning piece of equipment is in his dressing room dealing with a slight headache."

I nod in understanding.

"That is preferable," he continues, "to having him on the set where I am forced to deal with a major headache. I trust you will not quote me on that."

"Never heard a word you said," I tell him, raising my hand in the Boy Scout's three-fingered salute.

"It's a pity, really. He is a very nice young man and extremely talented. It's just that he comes to the set laden down with insecurities and reams of gobbledy-gook learned from those pretentious windbags in New York City and I really have no idea how to communicate with him." He shrugs philosophically. "Ah, well, I suppose if I could survive Mr. Laughton, I can survive anything."

He watches me carefully for a reaction. I've learned that Hitchcock says a lot of things he doesn't mean just to get a reaction. I don't disappoint him. I laugh. I relay Mackenzie Starr's request for a private interview. As I predicted he dismisses the idea. I tell him about the press dinner planned for Sunday evening at the hotel. This sparks a positive reaction. He will have an audience for his bon mots. He gives the dinner his blessing.

Just then Clift appears from a side door to the church. He is wearing a black cassock and with that handsome sensitive face he looks every inch a young Catholic priest. We've chatted a couple of times and he smiles when he sees me.

"Good morning, Joe," he says.

"Good morning, Monty," I say with his blessing. Clift may be a troubled man but he is not an elitist.

He turns to Hitchcock.

"Ready to go, Mr. Hitchcock."

"Excellent, Mr. Clift," Hitchcock says as he signals the Assistant Director who immediately starts barking orders. The set comes to life. The magic is about to resume.

Monty takes me by the arm and we move off to the side a few feet.

"Got a few minutes later today?" he asks.

"Sure," I say. "When you're finished, contact the production office. They'll find me right away."

"Good man," he says with a smile. "See you later." He walks over to Hitchcock and they start to converse quietly.

At 4:15 Monty and I are sitting on the rear terrace of the Frontenac next to the swimming pool. He's wearing dark glasses and a New York Giants baseball cap, the better to escape the attention of zealous fans. He needn't have worried. The temperature's in the low fifties and the pool isn't heated. He's sipping on an iced tea. I'm working on a Molson beer.

"I thought you were a bourbon man," I say.

"Scotch, actually," Monty says, "but I'm trying to cut back, especially when I'm working. A couple of times I've caught myself going over the top with that stuff. Not good for mind or body."

I nod. "I thought maybe those priests you're living with were turning you into a teetotaler."

He laughs. "Are you kidding? A couple of nights ago, we stayed up til past midnight discussing dogma and depleting the church's wine reserves. We had to pour two of the guys into bed."

After a few minutes of this, we get down to business.

"As much as possible, Joe, I'd like to keep a low profile during this shoot."

"Okay," I say.

"That means no civic luncheons, no appearances at the local universities, no phony dates with local wannabe actresses."

"Never crossed my mind," I say.

"Good," he responds. "Working with Mr. Hitchcock isn't the easiest experience I've ever had. I really need to expend my energy on the work."

"Press interviews?"

"Not if I can help it," Monty says. "Look, I know what you do is important and I want to cooperate but I feel really uncomfortable talking about myself. I know what they say, that I'm difficult, but for me it's the work and nothing else. Buttering up some stranger with a pad and pencil, it's just not me and never has been. But, look, if you really need me, I'll do the best I can."

"Can't ask for more than that," I say.

He hesitates. "There's something you can do for me."

"Shoot."

"I talked to Elizabeth last evening. She's going to try to fly in for a day without the world knowing about it."

I don't need to be told he's talking about Elizabeth Taylor.

"You know she's pregnant," he says.

"The world knows she's pregnant, Monty."

He nods. "Well, she's got her problems and I've got mine and when it gets like this, we like to talk. It helps a lot for both of us."

"I understand," I say.

"It would be nice if she had a decent place to stay in some out of the way first class pension where she could spend the night under an assumed name, not have to check in anywhere and uh, just be anonymous."

I nod.

"I'll have Sherry Shourds find the place and add Angela Vickers to the cast list."

Monty breaks into a huge grin.

"You're wicked, you know that?" he says.

"I know," I say.

Angela Vickers is the character Elizabeth played in their huge hit, 'A Place in the Sun'.

"Let me know when she's coming and I'll pick her up personally and whisk her off to her digs."

"Thanks, Joe. I knew I could count on you."

"Now here's one you can do for me and it may make things easier for you," I say.

I tell him about the press dinner. One big bash to answer a lot of questions, pose for a gaggle of photographs and after that, it's a series of polite no's and no thank you's.

"The difficult working relationship between you and Hitch? It's common knowledge, Monty. It can't be ignored. I have to deal with it."

He shakes his head, takes off the glasses and rubs his eyes. He sighs audibly.

"I love the guy, I really do," Monty says. "But he and I are from different planets. I guess you've heard the cattle story."

I tell him I have. Several years ago during the filming of "Mr. and Mrs. Smith", Hitchcock was quoted in the local paper as saying that all actors should be treated like cattle. The next day Carole Lombard showed up on the sound stage with a couple of oxen which she presented to Hitchcock and then promptly went home for the rest of the day.

"He didn't really mean it," I say.

"Maybe yes, maybe no," Monty says. "In either case, we are having difficulty communicating and we are doing our best to deal with it. If you can't kill the story, maybe you could minimize it or refocus it. "

"I'll do my best," I say.

He smiles and lifts his tea. "Well, all right, Joe. Here's to your dinner party. Let's hope it works." I raise my beer. We clink.

CHAPTER THREE

id I mention that Jeanne d'Arcy is a knockout? I lied. She is an explosion. I am standing by the entrance to the Chateau Frontenac. It is 7:29. As ordered I am wearing my most expensive tie, a silk Countess Mara. My gold cufflinks initialed J.B. are plainly visible in the inch or two of French cuff that shows from each sleeve of my expensive tailored suit. My shoes gleam like black opals. I am sure that all eyes are upon me, particularly the zoftig blonde out walking her lhasa apso. Twice I have caught her staring at me.

At 7:30 precisely Jeanne drives up in a spanking new Austin Healey 100 with the top down. Her flaming red hair is windblown but far from messy. She is a vision in form fitting white silk. Around her neck is a necklace of green emeralds and diamonds. At this moment I am sure no one is looking at me unless it is with a look of envy. She leans over with a smile and pops open my door. Despite her addiction to French tobacco her teeth are glistening white. I slide in. I am already trying to figure out how to shorten her few days of 'getting to know you' to a few hours. As we pull away from the entrance I raise my hand to my shoulder and without looking back, wiggle-wave my fingers to those I have left behind. One does not experience these moments often. I make the most of this one.

Clarisse is located in the oldest part of Quebec's old town. The building is constructed of hand-hewn stone. The massive main entrance features a wooden door with brass fittings. The only thing missing is a moat. Inside we are greeted by a maitre'd who fawns over Jeanne like an adoring father whose prodigal daughter has just returned to home and hearth. They babble in French and then, hoping to include me, he asks me something Gallic. My blank stare gives me away. He pegs me for an Englishman, or worse, an American. His attitude turns to one of frosty civility.

He leads us to an excellent table for two along a far wall, slightly separated from the throng. It is dimly lit and quiet enough for us to talk. He leaves behind two menus the size of the New York Times front page. I open mine and discover that I have the "lady's" menu, the one with no prices. Jeanne smiles as she lights up a cigarette and tells me I am the guest of the film commission. I don't argue. I am seldom taken on a date by a woman this vivacious and I like it. Now, how do I speed up that getting acquainted process?

We order drinks and dabble in small talk. Her silver cigarette case and lighter are on the table close at hand. She doesn't exactly chain smoke but it's close. I'm anxious to know more about this Ma'amselle but she fends off every personal query. She has hard and fast opinions on a wide range of subjects like American football, cajun cuisine, MGM musicals, war criminals (against) and the United Nations (for). I don't know her age though I guess at early 30's, same as me. Is she native born? What did she do, if anything, during the war? Has she ever been married? Does she have children? How about siblings? She answers each of my questions with a question of her own. I think maybe she's actually a lawyer but too ashamed to admit it.

An elderly white-maned waiter comes by and she orders for us both. My groundrules are no fish, no liver, no kidneys, and absolutely no snails. She speaks to the waiter in flawless French. I nod a lot, throw in a 'tres bien' or a 'bon' here and there and even do a jocular Maurice Chevalier laugh. The waiter is not fooled. He recognizes an ill-mannered kid from Oklahoma when he sees one.

She looks across the table at me as she lights up another Gitanes.

"I'm sorry about your friend Bunny," she says.

I'm taken aback. I can't even get this babe's hat size and she knows all about my tattered love life.

"It's a long story," I say and now I am the one being close-mouthed.

"I love long stories," she says. "Especially sad ones. I think it's the Irish in me."

Aha! A clue.

"Was your mother Irish?" I ask.

"Now why would you ask me a thing like that?" she asks. "Doesn't my hair give me away?"

"Then it's au naturel?"

"Why are you so curious?"

"Why are you so evasive?"

"Am I?"

"You answer questions with questions."

"Do I?"

"Are you hiding something?"

"Is that what you think?"

Quietly I grind my teeth. This is a losing battle. I am saved from the humiliation of surrender by the approach of a man to our table. His gait is slightly unsteady and if he weren't so drunk

I'd take him for a distinguished middle aged banker. He never takes his eyes off of Jeanne.

"Bonsoir, Jeanne," he says with a smile, leaning heavily on our table.

She looks up and it's obvious she is not pleased to see him.

"Good evening, Daniel," she says icily.

He responds in French. It's an attempt at charm. It fails.

"My dinner guest does not speak French," she says.

He looks at me apologetically.

"A thousand pardons, monsieur. Daniel Bruckner," he says putting out his right hand while still leaning on the table with his left. I take it and we shake. His hand is clammy.

"Joe Bernardi."

"Delighted to meet you," Bruckner says and promptly forgets all about me as he zeroes in on Jeanne. "We need to talk," he says.

"This is not the time," she replies.

"You do not return my phone calls."

"I've been busy."

"Yes, I can see that," he says coldly with a glance in my direction.

"Will you please leave me alone? I have no time for this."

He glares at her.

"I will not be dismissed so easily, mon cheri," he says.

She glares back.

"Very well, Daniel, if it's a scene you want, I'll accommodate you." She raises her arm and waves toward the maitre'd who has been watching this confrontation with interest.

Bruckner straightens up abruptly.

"No need," he says. "We will meet again soon under better circumstances." He looks at me and snaps off a perfunctory head nod, then turns and walks away, still unsteady on his feet.

I watch him walk away and then turn to Jeanne who is again lighting up. The maitre'd comes to the table.

"May I be of service, Mlle. d'Arcy?" he asks.

"Thank you, no, Henri. There is no problem."

Henri looks after Bruckner who is headed for the bar. He smiles.

"As you wish," he says and turns and goes back toward his station.

"I'm sorry you had to see that," Jeanne says, still angry.

"I'm sorry you had to endure it," I say.

She smiles.

"Tres gallant, mon ami," she says.

I shrug."We Italians take a backseat to no one when it comes to gallantry, mon cheri, particularly the French."

She laughs and lifts her glass in a toast and sips. She obviously has no intention of telling me what this little contretemps was about and why should she? The mystery that surrounds this woman deepens. I am fascinated.

Dinner is a delight. Jeanne has ordered lamb cutlets for us both with white asparagus on the side and a Caesar salad to start. For dessert, creme brulee and strong Turkish coffee. The conversation continues to revolve around trivialities. I do not discuss Bunny and she does not discuss the gentleman who barged into our conversation earlier on. By nine-thirty we are outside the front entrance waiting for the parking valet to deliver her car.

"The evening's still young," I say. "I'm game for an hour or two of frivolity at a local nightclub."

She smiles apologetically.

"Not tonight, Joe. Maybe later this week."

"As you wish," I say.

I hadn't seen him coming but there he was, appearing out of nowhere and clamping his hand on Jeanne's arm.

"We have to talk now," Bruckner says, even more drunk than he was before. He's also nastier.

"Let go of me!" Jeanne squeals trying to get loose from his grip.

I step forward and try to push him away. His head snaps toward me and there is fury in his eyes. He lets go of Jeanne and takes a roundhouse swing in my direction. He misses badly and, off balance, falls to the pavement. Jeanne leans down and tries to help him up, saying something in French. He responds angrily, also in French, as he gets to his feet. They go at it loudly, each angrier than the other. A hotel security guard approaches and tries to separate them but it's difficult. I back away. Something tells me this is a lovers' quarrel and I want no part of it. Just then the Austin Healey is driven up and the valet taps the horn lightly. Jeanne looks over, then storms toward the car grabbing me by the arm and pulling me along.

A couple of minutes later we are speeding down Wyndham Street and Jeanne is still angry.

"The man is a pig," she growls. "Une cochon in a thousand dollar tuxedo. Merde."

I stay silent in hopes that she will elucidate. She doesn't. There's a set to her jaw that wasn't there before and while she isn't driving recklessly, the rage within her is reflected in the way she pushes her little sports car to the max. Ten minutes later she whips up the entrance drive to the Frontenac and skids to a stop at the front door. She turns to me.

"I am sorry about this evening. I was terrible company."

I am about to say 'Oh, no' when she takes my face in her two hands and pulls it toward her own and plants a kiss on my lips.

Her tongue goes in search of mine and finds it. I feel a stirring in my nether regions.

"We will do this again, perhaps tomorrow or the next night," she says. "I have decided that I like you very much, Joe Bernardi. Now, bonsoir. A la prochaine fois, mon ami."

She reaches across and pops my door open. I get out, wishing I had a hat to disguise my excitement. As she drives away I find myself looking forward to our next encounter. I also find the nearby guests just looking.

It is the next morning. I have left a standing order for hot coffee and croissants and jam to be delivered to my room each day at 7:30. It is a more civilized way of awakening than an alarm clock and allows me to eat breakfast undisturbed. The morning edition of the Chronicle-Telegraph is part of the service. After I have showered and shaved and dressed, I sit down to eat and scan the front page of the newspaper. To my surprise I find a photograph of Daniel Bruckner in a position of prominence. In contrast to the night before he is well-groomed and clear-eyed. Next to him is a photo of a man identified as Louis Marchand. The banner headline reads: MARCHAND FRAUD TRIAL BEGINS.

I skim the story. Bruckner is a defense attorney representing Marchand, a public official high up in the provincial school system, accused of diverting food meant for school lunches to a supermarket chain that operates throughout eastern Canada, primarily Ontario. The chain is owned by two brothers named Gonsalvo who have ties to a known criminal organization operating out of Buffalo, New York. Marchand comes from a distinguished Quebec family and is well connected to the political hierarchy. This trial, which has been postponed three times, is an embarrassment to a great many people. There's more but I get the big picture. I wonder if this trial has anything to do with the scene I witnessed last evening at Clarisse.

I fold up the paper and take it with me to the production office. When I arrive I find the ladies of our staff all atwitter as they gather around Alma Hitchcock, our director's wife of 27 years. Alma, who was once Alfred's film editor and then his assistant director, goes wherever Alfred goes and he will be the first to admit that she is an invaluable collaborator and sounding board. From what I can gather, however, it doesn't appear that this hen party has anything to do with the picture. Sure enough, when I catch Sherry Shourds' eye, she comes over to tell me that Alma has just received news that their only daughter, Pat, is expecting early next Spring. I wonder if the old curmudgeon knows about it. I make a note to buy him an expensive cigar before I visit the set again. Hitchcock as a grandfather. It boggles my mind. His as well, I suspect.

I go back to my desk and dig out the list of entertainment editors and reporters in the province. Jeanne and I have already settled on this coming Sunday evening as the date for the press dinner. Now I can start making get-acquainted calls in advance of sending out formal invitations.

I've just knocked off Le Peuple Nevis and Le Nouvelliste de Trois Riviere when she comes waltzing in, apparently without a care in the world, smiling at everyone in general and me in particular. She's wearing a full navy blue skirt and a white cotton blouse underneath a baby blue vest which she has left unbuttoned and her hair has been pulled back into a pony tail. She is bubbling over with good humor and tells me she has shoved last night's regrettable events from her mind.

I laugh.

"The mood you were in, I was afraid you were going to go looking for him to knock his teeth down his throat."

She laughs back.

"No, no, nothing like that. I went straight home, plopped myself into a hot tub, took two pills to relax and then tucked myself into bed. How about you?"

"Straight to bed where I dreamed all night about this gorgeous redhead," I say.

"I'm flattered," she says.

"Rita Hayworth," I say with a wink.

"Aller en enfer," she snarls. Whatever she said wasn't nice but I laugh anyway and so does she.

I'm looking into her face and my eyes shift slightly as I peer over her shoulder toward the entrance to the office. Three men have entered and stopped by Connie Lederer's desk. One is a tall slim man wearing a camel's hair coat and a tan fedora. The other two are uniformed officers of the Surete Quebec. The tall gentleman looks off in our direction, then nods to Connie. He speaks quietly to the two uniforms who take up positions in the doorway and then he starts walking toward us. Jeanne sees that I have been distracted and turns just as the man reaches my desk.

"Mlle. d'Arcy?" he asks of Jeanne.

"I am she," Jeanne says.

He takes out his identification and holds it up for us both to see.

"I am Inspector Luc Villiers of the Surete Quebec." He looks at me. "And you, sir?"

"Joseph Bernardi. I work for Warner Brothers Publicity."

"Bien," he says with a slight nod and turns back to Jeanne. "I understand that you dined last evening at Clarisse in the company of an unidentified gentleman."

I raise my hand. He smiles at me.

"Excellent," he says. "One of the little mysteries solved." He takes out a small leather-bound notebook and writes something in it. Seven gets you five it's my name.

"And while you were dining were you approached at your table by a man named Daniel Bruckner?" the Inspector continues.

"I was," Jeanne says.

"And were angry words exchanged?"

"Yes, they were. Listen, Inspector, if Mister Hot Shot Lawyer is using his connections to harass me over a few well chosen and accurate words I may have used to describe him---"

"Monsieur Bruckner is dead, Mademoiselle," Villiers says. I can see him searching Jeanne's face for any sign of a guilty reaction.

"No. Impossible," Jeanne says, visibly shaken. "How?"

"He was stabbed to death," Villiers says.

"Mon dieu," she says. "He was so terribly drunk, he must have been an easy target."

"You think perhaps it was a robbery or, what do you call it, a mugging?" Villiers shakes his head. "No, Mademoiselle, he was not killed in the streets, he was murdered in his own apartment between one and two o'clock in the morning."

Jeanne shakes her head violently in disbelief.

"No. How could that be? The building where he lives it is very well protected. It couldn't have happened."

Villiers looks at her patiently.

"Oui, Madame, But it did."

"Do you know who is responsible?"

"Not yet," Villiers says. "That is one of the reasons I am here."

I frown, catching his drift immediately.

"You can't possibly suspect Miss d'Arcy," I say.

He looks at me coldly. Here is a man who does not like to be challenged.

"To the best of my knowledge, Mlle. d'Arcy and you as well, M. Bernardi, are among the last people to see M. Bruckner alive.

You can readily see why I am giving you my full attention. Now if you both would be good enough to accompany me to head-quarters where I can take your statements---"

"Sorry, Inspector, but I have work to do."

"M. Bernardi, I framed my request in the politest terms possible. I can rephrase if you wish or if you prefer, I can put you in cuffs and place you and the young lady under arrest. Your choice."

He smiles, awaiting my answer.

CHAPTER FOUR

The main headquarters for the Surete de Quebec is located in Montreal. The facilities here in Quebec City are smaller. Fewer offices, fewer personnel. I wouldn't bet my paycheck on it but given the deference shown to Inspector Villiers when we arrive, I would say that he is in charge of the operation.

The moment we walk in the door Jeanne and I are separated. I am stashed in an eight-by-eight windowless cubicle with one table and two chairs. They offer me coffee but I decline. I don't want my bladder distracting me from what I hope will be quick and concise answers to whatever questions they have in store.

The rickety wooden chair upon which I am sitting wobbles so I try the other one. It, too, wobbles. I lean on the table. Three for three. I'm sure there is a method to this madness but it escapes me. The door opens and a uniformed policeman enters. His chevrons identify him as a sergeant. He does not greet me. He is carrying a yellow legal sized lined pad and two slim paperback books. Oh, goodie. We're going to read. The sergeant kneels down and places one of the paperbacks under one of the legs of his chair. He places the second book under a leg of the table. Now I am the only one that wobbles.

The sergeant sits and takes out a couple of pencils which he sets down next to the pad. Then he reaches in his shirt pocket and takes out a pair of reading glasses which he puts on. Finally he looks up at me.

"Would you like some coffee?" he asks.

No, thanks, I say again.

"My name is Sergeant Fichtenau. I will be taking your statement."

"Bon," I say. "Where is Miss d'Arcy?"

He ignores my question. I wobble. It's getting annoying.

"Your name is Joseph Francis Xavier Bernardi, you are thirty three years old, unmarried and you work for the Warner Brothers motion picture company as a publicist. Is this information correct?"

I say it is.

"And you are good friends with Mlle. Jeanne d'Arcy, the director of the Quebec Provincial Film Commission?"

I shrug noncommittally.

"We are colleagues," I say.

He looks at me skeptically.

"As colleagues are you in the habit of kissing each other passionately in full view of strangers in a public place?"

"No, not really," I say.

"Are you lovers?" he asks.

"I only met her yesterday," I say.

"That does not answer the question," he says looking at me archly.

I tell him we are not. I do not tell him we are thinking about it. It goes on like this for about twenty minutes while I continue to wobble. Yes, I remember Mr. Bruckner coming to the table and later accosting us in the parking lot. No, I have no idea what the argument was about. I do not speak French. Yes, Miss d'Arcy drove me to my hotel where I went straight to my room. I give him the long version as opposed to the flippant version I told to Jeanne. I read for an hour and drifted off but awoke again just past midnight. I couldn't get back to sleep so I ordered hot chamomile tea from room service. Around one-thirty I again fell asleep and didn't wake up until room service knocked on my door with my morning coffee. During those hours I had a wet dream about a gorgeous redhead. It was not Rita Hayworth.

"And where did Mlle. d'Arcy go when she left you at your hotel?" Sergeant Fichtenau asks.

"That's a little hard for me to say," I tell him in frustration as I spit out each word of my answer, "since I went to my room, got in bed, read, slept, woke up, drank tea and then went back to sleep again. But maybe you missed that part."

Fichtenau looks at me deadpan.

"I should warn you, Mr. Bernardi, I have no sense of humor."

"I know. You're French."

He looks at me scornfully.

"Did Mlle. d'Arcy tell you where she had gone?"

"The same as me, Sergeant. Home to bed."

He pauses, then writes it down.

"Did she tell you if she had stopped anywhere? To get gasoline, perhaps, or some sort of car trouble?"

"Straight home. That's what she said."

He nods. Something about his expression tells me I have just stepped into a doggy deposit.

Ten minutes later I am ushered into Inspector Villiers' office. Jeanne is already seated there and Villiers is on the phone in the midst of a hearty conversation that doesn't sound much like police business.

"But I would be delighted to meet the Duchess, Jacques. I have heard she is quite charming." Pause. "Yes, I know the villa quite well. I spent several weekends there a year ago when it was still owned by the Prime Minister's cousin." Pause. "No,no, Godfrey. The fat one. The one that's into lumbering in New Brunswick. Yes, yes. That one." Pause. "Look, why don't you pick me up at my place at nine o'clock and we'll drive up together." Pause. "Oh, yes, I know Veronique very well. Shame about her husband." Pause. "Are you? Well, good wishes to you both." Pause. "Nine o'clock. Right. We'll have lots to talk about on the ride up. Au revoir."

He hangs up and stares reflectively at the ceiling, then turns and looks at Jeanne and me as if noticing us for the first time.

"Ah, Mlle. d'Arcy and M. Bernardi. My thanks for your cooperation. I have your statements here and will be reviewing them later today." He leans forward in his chair and regards us solemnly. "I must tell you, this murder of M. Bruckner, it is most disheartening. It cannot be allowed to stand. You expect this sort of thing from the rabble, but for a man of Daniel's standing in the community---" He shakes his head in frustration.

"May I presume we're free to go, Inspector?" I ask.

"Go? Yes, of course," he says rising from his chair. We do likewise and follow him to the door. He opens it and we step into his anteroom just as his phone is ringing.

He shakes my hand and nods to Jeanne. "Once again, my thanks for your cooperation.

His secretary interrupts.

"Inspector, the Deputy City Administrator is on the phone." she says.

I was about to say goodbye and wish him well but I am much too slow. He darts into his office like a dog in pursuit of a school bus. Jeanne looks at me and raises her eyes to the ceiling. As we head out we can easily make out his voice, loud and gregarious.

"Pierre, my good friend, so nice to hear from you!"

On the ride back to the hotel Jeanne and I sit in silence. We have nothing to say that our driver needs to hear. It is only when we enter the lobby that the questions flow. What did he ask? What was his attitude? Are you under suspicion? Am I? Was this just routine or something more?

As we step into the production office, Jeanne stops short and takes my arm.

"They asked me where I went and what I did after I dropped you off. What did you say?"

I shrug. "I said I had no idea. How could I?"

"Of course."

"When he pressed me, I told him what you had told me, that you had gone straight home to bed. Why? Should I not have told him that?"

"No, no, of course not. You did the right thing. I have nothing to hide. It's just that----." She stops.

"What?"

"It was the way that interrogator kept harping on my whereabouts after midnight, as if he suspected me of involvement."

I shrug.

"Cops think like that. It's part of their makeup."

At that moment Connie comes back into the big room carrying a container of hot coffee.

"Oh, Mr. Bernardi, I have two messages for you." She picks up a couple of pink memo slips from her desk and hands them to me. I scan them. One's from Charlie Berger, my boss. The other's from Phineas Ogilvy, the entertainment editor at the Los Angeles Times.

"I'm going to make these calls from my room," I say to Jeanne.

She nods. "I'll need that list of phone contacts." she says.

"Middle drawer of my desk," I say. "If you need anything, ask Connie."

"See you later?"

"You bet," I say. "Call me when you're ready to leave."

She nods and I head for the elevators.

Twelve-thirty my time, nine-thirty Charlie's. He's in early which means he had to drop his twin girls Daphne and Danielle off at the St. Sebastian School in West L.A. which means he has probably lost another housekeeper-chauffuer. Charlie is a walking advertisement for why you should never marry a woman twenty-five years your junior no matter how sexy she is. I feel sorry for him. I also envy him. He has a couple of kids. I would love to have a couple of kids and a wife I could grow old with but no such luck. That's why when Charlie starts bitching about the high maintenance costs of his two little darlings, I tune him out. I wish I had his problem.

His secretary puts me through right away.

"You have a traitor in your midst," he says as he comes on the line.

"Say again?"

"I just got a peek at an early edition of the Herald Examiner. That bitch has the whole story and then some. Listen to this. 'Clift and Hitch at swords points. Hitch fumes while Clift whines. Runaway production on the verge of shutdown."

That bitch is a 28 year old feline with claws for fingers named Astrid Ankers. A month ago she succeeded Harry Frakes as the paper's entertainment editor. She's out to make a name for herself like Hedda or Louella or Sheila but she hasn't the wit or the style to pull it off. Whereas Hedda draws blood with a scalpel, Astrid attacks with a sledgehammer. She's not fun to read and she won't last long but in the meantime I have to deal with her.

"She's got someone on the crew," I opine.

"That's what I think," Charlie says.

"Almost certainly someone we brought with us."

"Agreed,"

We have a hybrid crew. Most are Canadian professionals but a dozen or so are key Hollywood reliables. The camera operator, the Best Boy, Anne Baxter's hair and makeup girls, several others. Sherry Shourds can get me the list. Meanwhile this woman's story has to be discredited and it has to be done now.

"I'll handle it, Charlie."

"Do what you have to do."

"Will the studio back me with the unions?"

"Absolutely," Charlie says.

"I'll get back to you," I say and hang up.

I immediately return Phineas Ogilvy's call. I don't need a ouija board to know what he wants. Phineas can read and he needs to know if he's been scooped by the devil's concubine who works for the rival paper. This is not something he will countenance quietly. He is a big man, flamboyant in attitude, with a Mensa level intellect that he loves to show off. Half the town believes he's gay. His three ex-wives have sworn to me that he's not and I believe them.

He's not at his desk so I leave my hotel room number. While I am waiting to hear from him, I order a club sandwich and coffee from room service and pick up the morning newspaper and scan the front page. There's a photo of a sober looking Daniel Bruckner next to a photo of a patrician looking man named Louis Marchand. The headline reads MARCHAND MOB TRIAL STARTS TODAY. I skim the article quickly. Bruckner is supposed to defend this guy Marchand on charges of theft, embezzlement and conspiracy. I doubt the trial will start today with Bruckner toes up on a slab in the city morgue. This is something the paper could not foresee when they went to press very early this morning.

Maybe there's something about the Bruckner murder on the radio so I flip onto an English speaking news station. I'd rather flip on a television set but these Quebeckers are a little behind the times. There is no television set in my hotel room because there is no television station in the city of Quebec. Matter of fact it was only three days ago that the city of Montreal got its first TV outlet.

From the radio comes the voice of Inspector Luc Villiers. The radio stations and the newspapers have trapped him on the sidewalk outside Surete headquarters and he is doing his best to fend off questions. They have several good leads, Villiers tells them. One or two viable suspects. Only a matter of time before an arrest will be made. No comment. No comment. No comment. He's an adroit liar and a championship caliber evader. They send it back to the studio guy who reports that the widow, Marie Bruckner, is incommunicado at the law office with her husband's partner Claude Le Pen.

"Meanwhile," the news anchor is saying, "the trial of Louis Marchand has been postponed for seventy two hours by Chief Magistrate Michel Berglund. A meeting with the Crown Prosecutor and M. Bruckner's surviving partner, Claude Le Pen, has been scheduled for chambers late this afternoon."

At this moment, my phone rings and I quickly turn off the radio and hurry to answer the phone.

"Tell me, old top," comes Phineas' voice, "have I been bush-whacked by this poisonous Annie Oakley who toils for the opposition?"

"You have," I say, "although she greatly exaggerates the situation. And before you say something stupid that you will most certainly regret, I had nothing to do with it. In fact, she didn't even have the professionalism to give me a courtesy call before running it."

"Dear boy," Phineas says, "professionalism is not a word to be located in the child's limited vocabulary."

"Amen to that, Phineas. I'm pretty sure she has a spy working as a crew member. I'm going to root him out and send him packing. Meanwhile I am in need of serious damage control."

"Indeed you are," Phineas says.

"I would ask for your help, my friend, but I know how high your professional standards are and that you would never do anything to demean or humiliate a fellow journalist."

I hear a 'harumph' and then, "If you are referring to Miss Astrid Ankers, try me."

"Well, as I said, she wildly exaggerated everything and I can certainly give you an exclusive which is much closer to the truth."

"In return for?"

"You have such a natural talent for words, Phineas. If you could somehow report the facts accurately while at the same time painting a picture of Miss Ankers as an immature, inexperienced young lady, devoid of ethics, who will write any sort of nonsense to support a bogus story----"

"Yes, yes," Phineas interrupts. "Not to worry, old top. I will carve her up into tiny pieces of chum and feed her to the sharks. This is a marvelous opportunity. Absolutely marvelous. Now, Joseph, I have pencil in hand and paper before me. Please begin."

I feed him the story. Hitchcock and Clift come from different worlds but each genuinely likes and admires the other person. In these early days of filming they are learning how to communicate with one another. Based on the rushes, Clift's performance is brilliant and Hitchcock's direction is taut and spellbinding. The set is a happy one and production is only a few hours behind schedule. To intimate otherwise is arrant nonsense and bespeaks fuzzy thinking and a lazy work ethic. Phineas will make porterhouse out of this chuck steak and if we're lucky, Astrid Ankers will find herself in a cubbyhole somewhere in the rear of the Herald Examiner building reporting on the activities of the Beverly Hills Women's League. Phineas promises to send me a fax of tomorrow's column. I thank him. I can't wait to read it.

After I hang up, I head downstairs to the production office. This is a two pronged attack and I need that list of Los Angeles crew members right away. I'm going to confront the lot of them and while I don't expect anyone to raise his or her hand in meek surrender, I am going to deliver a message that no one can afford to ignore.

Sherry tells me she can have the list ready in ten minutes. Meanwhile I look around and see no sign of Jeanne. Sherry tells me that she has gone to the bar with a man who showed up about fifteen minutes ago. I head for the bar. Sherry promises to bring me the list as soon as it's compiled.

They are sitting at a table in the middle of the room. As I approach the table Jeanne says something to him and he rises from his seat as Jeanne introduces us. Claude Le Pen is a hefty man, well-dressed and well-groomed who looks to be in his fifties. At one time he might have been an athlete but middle age has not been kind to him and he is packing a lot of unwanted pounds. I suspect that exercise is not part of his daily regimen. His skin is pale and his hair cut on the long side, dark brown turning grey. He puts out his hand with a smile. We shake and I pull up a chair.

"The radio news report said you were with Mr. Bruckner's widow earlier in the day, Mr. Le Pen. How is she doing?"

He shakes his head.

"Not well, I'm afraid. On Villiers' orders, the police went out to her cottage by the lake and brought her back into the city. Back to the apartment, actually, where she had to look at the tape outline of her husband's body and the huge red stain on the carpet where he'd lost all that blood. Insensitive bastard. You can imagine her hysteria. The police very nearly had to hospitalize her."

Jeanne shrugs.

"I'm sure Marie was shocked but she is also given to theatrics. When necessary she can dredge up tears at a moment's notice," she says.

"Please, Jeanne. That was not necessary," Le Pen says.

"An observation, Claude. You know it's true."

Jeanne stubs out her cigarette in annoyance and looks over at me.

"The police suspect me," she says.

"Absurd," I say. "Where did they get that idea?"

Le Pen shrugs helplessly.

"It seems Inspector Villiers has a witness," he says.

"What kind of a witness?" I ask.

"I don't know," Le Pen says. "I got this in confidence from a close friend in the department. Jeanne, or someone who looks like her, was seen driving away from Bruckner's apartment building shortly before one a.m."

I look at her curiously. She shakes her head.

"It isn't true, Joe," she says. "I was in bed by eleven and fell asleep immediately."

"Did anyone see you?" I ask.

"No," she says petulantly. "It is terrible of you to ask that of me."

"The police will be even more terrible, especially that

ineffectual poppinjay Villiers," Le Pen says. "They tend to lose their good manners when they think they have a decent suspect in their sights."

"He's right, Jeanne," I say.

"If there's no conflict of interest with the Marchand case, I've offered to represent her if it comes to that," Le Pen says. "Marie will be displeased but I can't help that. It's what Daniel would have wanted."

I look at Jeanne. She looks away, extinguishing yet another cigarette. I think I get the picture but neither of them will say it in so many words. Last night at the restaurant, I think my instincts were correct. A lover's quarrel? Or a quarrel between ex-lovers? I have no idea which. Either way it is not good for Jeanne. Their spat attracted attention. The words were certainly acrimonious and while I don't speak French, it's a good bet many of the nearby patrons understood every word that was said. Le Pen was right to offer his services. Coupled with the so-called witness, this situation could turn ugly very quickly.

Just then Sherry approaches with my list. I get up and excuse myself. Company business beckons and it is a priority. I tell Jeanne I will call her later. She merely nods. The enormity of her situation is starting to settle in and she suddenly seems very frightened. I look over at Le Pen who has taken her hand in his. His expression tells me that he, too, is very troubled.

CHAPTER FIVE

itchcock has a thing for blondes which is why I am not surprised to find Anne Baxter, a natural brunette, in the makeup trailer sporting a first rate dye job. She arrived by plane early this morning and this is her first official day of work on the film. It won't be much. A shot of her on the street as seen through a window and then she's done for the day. The bulk of her scenes will be shot early next week including all of her flashbacks with Monty when her character and Logan, not yet a priest, were involved in a love affair.

I have introduced myself. She is warm and gracious. I know right away she'll be easy to work with. I tell her that I need to speak to Gwendolyn Haskell, her hair dresser, and Phoebe Schultz, her make up artist and I would prefer to do so in private if she doesn't mind. She tells me she does mind. She has been working with both these ladies since 'The Razor's Edge' for which she won the Academy Award. When she works they work. They are close personal friends and they are here in Canada as a part of the crew because it is stipulated in her contract. Unlike Baxter, both Gwendolyn and Phoebe have been with the company since Day One.

I try once more to persuade Baxter to give us some privacy

but she refuses, now more curious than ever. The two girls stare at me open-mouthed, visibly worried about what I have to say.

"Very well," I say, "I'll keep this short and sweet. I have already talked to the others who joined the crew in Los Angeles. You are the last two on my list. I will say to you what I said to them. This is not an accusation aimed at either of you. It is a statement of fact. Please listen closely. Someone affiliated with this company has been feeding scurrilous comments about our work here to a third-rate newspaper columnist back in Los Angeles. These comments have either been untrue or wildly exaggerated but in either case, the studio has been embarrassed and the picture making process has been seriously damaged. If and when we discover who is responsible for this betrayal, he or she will be summarily fired and sent back to Los Angeles. Every other studio in town will be apprised of the circumstances of the firing and I seriously doubt that this person will ever again be able to find work in the motion picture industry." I look from Gwen to Phoebe and then over to Baxter whose expression tells me nothing. I look back to the girls. "Are there any questions?"

"It wasn't me," Gwendolyn says.

"Me, either," Phoebe echoes.

Gwendolyn looks at her boss.

"I swear, Miss Baxter. I didn't do it," she says.

"Then you have nothing to worry about," Baxter tells her. She looks at me. "Is that it, Mr. Bernardi?"

"That's it, Miss Baxter."

"And if there were no more leaks, how long do you think you would continue to investigate this matter?" she asks.

"Not long," I say.

She nods. "Then we shall hope for the best," she says. "Disloyalty is something I personally cannot abide. Thank you for bringing this situation out into the open, Joe. And please call me Anne."

She smiles warmly at me. I smile back. I was right. This is one classy lady.

It is starting to get dark as I leave the trailer and head back toward my ride. By now Nate McIver has become my regular driver and he's as knowledgeable as he is entertaining. If he ever decides to give up chauffeuring, he could run for Mayor and win. As I approach, I see that he's standing by the car with a guy I've never seen before.

The stranger steps forward to introduce himself. He is a private investigator and his name is Phillippe Bachelet. I'd say he's close to my age, very tall, with wavy blonde hair and a neatly trimmed mustache. As we shake hands he tells me he is a private contractor but the bulk of his work is done for the firm of Bruckner & Le Pen.

"A sad day for us all, M. Bernardi," he says looking appropriately downcast.

I agree that it is.

The mourning done with, Bachelet gets down to business.

"I have been sent by M. Le Pen who hopes that you will do him the great favor of seeing to Mlle. d'Arcy for the next few hours. He remains closeted at the courthouse with the magistrate and the Crown Prosecutor. It has already been decided that the trial of M. Marchand will begin this coming Friday and there is much work to be done for both M. Le Pen and myself."

"Not a problem, Mister Bachelet. I'm delighted to help."

He smiles. "Bon. I will drive you to Mlle. d'Arcy's place where she awaits you. If she offers to cook, have her suggest a restaurant."

"That bad?"

"She is a lady of many talents. Cuisine is not one of them."

"Thanks for the warning."

I nod and tell Nate he's free to go back to the hotel.

On the way to Jeanne's I learn a little about Phillippe Bachelet. He's two years older than me and served with distinction during WWII. His unit, the 3rd Infantry Division was the first to land at Juno Beach on D-Day in '44. He was shot in the leg and the shoulder but survived and eight weeks later, unwilling to accept a medical discharge, found himself fighting his way across France into Germany. After eight years he still has no use for the Bosch. He is single, never married and carries himself like a man who is used to making the most of life's good times.

"The police have it wrong, of course," he says as we sit waiting for a red light to turn green.

"And how is that?" I ask.

"Mlle. d'Arcy had nothing to do with Daniel's death although I suspect someone is trying very hard to make it look that way."

"Sorry. I don't follow you," I say.

The light turns green. We continue on.

"Daniel Bruckner is--was a brilliant trial lawyer. In Daniel's hands Louis Marchand had an excellent chance of gaining his freedom. M. Le Pen is not of the same caliber. I do not say this to demean him. He will be the first to agree. I think it far more likely that Daniel was murdered by someone working for the Gonzalvo brothers or perhaps even the organization they answer to in Buffalo."

"A mob hit?"

He smiles. "Yes, I believe that is the term your television policemen use."

I shake my head. "Stabbing? Not their style, Mr. Bachelet."

He shrugs. "Which is precisely why I think they are responsible.

Most of the time these criminal killings are designed to send a message, a warning to others to toe the line. The small caliber pistol shot to the back of the head. Yes, next time this could be you. Do not defy us. But in this case, M. Bernardi, they wish no credit. Quite the opposite. And by eliminating Daniel Bruckner they greatly enhance their chances of surviving this trial."

I nod.

"An interesting theory," I say.

"Quite so," he smiles.

We are now driving through an upscale residential section of the city. The light of the full moon reveals big houses, huge lots, carefully manicured lawns, and well tended gardens. The street signs which are illuminated by curbside lamps are bi-lingual. Easily readable is the French version of the street we are traveling, 'Rue de La Jonquille', and below, smaller and less easily read: Jonquil Street. We continue on for several blocks and then take a left turn onto 'Rue d'Oeiller' (Carnation Street). We pass two houses on the left and then Bachelet turns into a wide driveway. The house is huge but totally dark. He continues past it and turns at the end of the driveway to reveal a small guest cottage which is lit up like St. Peter's square at midnight on New Years Eve.

"The house belongs to Avrom Pinchot, a very important film producer who rents out the cottage to Mlle. d'Arcy as a courtesy. M. Pinchot and his wife are currently vacationing at their villa outside Nice."

As the car comes to a stop, the door to the cottage opens and Jeanne appears, a drink in one hand and a lit cigarette in the other.

I get out of the car as they exchange greetings in French and then with a quick wink and a whispered "Bon chance", he drives away.

"Hi," I say as I reach the doorway.

"Hi, yourself," she says.

"Let me introduce myself. I am your designated escort for the next few hours."

"Yes, Claude phoned me. I'm delighted."

We go inside. The main room is cozy and furnished in French provincial. To the left I see a small dining area next to the kitchen. Toward the back a short corridor and a couple of doors, most likely the bathroom and the bedroom.

"Drink?" she asks standing by the wet bar and holding up a glass.

"Beer. Cold. In the bottle," I say.

She puts the glass down, rummages in the small refrigerator and produces a Molson. She uncaps it and hands it to me. I raise it in salute. She picks up her own glass which has been sitting there half-filled.

"A votre sante," I say and down a large gulp.

She laughs and takes a deep swallow.

"So you do speak French," she says.

"That was it," I tell her, "with the exception of a few very effective phrases I memorized during the war when fraternizing with various juene filles. I won't bother to repeat them here."

"Merci," she says coyly.

"This is very nice," I say looking around the room.

"Better than 'very'," she smiles. "Rent free."

I nod appreciatively.

"M. Pinchot must, uh, admire you very much," I say.

She laughs.

"Avrom Pinchot is a sixty-five year old Kris Kringle. His wife has been a movie buff all her life and she is a huge supporter of the Film Commission. This is her idea, not his."

She picks up a couple of sheets of paper from her desk and hands them to me.

"While you were off chatting up Anne Baxter, I polished off that list of reporters and columnists we'll be inviting to the press dinner."

"How'd we do?"

"Thirty four acceptances, one turn down."

I look at her in mock disbelief.

"A turndown?"

She nods.

"Dead."

"Too bad. Nothing serious, I hope."

"Two days ago. Trying for 90. Never made it."

"Sad."

"Very," she says, getting up. "Let's go."

"Where to?"

"Le Coq Rouge. We have reservations."

I shake my head.

"First we talk, then we eat."

"The reservation is for seven-thirty," she says.

I check my watch.

"It'll keep. Sit down."

She hesitates for a moment, then sits. She stubs out her cigarette.

"This sounds serious," she says.

"It is," I say.

She's sitting on the sofa. I sit down in an easy chair opposite her.

"Tell me about you and Daniel Bruckner."

She hesitates.

"You assume there is something to tell."

"I know there is. Look, Jeanne, there's a lot of work that

needs doing on this location. More than I anticipated and I am going to need your help and that means your total cooperation, physical and mental. This murder has roiled things up and maybe made you useless. Since I don't want any surprises, I say again, tell me about you and Bruckner."

She takes a deep drag on her cigarette, It's an old trick. Professors do it with a lit pipe, politicians with a cigar. Stalling for time to formulate an answer.

"We were lovers," she says finally.

"I thought as much," I say.

"It started a year ago. It ended last month."

"His idea or yours?"

"His."

"Hard to imagine," I say.

"There was a time when he talked of divorce despite the religious problems. He has been married in name only for many years but Marie refused to let him go. Then several months ago he was approached about running for a seat in the National Assembly, something like your state legislatures, and he agreed. At that moment, divorce became impossible. So did our future."

She says this last bitterly and takes a deep swallow from her glass. I'm not sure what's in her glass but it could easily be straight scotch.

"Now here is the ironic part," she says. "At one point several weeks ago, Marie had relented. She was willing to grant the divorce because I think she had something going on the side. But of course, by then it was too late. Who was it called all this the human comedy, Joe? In some ways it really is quite funny."

She drains her drink and plunks it a little too loudly on the table. It's become obvious she has a head start on me. I wonder how many she's put away. Too many, I suspect.

"When was the last time you were in Daniel's apartment?" I ask.

Her eyes narrow. "Why? You think I had something to do with his death?"

"Not at all," I say, "but I know that in some cases fingerprints can remain on a surface for weeks, even months. A door handle, a desk drawer, the lever on a commode."

"Five weeks ago," she says in annoyance. "But I am sure they have been wiped away by now. I have been told that his housekeeper is very efficient." She looks away.

"Look, Jeanne," I say, "I can see how you would feel betrayed and very, very angry. Inspector Villiers will probably see it that way as well."

She looks back at me, fury in her eyes.

"I did not kill him," she says emphatically. "Believe me or not, as you choose."

"I believe you, Jeanne," I say. "I was merely pointing out how the police and the prosecutors will look at it."

"Let them look all they like," she says.

She looks at me with determination. It's then that I notice the little trickle of red coming from her left nostril.

"Jeanne," I say touching my upper lip just blow the nostril.

She frowns and mimics me, then pulls her finger away. It is red with blood.

"Zut alors," she says in annoyance. She goes to the bar and grabs a cocktail napkin. She presses it against her nose. "Ever since I was a little girl, I get upset and my nose bleeds. The day I married, it bled when I said 'I do'."

She laughs and I do, too. She takes a piece from another napkin, balls it up, dabs it in her drink to moisten it and shoves it into her nose.

"Pretty, n'est pas?" she says.

"Will you be okay?" I ask.

"It will stop in a minute."

She drains her drink and stubs out her cigarette.

"Let's eat. I'm hungry."

We leave a note taped to the front door directing Le Pen to Le Coq Rouge in case he arrives before we get back. The temperature is brisk now but Jeanne leaves the top down and despite the chill I find the air invigorating. I try to convince her that I should drive but she won't hear of it. It turns out my fears are unfounded. Drunk or sober she's a good driver.

As predicted, her nose stops bleeding and she tosses away the napkin stopper. We miss our reservation by twenty-five minutes but the maitre'd still finds us a very nice banquette with a view of the room. The restaurant is not particularly large but the atmosphere is welcoming and the wait staff particularly friendly. It's no secret she's something of a regular and well-liked by everyone.

She's just finishing up her lobster thermidor and I am only halfway done with my beef bourguignon when she jams an elbow into my rib cage and nods toward the bar across the room. I spot him immediately. Mackenzie Starr, the rude reporter from the Chronicle-Telegraph, is watching us watching him and when we make eye contact, he gets up and starts toward us, drink in hand.

"Now what do we do?" Jeanne asks.

"Be polite," I say. "Maybe he'll go away."

"I tried being polite to my ex-mother-in-law. It didn't work," she says out of the side of her mouth as Starr reaches our banquette.

"Good evening, Mr. Starr," I say with a smile.

"It is now," he smiles back. "Nice little party we have going here."

"Just dinner," I say. "That's all."

"That so?" he says. "Thought you two ought to know, a pal of mine in Los Angeles read me a column by this woman with the Herald Examiner. Seems I had it right about Clift and Hitchcock. You'll be reading all about it in my piece tomorrow morning."

"I'd hold off on that if I were you, Mr. Starr. There's an article set to appear in the L.A. Times tomorrow morning which will put the lie to the things that woman wrote and make anyone who believed her look like a fool."

"You'll forgive me if I don't believe you, Mr. Bernardi," he says, draining his glass and putting it empty on our table.

"Suit yourself," I say, "but people like you astound me, Mr. Starr. You come to me looking for an exclusive interview with Mr. Hitchcock or Montgomery Clift and meanwhile your uncooperative and combative attitude tells me, why should I?"

He looks puzzled as if the booze has dimmed his thought processes.

"I didn't ask you for a personal interview," he says.

"I know, but if you had," I say. It's the old carrot-and-stick approach. I use it often with brain dead writers like Starr.

"You mean, if I play ball, I get a sit down with Hitchcock?"

"He listens to me," I say which isn't exactly an answer but he takes it for one.

Just then I look over to the entranceway and see a sight I really don't wish to see. It's Inspector Villiers again, still elegantly dressed, accompanied once more by two uniformed officers of the surete. They may even be the same ones who were with him earlier this morning. Villiers looks toward us and begins to approach with the officers at his side. This I like even less. It means he's not here to chat.

"Good evening, Mlle. d'Arcy. M. Bernardi."

He smiles as he says it. We smile back for all the good it will do us.

"Forgive me for interrupting your dinner but it is most necessary, Mlle. d'Arcy, that you accompany me to headquarters."

"Am I under arrest?" she asks.

"You are not," he says. "Not at the moment but I have more questions for you. If you refuse to cooperate then, of course, I will place you under arrest,"

Starr is flabbergasted. He looks from one to the other to the other as if following a tennis match at Wimbledon.

"In that case," Jeanne says, reaching in her purse for the keys to the Austin Healey, "Joe, will you drive my car back to my house?"

She tries to hand them to me but Villiers snatches them from her hand.

"Forgive me, but in addition to a warrant for your arrest, I also have a warrant to search your car. Apres vous," he says, stepping aside so that she can get out of the booth.

I start to slide out to accompany her but Villiers fixes me with a hard stare.

"Your participation is not required, Mr. Bernardi. Have a good evening."

I watch as he and the two uniforms lead Jeanne toward the entranceway. I look over at Starr who is still stunned by what he has just witnessed. He turns to me quizzically and then smiles.

"And just when I thought I didn't have a story for tomorrow's edition," he says.

CHAPTER SIX

It's well past midnight. I'm sitting on a bench on the second floor of Surete headquarters outside of Inspector Villiers' office. He is down the hall in an interrogation room questioning Jeanne. Le Pen is with her. I hear no screams of agony. Quebec City is not Chicago. The sergeant on the desk in the lobby has come upstairs twice to tell me that Inspector Villiers will not be able to see me tonight. I thank him for his kindness and ignore his warning. If I have to punch the Inspector in the nose to get him to arrest me, I will do so but the one thing he will not be able to do is ignore me.

I hear voices and look down the corridor. Jeanne and Le Pen and the Inspector are exiting the interrogation room. I stand as they approach. Jeanne spots me and hurries to me, throwing her arms around me.

"Joe, you are so sweet," she says, "but you did not have to wait for me." I don't tell her she's not the one I'm waiting for. I return her hug.

"I wouldn't be able to sleep until I knew you were all right," I say. She buys it.

Villiers and Le Pen are shaking hands.

"Mlle. d'Arcy will be available to you at a moment's notice, Inspector," Le Pen is saying. "Thank you for your kindness."

Villiers shrugs.

"Il n'y a rien," he says.

"Good night, then," Le Pen says. He looks at me. "Mr. Bernardi, may I drop you?"

"Thanks, no, Mr. Le Pen. I need a few minutes with the Inspector."

Villiers shakes his head.

"I have no time for you tonight, M. Bernardi," he says.

I plaster on my most winning smile.

"But of course you do, Inspector," I say. "Otherwise tomorrow is going to be a most unpleasant day for both of us."

I look him in the eye and I don't flinch. He doesn't either. Finally, he shrugs.

"As a courtesy I will give you ten minutes. Come into my office." He starts in. I follow. Before I shut the door behind me I throw Le Pen a wink, as if I know what I'm doing.

Villiers is already seated behind his desk.

"Get on with it, monsieur," he says. He does not invite me to sit.

"I would like to know the nature of the case against Miss d'Arcy."

"That is none of your concern."

I shake my head. "Wrong. It is the concern of my employer, Warner Brothers Studio, which is shooting a film here, contributing American dollars to the city's economy and giving employment to at least 50 of your citizens that I know of. It is of concern to Jack Warner, one of the most powerful men in the movie business who will doubtless be asked many times what it was like to film in Quebec and I have no doubt you would prefer that his assessment be favorable. And finally it is of particular concern to M. Avrom Pinchot in whose guest house Miss d'Arcy resides and with whom Miss d'Arcy has a very special relationship. I hear that M. Pinchot is not a man to suffer fools gladly and I suspect that when I call him overseas tomorrow and then he immediately calls you, you will have something to say to him that is slightly more helpful than 'None of your business'."

This last part is a total fabrication but I am betting that Villiers doesn't know what Jeanne's relationship to Pinchot really is.

I guess right. He gestures to a chair.

"Sit down, M. Bernardi," he says and then proceeds to tell me what they have so far.

"First we have the witness who saw Mlle. d'Arcy running from the Bruckner apartment house."

"Or someone who looked like her."

Villiers puts up his hand to shut me up.

"Second, we have found several of her fingerprints at the Bruckner third floor unit."

"That means nothing. She could have been at a party there some months ago. Fingerprints linger for a long time."

Villiers shakes his head with an expression of wounded patience.

"Please, M. Bernardi. We have spent many hours today interviewing staff and guests at Clarisse. The loud argument between them leaves no doubt that until recently they were having an affair."

"She told me she hadn't been in his home for at least a month, maybe longer," I say.

"She told me the same thing. In the ashtray on the coffee table were four cigarette butts. They were Gitanes, her brand of choice."

"Plenty of people smoke---"

"On the table by the ashtray was a Ronson Queen Anne table lighter which M. Bruckner had purchased two days ago. Mlle. d'Arcy's fingerprints were on that lighter."

That one shuts me up.

"Finally, upon searching Mlle. d'Arcy's automobile, we found the letter opener missing from M. Bruckner's desk. It was secreted beneath the driver's seat. It was covered with blood and fingerprints. Again, these fingerprints belong to Mlle. d'Arcy."

I shake my head violently.

"Surely you realize that----"

Again he raises his hand and this time his tone is harsher.

"Sil vous plait, M. Bernardi, you asked for a precis of the case against Mlle. d'Arcy. Allow me to continue without interruption. The presence of the letter opener tells me one of three things. First, that the lady is extremely stupid. This I do not believe for a moment. Second, that she is extremely intelligent and is fabricating a scenario which makes it appear that she is being framed for Mr. Bruckner's death. I find this far more likely. And third, M. Bruckner was killed by someone else who planted the letter opener in a clumsy attempt to implicate Mlle. d'Arcy. This is possible but far fetched."

"'She always kept the car top down. Anyone could have put the letter opener in the car----"

"Yes, yes, I understand," Villiers says, "and for that reason, among others, I did not arrest Mlle. d'Arcy this evening. I have two more things I must check on. First, the lady has agreed to appear in a lineup for the benefit of my witness. Perhaps I will discover that the witness is mistaken though I doubt it. Secondly, a small amount of blood was found at the scene which does not match the victim's blood type. Mlle. d'Arcy provided us with a saliva sample which will enable us to determine her type. Those are the things I am waiting on, M. Bernardi, and now if there is nothing else---"

He gets up. I am being dismissed. I get up and head for the door. I turn back to him.

"You don't have much, Villiers. I hope you know that," I say.

"On the contrary, monsieur, we both know I have more than enough to secure an indictment. Bonsoir."

I bound down the stairs and out the main entrance into the clear night air. There is a taxi rank across the street and I climb into the first in line and tell the driver to take me to the Frontenac. Villiers has given me a lot to think about. Too much, in fact, but if there is one thing I know with certainty, it is that Jeanne d'Arcy did not kill Daniel Bruckner.

Or so I keep telling myself.

Breakfast the next morning is an ordeal. The coffee is fresh as is the toast and the fruit juice is tangy but I find it inedible as I try to eat while reading Mackenzie Starr's vitriolic and florid front page story in the Chronicle-Telegraph. Not content with the melodramatic scene at Le Coq Rouge, he waited outside of Surete headquarters on the chance that Jeanne would appear. Which she did. His photographer grabbed a shot of Jeanne trying to cover her face while Claude Le Pen reached out to push the camera away. The only thing that would have made her look more guilty would have been prison garb and shackles. He also fired a lot of damning questions at her to which she either remained silent or said things like 'no comment', 'get out of my way', 'none of your business', and 'stuff it'. Things like that.

I make a mental note to deal with Mackenzie Starr in my own way sometime in the near future and then I head downstairs.

True to his word, Phineas has send me a fax of his morning column and it is a pip. Part Wilde, part Mencken, part Shaw, he uses the English language as a rapier to reduce the arrogant Miss Ankers to a clueless schoolgirl. How dare this illiterate scribbler with a single digit IQ dare to judge two of Hollywood's most revered icons. She is a 28 year old adolescent whose limited talents qualify her for proofreading Betty Crocker recipes and nothing more. One can understand hiring such a nonentity during the exigencies of wartime but Johnny came marching home years ago and there are thousands of Johnnies out there infinitely more qualified to replace her. One would hope that management would wake up before this laughing stock threatens to infect the entire newspaper. Okay, so maybe it's a little over the top but with someone like Astrid Ankers, subtlety is totally ineffective.

I lean back and finish off my coffee, then rummage in my desk for Jeanne's phone number. I call but there's no answer. There's a good chance she is sleeping in this morning and muted the ringer. I wouldn't blame her. Yesterday was rough all around. If she shows, she shows. If not I'll muddle along. And speaking of muddling I realize that I need to contact Bella Zwick, the hotel's catering hostess, who has been after me for a head count and a final decision on the menu for next Sunday's press dinner. No time like the present, I think, and get up from the desk.

But just then I spot Connie Lederer waving at me from her desk by the entrance to the room. I head over to her.

"What's up?" I ask.

"Trouble," she says. "Clift's missed his morning call. He's still at the church and he wants to see you."

"Me?"

"That's what he said. There's a car outside waiting to take you to the church."

I nod and hurry to the front entrance. Nate McIver is standing by his Peugeot and when he sees me he throws me a smile.

"Morning, boss," he says, opening the rear door for me.

"I'll sit up front, Nate", I say as I let myself into the passenger seat.

"Whatever makes you happy," he says.

He tears away from the entrance endangering anyone within fifty yards of us. He zips through the streets, weaving in and out of lanes with the precision of an Indy driver. After a mere eight minutes, he turns onto Rue St. Joseph and there in front of us is Eglise Saint-Roch, the largest church in the city, a massive edifice built with grey stone in neo-gothic architecture. Nate bypasses the church and pulls up to the nearby rectory where Clift has been living midst the priests for the past several days. I get out. I ask Nate to wait and hurry up the steps to the front door and go inside. I am in a small foyer and off to the right is a comfortable looking vestibule. Monty is seated in a high backed chair by a window staring off into space.

"Monty?" I say.

He looks over at me with a smile and gets up.

"Hey, Joe, thanks for coming." he says. He puts out his hand and we shake. He's uncomfortable. "I know I'm acting like a jerk."

"No," I say.

"How about some coffee?" he suggests. "They're real informal around here. Help yourself to whatever you need. Good system. I like it."

We go into the kitchen. He introduces me to Father Leo who is preparing some kind of soup for the luncheon meal. He is a rotund happy looking man with greying hair and a pixie-like smile on his face. Off to the side is a large percolator still half-full of coffee. Monty pours and we sit down at the little pine table by a window that overlooks the garden at the rear of the rectory.

After sipping his coffee, Monty says to me, "I got a phone call last night from a friend in L.A. He read me the story in the Herald Examiner."

"That drivel," I say.

"Joe, I'm a professional. I don't want to foul up this picture. I certainly don't want to offend Mr. Hitchcock. I just want to do the very best I can the only way I know how but if I can't, maybe they should replace me."

"Don't be ridiculous."

"I'm perfectly serious. Is there anything you can do about that story, maybe get her to rethink it? I mean, I'll talk to her on the phone if it'll help. Whatever it takes."

I reach in my pocket and take out Phineas' fax. I hand it to him.

"This appeared in this morning's L.A. Times."

He takes it and hesitantly starts to read. Then he smiles. Then he smiles more broadly and looks up at me.

"Hey, this is good," he says.

"Better than good, Monty," I say. "I think we've heard the last of the lady. And believe me, you're not hurting the picture. Take ten or fifteen minutes and sit down with Hitch. You two are both intelligent and you both want what's best for the film. I have no doubt you can work things out."

He gets up.

"Yeah. You're right. Let's go," he says and I follow him out.

On the way to the set we chat amiably and I realize that Astrid Ankers has probably done us a great favor. Thanks to her attack I am pretty sure that Hitchcock and Monty will start to bond, at least long enough to get the picture finished. I hope I'm right.

Back at the production office I try to keep busy. I try Jeanne again. Again no answer. I call Claude Le Pen at his office but he is not there. I leave my name and number. I spend an hour with Bella Zwick going over the arrangements for Sunday evening's press dinner. I suggest chicken for the entree. She asks me what kind. I say any kind but rubber. She looks at me oddly. Obviously she has never attended a monthly meeting of the Kiwanis. We finally settle on capon which is chicken with a college diploma. She guarantees that it will be 'tres bon'. I let her fill in the rest. We will have five tables of 8 and someone from the film will be seated at each of the five. Karl Malden at one. Brian Aherne at another. Then Hitch and Alma, Monty, and Anne Baxter. Jeanne and I will float. An open bar should get everyone well lubricated and if the jackals are on their best behavior, it should be a successful evening. Press kits will be handed out as each one leaves. Inside he or she will find all sorts of helpful information, witty quotes and a half dozen glossy photographs including one of Hitchcock and Monty with their arms around each others shoulders. Feud? What feud? Les Americains are just one big happy family.

All in all it is a peaceful and productive day, right up until five thirty when the 'merde' hits the fan. I am in the bar enjoying a beer and going over the newest script revisions when Claude Le Pen finds me. I look up at him. His expression is grim.

"She's been arrested," he says. "Murder in the first degree."

I can't say I'm stunned. I half expected it. Still, the enormity of the reality hits me hard.

"My God," I mutter quietly.

"Oui, mon ami. Mon dieu," Le Pen says. "We must talk."

CHAPTER SEVEN

A nd talk, we do.

It's Thursday morning and we're gathered in a conference room at Bruckner & Le Pen. There's Le Pen, of course,
and two of his subordinates whose names I did not get. There is
also the private investigator, Phillippe Bachelet, and one of his
operatives. A court stenographer is at Le Pen's elbow recording
the proceedings for future reference. And further down the table
is Esther Laval, a matronly woman in her late 40's to whom I
was introduced as soon as I arrived. Le Pen describes her as one
of the three best defense lawyers in the city and he has retained
her to represent Jeanne. After long deliberation he has decided
he cannot represent her himself, he tells me, because of a possible
conflict of interest and because his defense of Louis Marchand
will claim too much of his time and energy.

Last evening I had asked him why he was inviting me to this
morning strategy meeting and he simply said it was because
Jeanne wanted me.

"She tells me you are amazingly adept at dealing with the
press," he says. "This is the sort of help we will sorely need in
the days to come."

I shake my head, almost laughing.

"Mister Le Pen, I deal with gossip columnists. They are clueless, narcissistic star fuckers and easily manipulated. I doubt hardboiled crime reporters fall into the same category."

"Nevertheless, she wanted you. And don't you think it's about time you and I began addressing one another by our Christian names, Joe?"

"I do, Claude."

"Include me in that," Phillippe pipes up from across the table.

"Mais oui," Claude says and looks down the table at Esther Laval who has been poring over a sheaf of papers. She looks up to find us all looking at her.

"And you college boys can call me Mme. Laval," she says sternly and then immediately breaks into a smile before going back to her papers.

I slept very little last night, tossing and turning in my bed as I tried to sort out the forces arrayed against Jeanne. She says she is innocent and I believe her. We have no history. I have known her for three days. We have worked together briefly so my defense of her is not borne of lifelong acquaintanceship but out of a gut feeling. I could be wrong about her. I am certainly not infallible but until proved otherwise I am working on a hypothesis of innocence.

And therefore the next logical question is, if not Jeanne, then who? The who is most certainly the person or persons who hid the bloody letter opener in her car and that opens up the question of who had access and the answer to that is, just about everyone.

I need to know who else stood to gain by Bruckner's death and immediately I think of the trial which starts tomorrow morning. What I know of it is cursory. I need to know a lot more so the first thing I did when I arrived this morning was to pull Claude Le Pen and Phillippe Bachelet aside and have them explain to me in detail what this trial is all about.

Some things I know because Le Pen had let me read all of Bruckner's notes on the case. Marchand was in a position to divert foodstuffs for school children to the Ontario based Gonsalvo brothers who, it is generally acknowledged, are in league with the Maggadino crime family in Buffalo, New York. Marchand comes from a highly respected Quebec family but bad investments had cost him the family fortune and with a wife and young son to support, in desperation he agreed to the scheme to remain solvent. Marchand now realizes what a horrendous mistake he made and is determined to make amends.

"Here's where Daniel's brilliance came into play," Claude told me. "Louis Marchand could easily have pleaded guilty to the charges. He could have made sworn statements implicating both the Gonsalvos and the Maggadinos but affidavits are dull reading and in a corrupt world, strange things have been known to happen outside the scrutiny of the public eye."

"Ah, justice Chicago style," I had said.

Bachelet smiled.

"Precisely," he'd said.

"And this is why" Claude had said, "Daniel pleaded Louis not guilty and brought him to trial. This made the Gonsalvo brothers very nervous and several times by phone and in person, they tried to persuade Daniel to change Louis' plea. Daniel refused because he had already convinced Louis to get up on the stand and tell the world the whole sordid story. This ensured nationwide press coverage. Scandals make good reading and everyone wallows in them whether they will admit it or not. The Gonsalvos would not be able to hide from the accusation. More importantly, the Ontario prosecutor who had been loath to go after the Gonsalvos with the evidence he had, now in the glare of Louis' accusations under oath, will be left with no choice."

I nodded. Clearly both Bruckner and Louis Marchand had balls of steel and just as clearly they were risking their lives by planning to reveal the Gonsalvo brothers' involvement.

I had looked Claude in the eye and said, "And now that Daniel Bruckner is dead, I imagine that Mr. Marchand is having second thoughts."

"As a matter of fact, he is not," Claude told me. "If anything he is now more determined than ever to tell the truth because Daniel was not only his attorney, he was his friend."

It is now ten past ten. Esther has briefed us on Jeanne's situation. The Crown Prosecutor has agreed that a charge of first degree murder is appropriate and the case will go forward. Esther has not yet talked to Jeanne but will visit her at the jail later today. She should have a copy of the police report and the autopsy report within 24 hours, perhaps sooner. At present Jeanne is being allowed no visitors other than counsel. Esther will let us know if and when that changes.

Now I am sitting and listening as Claude outlines our strategy. We will do whatever it takes to cast suspicion on the Gonsalvos. Phillippe's investigator will travel to Ontario and get a timeline on the brothers' activities for the time of Bruckner's death. We hope to discover that one or both was out of town at the time of the killing but even if they were not, they could easily have hired someone, perhaps even someone from the Maggadino family, Despite the circumstantial evidence against her, we take the position that Jeanne has been framed for this killing and it will be up to us to discredit the trumped up evidence, piece by piece. My job will be to encourage stories that point to Jeanne's innocence and to counteract, as best I can, any negative press that develops.

We are just winding down when suddenly the door flies open and Marie Bruckner enters without bothering to knock. Her expression is stony as she surveys the room, finally fixing her gaze on Claude.

"Why was I not informed about this conference?" she demands to know. "Claude?"

The gentlemen have all risen in her presence.

"We saw no need to trouble you, Marie," Claude tells her. "And really, there was nothing you could have contributed."

She steps to the end of the long table and leans on it. She stares at Claude angrily.

"I could have contributed my strong objection to the nature of this meeting, Claude. The subject is Miss d'Arcy, I presume."

"It was but the meeting's over, Marie."

"I will not have this firm representing the little trollop who killed my husband."

"We are not. That is Mme. Laval's job."

Esther smiles sweetly up at Marie. It has no visible effect on her disposition.

"Besides," Claude continues, "whatever the firm decides to do is no concern of yours."

"I am a partner!" she says indignantly.

"Marie, we have had this discussion. You refuse to accept it. My agreement with Daniel provided that whichever partner survived the other, that partner would inherit complete ownership of the firm."

She shakes her head violently.

"No!"

"Yes," Claude says firmly. "Daniel provided for you well in a dozen different ways but not the law firm. Now I am not going to have this discussion with you again. If you don't believe me, hire yourself an attorney but I assure you, you will just be wasting your money."

She continues to stare angrily at Claude, then switches her gaze to me as if seeing me for the first time. I don't look away and after a moment she turns and storms out of the room.

We've all resumed our seats but Claude is still standing.

"Strange behavior for a woman who is being serviced by a man half her age," he says. He sees my surprised expression. "The assistant tennis pro at the country club. It's been going on for months."

"She sure doesn't act like it," I say.

"No, she does not. Pity. When it comes to Jeanne d'Arcy, there is real venom in that woman. We must do whatever we can to keep her from spreading it to the press." He looks at me quizzically. "Have you any free time from your busy schedule?"

"I may," I say. "Am I volunteering for my first assignment?" I ask.

"It appears you are," Claude says with a smile. He tells me that Marie Bruckner is registered at the Manoir Victoria Hotel in the old town. He also tells me that she is American, born and raised in Joplin, Missouri. Maybe we speak the same language. Maybe. He can only hope. I tell him I will try to reach her this afternoon.

It's eleven thirty when I get back to the hotel. These cab rides are killing me but I can't very well call up a company car for a meeting I want Jack Warner to know nothing about. As I'm crossing the lobby I hear my name and turn as Alma Hitchcock bustles toward me.

"Mr. Bernardi," she says, "I have been looking for you all morning."

"Keeping busy, Mrs. Hitchcock," I say.

"And doing a fine job of it, too," she says. "Alfred wishes me to convey to you his deepest thanks for your help with Mr. Clift. Great progress is being made on the set and the young man is doing his level best to accommodate Alfred's suggestions."

"I'm pleased," I say.

"And well you should be," she says with a warm smile. Then the smile fades. "Now, as to Miss d'Arcy, what is happening?"

"She's been arrested," I say.

"So I gathered. Alfred and I are quite taken with her. I assume this is all some sort of mistake."

"I hope so."

"I know so," she says. "That sweet child wouldn't hurt a flea."

"I agree," I say.

"Well, if needed, Mr. Bernardi, Alfred and I stand ready to help in any way we can. Don't hesitate to ask."

"That's very kind of you, Mrs. Hitchcock. I know Jeanne will be very grateful for your support."

"De rien, Mr. Bernardi. De rien. For generations, it's what we British have been taught to do."

She smiles and off she goes. Things are looking up. Now if Warner finds out what I'm doing and tries to yank me back to the States, I may have an ace in the hole with Hitch who may not want to let me go.

When I enter the production office I see him sitting in my chair, feet upon my desk, sipping on a soda can while he reads the newspaper. When I get to the desk I grab his legs and swing them off my desk. Mackenzie Starr nearly falls out of my chair.

"Hey, what's the matter with you?" he whines.

"Get out of my chair," I say.

"Now, look---"

"Out, or I'll throw you out of the office and then I'll have security toss you out of the hotel."

"You've got no manners, friend," he says, getting up and out of the way.

"And you do? What are you doing here, Starr? And how'd you get past Connie at the door?"

"I showed her my press card and told her we had an appointment."

"Well, we don't, so goodbye," I say sitting down.

"I'm the press. I have a right to be here," he says.

"You have the right to get your ass kicked," I say.

He smirks.

"Guess you read my story in yesterday's paper. Sorry if the facts get in the way of your fascination for the little lady."

"What do you want?"

"I'm writing a follow up for tomorrow's edition. I'd like to get some quotes even if they're only 'No Comment'."

"Not interested," I say. "I'm calling security." I pick up the phone.

"Tell me about the meeting this morning," he says.

I pause and then replace the phone.

"What about it?"

"Is Esther Laval going to take her case?"

"Why don't you ask her?"

"She's next on my list. Why were you there? What do you know that my readers should know? By the way, have you been sleeping with her? I wouldn't blame you. That is one luscious piece of ass."

I rise up out of my chair and grab him by his egg-stained tie.

"Let go of me!" he says.

I tug at him pulling him toward the entrance to the room.

"You can't do this! This is assault!"

"Actually, it's merely battery," I tell him. "What kind of a reporter are you, anyway?"

I stop at Connie's desk, still clenching Starr's tie.

"Connie, call security. Tell them I'm taking this guy to the main entrance and throwing him out on the curb. If he tries to get back in the hotel, call the cops and have him shot or at the very least arrested."

She stares at me wide-eyed.

"Okay," she says. "On what charge?"

"Making a lewd proposition to a member of the same sex in a public place. If sodomy's not a crime here, think of something else."

I yank at his tie and pull him across the lobby while he sputters and protests. I'm a lot stronger than he is. It's no contest. When I finally am able to shove him through the front door, I give him one last dirty look and walk back inside. He doesn't follow. Score one for the good guys.

Back at my desk, I call the Manoir Victoria Hotel and within a minute or two I have Marie Bruckner on the phone.

"Bernardi?" she says. "I don't believe I know the name."

"Actually we haven't been introduced, Mrs. Bruckner. I was at the meeting this morning when you dropped in."

There's a pause.

"The tall good looking man in the grey suit."

"If you say so."

"What can I do for you, Mr. Bernardi?

"I'd like to sit down and chat with you if you have a few minutes."

"I don't. In fact I have a cab waiting for me downstairs. I am going back to our cottage by the lake where I've spent the last couple of weeks."

"Not a problem," I say.

"It's a considerable distance north of the city in the outlying countryside."

"Tell me exactly where and when and I will be there."

Surprisingly she agrees and I write down detailed directions on a scratch pad. The trip should take no more than forty minutes, she tells me. We agree on 2:30. I grab a quick lunch and then return a call from Charlie Berger. Charlie tells me that Warner is pleased by the dailies, despite the rumblings he's heard of discord on the set. Charlie also says that Warner spent fifteen minutes on the phone this morning with Hitchcock who apparently had nothing but nice things to say about yours truly. Now if I can keep from disappointing Hitch, I'll be in fine shape.

At 1:20 I call transportation and tell them to send around Nate McIver and his Peugeot. A cab ride to this far away address is out of the question, not if I want to keep any part of my per diem money. My gut tells me that Nate is a good guy who knows how to keep his mouth shut. At 1:30 he appears, I hop in the front seat and off we go. As we turn onto Rue St. Louis, I spot a late model Cadillac parked across the street with a man behind the wheel. I think I recognize him. When I look back and see him start up and make a U-turn to follow us, I am sure of it. Mackenzie Starr, ace reporter, is in hot pursuit of a story.

"You see that Caddy on our tail?" I say to Nate.

He glances into his rearview.

"Got him."

"You think you could lose him?"

"Sure."

"Could you lose on him in such a way that his car might not be fit to drive for a day or two?"

Nate grins and then slowly nods.

"I can try," he says. "You don't have problems with high speeds, do you, boss?"

"Hell, no," I say.

He puts the accelerator to the floor and the Peugeot leaps forward. I look back. The Caddy speeds up. It has a powerful engine and we can't outrun it but I'm sure Nate has something else in mind. I glance down and see that his trouser leg has hiked up several inches and a hint of leather is peeping out from below his cuff.

"So, Nate, would that be a holster down there wrapped around your calf?"

"Sure is," he says with a grin.

"And would there be a weapon in that holster?"

"You bet. Smith & Wesson snub-nosed. 38 police special."

"I'm surprised," I say, "but not complaining."

"We have a loony element here in Quebec that thinks we should break away from Canada and become our own country. There aren't many of them, at least not yet, but they've pulled some bizarre stunts to get attention. I think the last thing we'd want is to have a bunch of them kidnap Mr. Hitchcock or one of our stars to make a political point."

"I agree. And the pistol, I assume you know how to use it."

He glances over at me and just laughs.

As we head north the streets start to narrow and we are coming into an older part of the city. The shops are smaller, the sidewalks narrower and suddenly ahead of us I can see several blocks of roadside stands. As we speed forward, Nate leans in the horn and the crowds give away when he shows no sign of slowing. Mackenzioe Starr at the wheel of the Cadillac is right behind us."

"Hold on!" Nate shouts and suddenly he yanks the wheel to

the left and the car does a controlled skid and then lurches left into a narrow alleyway. The Caddy never had a chance. Starr tries to follow but his big lumbering sedan skids and crashes into a vegetable stand and then plows into a telephone pole, front end first. The last thing I remember seeing is steam hissing up from under the hood.

I look over at Nate. He smiles back at me and shrugs.

"I have two cars in my garage at home. One is an MGB roadster," he says.

With no further need to risk life and limb, Nate slows down and we pick up Route 175 heading north, looking for signs to Lake Clement. The scenery changes quickly from urban to the suburbs and then to something more pastoral. It is an unspoiled area of tall pines and thick forests interspersed with productive farmland. For those seeking a slower, gentler life style, you could probably not do better.

The lake appears on our left and the next left turn is Rue Clement. We follow it around the lake, passing various cottages and cabins and hunting lodges. We finally come upon the number I have been looking for and we turn into the driveway and pull up to the front door of the small cottage.

"I'll try not to be long," I say as I start to get out of the car.

"You never did say what this was all about, boss'" he says.

"Business," I tell him as I head for the front door.

I press the doorbell and wait. After a moment or two, the door opens and Marie Bruckner is standing there wearing nothing but a welcoming smile and a pale yellow negligee.

I look back at Nate who grins and gives me an enthusiastic thumbs up.

CHAPTER EIGHT

She offers me a drink. I accept. What really has me worried is what else she is planning to offer me. It's two thirty in the afternoon and she's dressed like a San Francisco harlot at midnight. Her make up has been carefully applied. The trouble is, there's enough to supply Phil Spitalny's all-girl orchestra and still have enough left over for the Dolly sisters. There have been times in my life when a woman has come after me so subtly that I never realized I was prey. This is not one of those times. I fear this encounter is not going to be constructive.

She hands me a cold beer. For herself, she pours four fingers of gin into a lo-ball glass and adds one very small ice cube. She raises her glass and then polishes off half its contents in two swallows.

She waves her hand around the room.

"So, Mr. Bernardi, how do you like my little home away from home?"

"Cozy."

"I have been staying here for the last several weeks. Certainly more peaceful than rubbing up against my husband at all hours of the day and night." She frowns. "You know, if I had been staying at home, he might not have been able to invite the little minx into his parlor and he might be alive today. Hmm. Hoist on his own petard. Is that how they say it?"

"Some do," I agree.

"Now, tell me, Mr. Bernardi, you work for Warner Brothers Pictures?"

"I do."

"And how long will you be staying with us here in Quebec?"

"At least another two weeks," I tell her.

She nods and finishes off her drink. She immediately fixes a new one.

"Are you here alone?"

"I'm expecting my fiancee any day now," I lie.

"Pity," she says as she moves to the sofa and sits down letting the negligee fall away from her legs in a provocative pose.

"I was hoping to talk to you about Jeanne d'Arcy," I say.

"What is there to say? She is a self-centered little bitch who has made a career out of stealing other women's husbands."

"That seems a little harsh."

She laughs. "Harsh? Give me a half an hour and I'll show you what harsh is really like."

More gin disappears into her gullet. I take another sip of beer. Out of self defense I am going to nurse this beer until sundown if necessary.

"Sit down, Joe, you make me nervous standing like that."

She pats the other end of the sofa. I prefer to sit in an easy chair on the other side of the coffee table, especially when she starts calling me Joe. She frowns at me petulantly.

"I'm sure you have every reason to be angry with Miss d'Arcy," I say. "It's particularly hard to lose the affections of one's husband if one is a vibrant attractive woman such as yourself."

"You're damned right," she growls angrily. She points to the bar. "Grab the bottle and the ice and bring 'em over here, Joe. I don't want to have to keep jumping up."

I do as I'm told and then resume my seat.

"Danny ran me out of his life ages ago," she says, "but at least he had the decency to keep it quiet. We got married young. Much too young. Did you know that I put him through law school? Yeah, I did. I was a court steno. You know what that is, don't you, Joe?" I admitted that I did. "I was three years older than him, making a good living. I paid the bills. He studied. He passed the bar. I paid the bills. He started a little practice that went nowhere. I paid the bills and then when he finally got established, he didn't need me to pay the bills any more. Matter of fact he didn't need me for anything."

She finishes off her drink and starts another. If she's getting drunk I see no sign of it. Not yet.

"Before long he comes to me looking to get a divorce. A divorce! Jesus Christ, I spend six or seven years supporting the bastard so he can become somebody and all of a sudden he wants a divorce. I tell him no as impolitely as I can. Not now. Not ever. If you don't like it, you know where the courthouse is. Quebec ain't Reno. You need grounds in this province. That's when he starts cattin' around in earnest. Funny thing about these Frenchies. Divorce is a tool of the devil but if a man takes a mistress, well, that's to be expected."

She puts down her drink and I think, has she decided she's had enough? But no, she takes a cigarette from a box on the table and lights it with a table top lighter. She takes a long enjoyable draught before she blows out the smoke. She points to the box.

"Want one, Joe? Help yourself. Camels. None of those Frenchie weeds for me."

I shake my head and tell her I don't smoke.

She smiles. "Tell me, have you any vices at all aside from the occasional beer?"

"I sing off-key in the shower," I say.

"That's a start," she says. "There are a few others I can think of. And I give lessons."

I shake my head and lean forward as if I have been hanging on her every word. "Tell me more about this divorce thing. I'm fascinated."

She hardly misses a beat.

"So now he makes no secret of his indiscretions, particularly with the carrot topped tramp. Then a funny thing happens, Joe, and you will like this. Oh, yes, I think you will like this very much. Around this time he decides to go into politics. Poor deluded man, I think he actually had his eye on the prime ministership. Well, naturally, this changes everything. Now he doesn't want a divorce. No, no, no, that will never do. A divorced man could not get elected Supervisor of Sewers, not in Quebec. Now I tell him that I want a divorce and I will take him to court if I have to. He squirmed like a wounded eel. You should have seen him, Joe. He was in a total panic. And here's the best part, he has to go to the ever-amorous Miss d'Arcy and tell her that the affair is over. He cannot marry her, now or ever. His political career comes first. Hah! I can only imagine her reaction. A woman scorned and all that."

She is now halfway through her fifth gin or rather, the fifth one I know about. Her speech is slowing down and she's starting to slur. I think one more drink, two at the most, and my virtue is safe.

"Well, Marie," I say trying to engage her understanding, "I can only imagine the terrible heartaches you've endured at your husband's hands and inadvertently by Miss d'Arcy."

"Nothing inadvertent about it, chum," she says, laying her head back and staring up at the ceiling. "Fuckin' bitch," she mutters.

"Yes, that may be but that doesn't mean she's guilty of murder. In fact Claude and I believe she's innocent."

"Hah!" Marie laughs. "Innocent. Oh, that is funny, Joe. All that evidence and you two geniuses think she didn't do it. Unbelievable."

"She didn't, Marie, and I'll tell you how we know. Because she is obviously being framed. Only an idiot would remove the letter opener from the body, preserve the blood and her fingerprints and then put it under the front seat of her own car for anyone to find. And Jeanne d'Arcy is no idiot."

Marie shakes her head.

"You are wrong. A woman in love who has been spurned is capable of any stupidity. Believe me, I know. I have spent the past twenty years proving it over and over again."

"It's only a matter of time, Marie. Inspector Villiers is no fool. He will be looking beyond the obvious and sooner or later he's going to come up with whoever staged this clumsy attempt to send Jeanne to the gallows."

Marie chuckles.

"Men. Amazing how you allow a pretty face to fog up your brain cells." She leans back again, her head resting on the back of the sofa as her eyes close.

I hesitate. I had come here hoping to enlist her cooperation, maybe not in support of Jeanne but in the hope that she would do nothing to poison the waters. From what she has said, I realize this is a fool's errand. Her hatred of Jeanne is deeply rooted. Nothing Claude or I could say will ever change that.

Then I notice that she hasn't moved. I lean closer and stare at her intently. A little snort escapes her lips. I look even closer. She's dead asleep. I get up. Quietly I head for the door and even more quietly I let myself out.

I climb into the Peugeot and settle in as Nate gives me a smile.

"Man, you are fast," he says.

"Drive," I growl.

Traffic's bad so it takes an hour to get back to the Frontenac. I check with Connie for messages. I have none except for Glenda Mae who called while I was out. This is my ever loyal secretary of six years without whom I cannot survive. A one time runner up for the title of Miss Mississippi she has the face of an angel, the figure of a Venus de Milo (with arms) and the brain of a Harvard PhD. Why she hasn't left me to run the studio I will never know. Maybe she's secretly in love with me and too shy to reveal her feelings. Naw, I think. Shy? Hardly. Besides she idolizes her husband Beau who, I have to admit, is a real hunk and a genuinely nice guy.

"Hi, it's me," I say to her.

"Hi, you," she says.

"What's up?" I ask.

"Nothing. I just wanted to hear your voice," she says. "Usually I get a call a day just for the hell of it. Not this time. Maybe you've caught up with a cute Canadian chick."

"No chance. I've just been busy."

"What happened? Somebody die?" she asks, almost laughing. I stay silent for just a second too long. "Oh, my God, you're kidding. Joe----"

"I'm okay. I've just gotten myself into the middle of something. It's nothing."

"I'll bet."

"I'll tell you all about it when I get back."

"If you get back. My God, boss, what is it with you and dead bodies?"

"Believe me, beautiful, I don't go looking for them."

I casually pick up a copy of Wednesday's Chronicle-Telegraph, the one that has Starr's lurid story on page one and I scan it as I talk.

"What's new on your end?" I ask.

"Nothing," she says. "Guess you heard about Gertrude Lawrence."

I frown.

"No, what about her?"

"Oh, Joe, I really thought you knew. She died last Saturday in New York. Cancer. The funeral was yesterday morning in New York.

"My God," I say quietly. It's hard to believe. She was the toast of Broadway in 'The King and I", her biggest hit ever. I'd been told she'd gone in for tests but when I heard no more about it, I assumed everything was okay.

"I sent flowers," Glenda Mae says.

"Good girl," I say. Miss Lawrence and I had worked together a couple of years ago on 'The Glass Menagerie'. She was theatrical as hell but at heart was a genuinely nice person. And young. That's what I can't get over. She can't have been more than fifty. How fleeting are the years.

After I hang up I sit back in my chair and continue to read over Mackenzie Starr's article. Something has caught my eye and now I realize what it is. I dig into my bottom desk drawer and pull out my Merriam-Websters dictionary which every self-respecting writer should have close at hand and I look up a definition. My suspicions are correct and I place a call to Claude Le Pen.

"How did you make out with Marie, Joe?" Claude asks when he comes on the line.

"Funny you should phrase it that way, Claude. She was set to ply me with booze so she could have her way with me but she miscalculated her own capacity for gin. I did discover what a miserable life she had with your partner and also the depth of her hatred for Jeanne, but, no, I never got to sweet talk her into laying low during the trial. I left her passed out on the sofa out at her cottage on Lake Clement."

"Disappointing," he says.

"If I can get her into a public place, I'll try again. Meanwhile I have a little chore for you."

"At your service."

"If you've still got the Wednesday morning paper with that diatribe by Mackenzie Starr, re-read it. He specializes in purple prose and this time he let it get out of hand. Somewhere near the bottom of the page he refers to Jeanne as a harlot. Now, Claude, there are a lot of terms he could have used like courtesan or mistress or gal-friend but he chose to call her a harlot and according to every dictionary that I've ever used, harlot is a direct synonym for 'prostitute'."

"Yes?" he says, not getting it.

"Whatever Jeanne may have been to your partner, she was not a prostitute and with her arrest and possible trial on murder charges, this story on the front page is not only defamatory but also prejudicial and greatly diminishes her chances of receiving a fair trial."

Claude perks up.

"Yes, I see. We demand a retraction."

"No, Claude, we sue for millions."

"Oh, no, I do not think---"

"Listen to me. We need to shut this jerk up and nothing succeeds like a good old fashioned lawsuit, particularly a sure winner like this one. Trust me, the paper will be very, very careful about what they print in the future and I can guarantee that whatever it is, it won't be written by Mackenzie Starr."

Still he hesitates.

"I don't know, Joe----"

"And then we let it be known that if the newspaper is even-handed in its coverage of Miss d'Arcy's trial, if there is one, we would seriously consider dropping the lawsuit as a gesture of good will."

More silence and then he says, "And this is how things are done in the United States?"

"If necessary," I say.

"Interesting," Claude says."So, Joe, you are what they call a hard ball player?'

"When I have to be."

"I will call Esther immediately. She will confer with Jeanne. I see no problem."

"Merci, mon ami,"I say.

"Il n'y a rien," he responds.

I hang up, pretty darned pleased with myself. We will be holding the city's largest newspaper at bay, Starr will no longer be writing slanted and scurrilous "news" stories and at least one automotive body shop specializing in Cadillacs will be making a few bucks at Starr's expense. All in all, a very satisfying moment.

I look up as Connie drops a large manila envelope on my desk.

"Hand delivered for you, Joe. I signed for it," she says.

"Thanks," I say to her back as she heads for her desk.

I pick up the envelope. In the corner is the return address, The Law Offices of Esther Laval. I open it up and take out a dozen sheets of paper. One looks like a police report. The other looks like the autopsy findings. I can't be sure because they are written in French. I am getting more than a little annoyed by this place. Road signs in French, menus in French, movies in French with English subtitles. I'm amazed they don't have the Home Guard posted at water's edge ready to repel an attack by the Germans. I wonder if Queen Elizabeth knows about this situation. The last time I looked Canada was a part of the British Empire, not a French colony like Bora Bora. I am annoyed no end until my gaze falls on Claudette, our bi-lingual typist-stenographer busily working away at her desk in the rear of the room.

I get up and walk over to her.

"Claudette?"

She looks up at me.

"Oui?"

"Sorry, I don't speak French," I say.

"If you did, I wouldn't have a job," she says. "And if I had no job, monsieur, my two little boys would go hungry and soon the bank would take away my house and I would be in the street, begging like some hag from 'Les Miserables' so thank you very much, M. Bernardi, for not learning French. I am in your debt."

I stare at her in disbelief. I'm not sure my mouth is wide open but it could be. After a moment, she breaks into a hearty laugh.

"Sorry, I couldn't help myself." she says. "I toil over here hour after hour in this deadly dull job. I just needed a moment of fun."

"Well, you got me good, Claudette."

"So what can I do for you?" she asks.

I hand her the sheets.

"Could you read these to me in English?"

She scans the sheets.

"This concerns Mlle. d'Arcy."

"Yes,"

"This is not company business," she says.

"No, it's my business."

"I have a special rate for personal business," she says. "That part about two young boys, that was all too true."

I nod and reach for my wallet I take out three 20's and lay them on the desk. She nods and scoops them into her purse.

"My workday ends at six. I will stay on and type these up in English and slip them under your door before I leave. "

I thank her and give her my room number and then start to walk away.

"M. Bernardi," she says.

I turn back toward her.

"I have known Mlle. d'Arcy for several years. She is a decent woman. She is not capable of this."

I nod and thank her again.

The phone rings at 11:20. I am already under the covers, half-asleep with the lights out. I don't want to answer it because at this hour, the call can only be bad news, but half my job is trouble shooting and so answer I must. I flip on the bedside lamp and lift the receiver.

"Yes?"

"Bernardi?"

"Who is this?

"You son of a bitch, you got me fired, you and that fat turd of a lawyer."

Now I recognize his voice.

"Go to bed, Starr. You're drunk."

"Wrong, fella, Very wrong. And tomorrow or maybe the day after I am going to prove it to you. I've got you in my sights, Bernardi."

"I assume that's supposed to be a threat."

"No, it's a promise. And you won't see me coming."

"You're an idiot," I say. "I'm hanging up."

"You cost me my job!!" he screams.

"You should have thought of that before you wrote that lousy story."

"I'm a reporter," he shouts just as loudly.

"Not around here you're not," I say.

There's a moment's silence. Then he speaks very quietly.

"Keep looking behind you, Bernardi. You won't see me but I'll be there and when I'm finished with you, I go after that lawyer."

"Whatever you have in mind, Starr, you can't get away with it."

"Sure, I can," he says and I can hear the smile in his voice. "You'll never even know it was me."

Click. He's hung up.

I replace the receiver, flip off the lamp and again curl up under the covers. This time sleep doesn't come as quickly.

CHAPTER NINE

I f this be a zoo, then the animals are in charge. The main floor of the Quebec Courthouse is alive with reporters, attorneys, voyeurs, and curious citizenry from every strata of society. Security is trying to keep order but the going is tough. Toes are being trampled, shins scraped, ribs jabbed with flying elbows and eardrums deafened by the noise level. These are the lucky ones.

Most will find a seat in the gallery when the Marchand trial actually gets underway. Out on the street are another hundred or so protesters with their signs (in French, of course) vilifying the defendant for literally taking the food out of their children's mouths. Or at least, this is what Claude tells me they say. I have no reason to doubt him.

The time is quarter past nine. Claude and I are standing off to the side by a door guarded by one of the security people. Claude is accompanied by one of his juniors who will sit second chair. In a few minutes the doors to Courtroom 3 will let the public enter in a controlled and orderly manner. At least that is the plan. I have no reason to worry. I have a seat reserved directly behind the defense table where I can watch the proceedings up close. I am curious about this trial, about Louis Marchand and about the peripheral people involved such as the Gonsalvo brothers and the Maggadino family from Buffalo. If I am to help point the finger of guilt in Daniel Bruckner's murder at one or more of them, I need to know more about this case.

Just then the door opens a crack. A security guard on the other side whispers something and our man nods, then taps Claude on the shoulder. He opens the door and the three of us are admitted. The courtroom itself is large and airy and except for the Crown Prosecutor and his team, it is empty. They are sitting at a table at the far end of the room. The defense table is directly ahead of us. Claude indicates the seat that has been reserved for me, then goes to the table with his assistant and lays down his briefcase. He crosses the room and he and his counterpart shake hands and exchange pleasantries. I have been told there will be no acrimony in this trial. Marchand has waived his right to a jury and his fate will be decided by Chief Magistrate Michel Berglund. According to Claude, the Crown will present it's case quickly and efficiently with a minimum of interruptions. Then Claude will put Marchand on the stand and will lead him point by point through an elaborate revelation about the workings of the fraud, naming names including dates and places of meetings with the Gonsalvos and two other men who worked for the Maggadinos.

I look back into the large gallery which is filling up quickly. I'm surprised to see Mackenzie Starr back in the section roped off for members of the press. Did I dream last night's phone call to my room? Maybe the news of his firing hasn't caught up with courthouse security. He turns his head slightly and sees that I am staring at him. He gives me a look that is more sneer than smile and then looks away.

At that moment, my eye is caught by two immaculately dressed men in expensive Italian silk suits who come down the middle aisle accompanied by one of the security guards. He leads them to two seats in the first row directly behind the prosecution table. If these men are who I think they are, they are getting a lot of courtesy from the courtroom staff and I wonder why.

I watch as Claude sees them and his body visibly stiffens. One of the men, the taller of the two, reaches across the railing, hand extended, but Claude ignores it. Words are exchanged. The man reaches to touch Claude's arm but Claude angrily shoves the man's hand away. He turns and grimly strides back to our table. He leans close to me.

"The Gonsalvo brothers," he says quietly.

"I thought so. Did he threaten you?"

"He offered condolences over Daniel's death. Such a tragedy, a man as young and vital as Daniel, he said. It goes to show, he said, that you never know when your time will come."

I shrug.

"Sounds like a threat to me," I say.

"And a not so subtle one, my friend."

"Maybe we should take them seriously," I say.

"I take my golf game seriously," Claude says. "Those two, let them rot in hell."

Now another door opens and a man is led in by a guard. He is well dressed in a dark blue suit and while he is not manacled, I don't need a name tag to tell me that this is the defendant, Louis Marchand. He is average height with ash-blonde curly hair and pale skin. His eyes have a watery look and his expression says it all. He wants this thing over with. He sits in a chair directly in front of me but pops right up, as does everyone else, when the clerk introduces the judge.

"All rise for the Chief Magistrate of the Court of Quebec, the Honorable Michel Berglund."

The judge appears from a door behind the bane and he takes his place in his high backed chair that overlooks the courtroom.

"Call the calendar," he says.

"Docket Number 185463, the Crown versus Louis Alfred Marchand."

"Ladies and gentlemen, you may be seated," the Judge says as he flips open a yellow lined legal sized pad which he will keep in front of him for the duration of the trial.

First come the opening statements. The Crown leads off. The prosecutor lays out the case in terms a first grader could grasp. He outlines what transpired, names Louis Marchand as the guilty party, and promises to present evidence that will leave no doubt as to Marchand's culpability. While he is speaking I glance over at the Gonsalvo brothers. From Bruckner's extensive notes on the case, I know that the tallest of the two is named Vito. He is also the oldest by two years. Dark in coloring and visage he is reputed to be the "smart" brother. He is the less violent of the two having been arrested a mere three times for assault and only once for attempted murder. He has never spent a day in jail. Potential witnesses against him have always had a propensity for disappearing at the most inconvenient times.

Vito's younger brother is named Salvatore. At five foot eight and two hundred and fifty pounds, he is called "Fat Sally". He has a pleasant face and smiles a lot. He is a patron of the arts, invests in musical comedies, serves on the board of the St. Catherines Ballet School for Young Ladies and tries to kill people who disagree with him. He, too, has a long arrest record for crimes of violence but no convictions. Together with his brother he owns a large chain of supermarkets in Ontario Province. The tax people have never laid a glove on either of them.

As the prosecutor winds down, I take one last look over at

the two of them. As I do, Vito turns his head and meets my gaze. He does not look away and I see something in his eyes that gives me a chill.

Now it's Claude's turn. He stands, glances at the gallery and then faces the judge.

"If it pleases milord, it is my privilege to stand here in this courtroom this fine Friday morning to defend a man who at his core is a decent man who may have acted unwisely but not with evil intent. We shall prove to you that Louis Marchand was duped by outsiders to betray the trust of his fellow citizens. We will name these outsiders and demonstrate to the court the frightening web that can threaten to strangle the best among us when evil men gain control of their lives."

I again look over the Gonsalvos. They are staring straight ahead their expressions betraying nothing.

By noon the first day is over. Confined entirely to opening statements this morning, the trial will start in earnest Monday morning at ten a.m. I am standing in the spacious lobby waiting for Claude who needs a few minutes with Marchand. I look around for the Gonsalvos but they are nowhere in sight. Phillippe Bachelet comes through the main entrance and waves as he spots me. He is here to drive us back to the law offices. He is not exactly a bodyguard but with tensions as high as they are, Claude is taking no chances. Phillippe is licensed to carry and he is carrying. He asks how things went. I told him well, though I'm no expert on the workings of the law.

Claude appears, ready to go and the three of us head for the main entrance. As we step outside, we find the Gonsalvo brothers waiting for us. Instantly, Phillippe interposes himself between Claude and the two brothers.

Vito manages a mirthless smile.

"Relax. We want no trouble," he says. "We'd just like to talk."

"We have nothing to say to one another," Claude tells him.

"I disagree, Mr. Le Pen," Vito says. "My brother Sal and I feel very badly about the mistakes Lou made while we were doing business and we would like to set up a substantial trust fund for his family as our way of supporting him in this dark time."

"Provided, of course, that he keeps his mouth shut."

I look around to see who said that and then I realize it was me. It's a terrible failing of mine. When someone is pitching bullshit, I just can't keep my mouth shut.

Vito looks at me, eyes narrowing. "And you are?"

"Joe Bernardi."

"Italian?"

I nod.

"And proud of it. How about you, Vito?"

His eyes narrow a little more. I don't think I've made a big hit with this.

Claude jumps in.

"Mr. Bernardi is a personal friend. He has nothing to do with all of this." Sal Gonsalvo steps forward edging his brother aside and bellies up to me. His eyes bore into mine and it's readily apparent that this is a man who enjoys inflicting pain.

"Then he would do well to keep his thoughts to himself," Sal says. "Back off," I tell him.

He doesn't move. He allows himself a knowing smile.

Vito puts his hand on his brother's shoulder. Quietly, he says, "Sal. Not now."

A moment and then Sal steps back, never losing eye contact. "And so, Mr. Le Pen," Vito says, "can we reach an agreement? Naturally there would be some sort of incentive in this for you."

"How many ways can I say I am not interested, Mr. Gonsalvo?

Now step aside and stop harassing me or I will summon the police. In this province, interfering with an officer of the court in the performance of his duties is a felony,"

Vito hesitates, then forces a humorless smile.

"We will meet again soon, perhaps. Good day."

He turns and walks away, his younger brother tagging close behind. They get into an obviously new white Citroen sedan parked across the street and drive away.

"Nice fellas," I say.

"Oui, tres jolie," Claude concurs, dripping sarcasm.

I am about to turn away when I see Mackenzie Starr across the street. He's been watching us and now his gaze is focused on the Citroen as it goes down the street. He looks back at me and then without acknowledgment, he turns and walks away.

Phillippe drives us to the law office. Nate McIver meets me there and takes me back to the Frontenac. By now he has become my official driver and I'm very glad to have him, both he and his snub-nosed .38 police special.

I check the production office for messages. There are none and so I go to my room and order a sandwich and coffee from room service. Last night, true to her word, Claudette delivered the translations to my room and I settled down to read them. I didn't get far. Exhaustion had caught up with me and so I laid them aside and went to sleep. Now I will study them in detail.

I take the police report first. The body was discovered shortly before seven a.m. by the housekeeper, a Mme. Brauner who immediately called the police. The police arrived at 7:18 and secured the crime scene. Inspector Luc Villiers arrived at 7:50 followed by members of the forensic team and the medical examiner. The initial time of death was set between one a.m. and two a.m. subject to revision upon closer examination. The cause of death was a single knife wound to the abdomen. The victim's loss of blood was substantial. Under "Blood" I find this additional notation. Examination of the blood at the scene revealed two types. Most of the blood was Type A, consistent with the victim. There was also a substantial amount of Type 0 Positive, source unknown.

The fingerprint team found three different sets throughout the apartment. One set belonged to the victim. The others are as yet unknown. An ashtray on the coffee table contained four cigarette butts. The brand was identified as Gitanes. On the table was a Ronson Queen Anne table lighter with one set of prints, person unknown. The lighter was bagged in evidence to be brought to the lab for further inspection. On the desk is a leather covered stationery ensemble consisting of a pencil caddy, a tray for note papers and a sheathe for a letter opener. The letter opener is missing.

Neighbors in adjoining apartments were queried. None saw or heard anything of value. (A note is included indicating that the apartment is exceptionally high-end with thick walls that effectively muffle sound from unit to unit.) The night receptionist in the lobby says that no one, other than residents, entered the building that evening. However, he did point out that someone with the proper key could enter the building from the underground parking facility and take an elevator to any floor, bypassing the lobby. Shortly after 9:30, Inspector Villiers ordered that Mme. Bruckner be located and brought to the apartment for questioning. She was found at a cottage on Lake Clement north of the city and brought to the apartment shortly after eleven a.m. She demonstrated shock at her husband's death but in no way indicated by word, deed or reaction that she had anything to do with his demise. This, according to Inspector Villiers.

There is more. Small details. A lot of obligatory police

department verbiage but I think I have the picture. I wonder how much strength it would have taken to thrust the fatal stab wound. I find my answer on the second page of the autopsy report. It was a soft tissue wound. Either a man or a woman would have been equally capable of inflicting it. The assailant appears to have been left handed. Jeanne is left-handed. The report goes on to say that the blade missed all vital organs and that the actual cause of death was loss of blood. It should have been a non-fatal wound and eminently treatable. The description of the wound would be compatible with the missing letter opener. The victim had scratches across his right cheek, possibly caused by a woman's fingernails. He has a badly bruised scrotum, indicating a physical confrontation.

There's more. Body temperature, extent of rigor mortis, weights and sizes of internal organs. Absence of foreign substances such as drugs or poisons. Alcohol content was cited as. 09%. Under anomalies, I find two curious notations. One, a minute amount of bandage adhesive was found on the left side of the victim's lips possibly indicating some sort of wound although none was found. And two, the victim's wrists showed minor abrasions as if he had been tied up at some point. Possible sex play is postulated.

I put aside the reports and rub my eyes. I am not a detective and I am not a forensic expert. I'm not exactly sure what I have just read and whether or not it helps or hurts Jeanne. If she is not being framed, fingerprints seem to place her at the scene unless the killer is a whole lot smarter than I am. I am logy and in need of exercise. I remember the swimming pool out back with mixed feelings and finally decide that, cold or no cold, I need to prime my system. I slip into sandals, a pair of swim trunks and a terry cloth robe and head downstairs.

Cold isn't the word for it. I feel like a Titanic survivor, treading water in the icy Atlantic with the ship going down behind me, chunks of the frozen berg floating all about me. I do two laps. I now have lost track of my fingers and my toes. I am stubborn but not crazy and I swim to the nearest ladder and haul myself out of the water.

Karl Malden and Brian Aherne are sitting at a nearby table enjoying a libation and smiling in my direction.

"Not cold, are you, Joe?" Karl says laughing.

"Invigorated," I say.

"Yes, I can tell by the icicle forming at the end of your nose," he says. Meanwhile Aherne has grabbed a towel and brought it to me.

"Thanks," I say.

"You're a braver man than I am, Joe," he says.

"Merely brain dead," I say toweling off.

"Well, my friend, you've proved that Lex Barker has nothing to worry about," Malden says. "Can we order you a drink?"

"Johnnie Walker neat," I chatter slipping into my robe and sandals. Malden signals the waiter while I walk around flapping my arms like a rabid chicken trying to get my circulation going. By the time my drink arrives I'm feeling pretty good and down half of it in one swallow. I pull up a nearby chair and sit.

"How goes the set?" I ask.

"If you mean how goes Mr. Clift," Aherne says, "I'd say quite well."

"For now," Malden says quietly.

I look over at him.

"I'm not sure I like the sound of that," I say.

"Maybe it's nothing," Malden says, "but Monty took a long distance call around three o'clock and when he returned to the set, he was very quiet. I might even say morose."

"Who was the call from?"

"Don't know and didn't ask."

This is not good. Monty when moody can be even more difficult to work with. I hope that the fragile detente I've created between him and Hitch is not in danger of collapsing.

I wish my companions well, drain my drink, and head inside, dreaming of a nice hot shower. When I walk into my room I find that a note has been shoved under my door. I open it up. It's from Claude. "Call me at office immediately. Urgent." It's not so urgent that I don't take my shower first and slip into something more comfortable than a business suit. Then I make the call.

"What's our problem?" I ask when he comes on the line.

'I'm not sure," he says." I got a call from Marie. She wants to talk. I think she has some sort of proposition."

"I'm not sure I trust her, Claude," I say.

"Well, it can't hurt to listen," he says. "Tonight. You and I. Her cottage by the lake. Eight o'clock."

"Why both of us?"

"I don't know. If what she has in mind helps Jeanne, fine. If not, we forget it."

I agree. He says he has more work to do at the office, that they will phone out for food. He suggests I pick him up as Phillippe is unavailable, due to a previous engagement with a very attractive real estate agent he met several months ago. At least that's who Claude thinks it is. Phillippe, it seems, is a very desirable bachelor in Quebec's social circles and steadfastness to one woman does not seem to be one of Phillippe's outstanding traits. I promise to be there at seven sharp which will give us an hour to get out to the lake. I call Transportation and get through to Nate. He promises to be out front at 6:45, not a minute later. I tell him to bring his friend. He knows which friend I mean. Always, he says.

True to his word, Nate is there with the engine running when I come through the door. I get in front and we take off. By now he's part of the team so I tell him what we're up to. He listens intently. I think he likes the intrigue. We pick up Claude just before seven and he slips into the rear seat of the car. He seems tired and I think he needs a break. He's worried about Louis Marchand and now Jeanne, and finally, we have this business with Marie, whatever it is, to deal with. I suggest he sleep in all weekend and recharge his batteries. He just laughs.

We pull away from the curb and head toward Rte. 175.

If I had been paying attention, I might have seen the white Citroen parked in the next block also pull away from the curb and start to follow us, a discreet twenty car lengths farther back.

CHAPTER TEN

At first the traffic is heavy. Fridays in Quebec City are probably like Fridays everywhere. Young men and women, through with work and looking forward to the weekend, primp for a date. Young marrieds may be heading for the local movie theater. If they have kids it may also involve hot dogs and hamburgers at a local diner or family restaurant. Whatever the cause, cars are on the road and the going is slow. It isn't until we reach the outer limits of the suburbs that we finally are able to pick up a little speed.

We haven't talked much. There isn't a lot to talk about until we hear what Marie Bruckner has in mind.

"Seems kind of funny," Nate says, "you two going to see the lady at this time of the evening way out in the middle of nowhere."

Claude shrugs.

"We need her. She doesn't need us. She gets to call the tune."

"I suppose," Nate says, checking his rear view for the third time in less than a minute. "Would you by any chance have back up following us, just in case?"

"No. Why?" I say.

"Because there's a white Citroen back there that's been following us ever since we picked up M. Le Pen," Nate says.

I turn and look through the back window. So does Claude. We are quickly losing the light but I can see well enough to know that Nate is right. I can tell from the expression on his face that Claude agrees. Moreover we both know who was driving the white Citroen at the courthouse this morning.

"Can you outrun him?" I ask Nate.

"I don't know," he says. "That's the new Traction Avant model. Lot of horses under that bonnet."

I look at Claude.

"What do you think?"

He shrugs.

"If it's them, and I think it is, then we give ourselves away by trying to speed away."

I nod in agreement.

"On the other hand we can't just lead them to Marie's doorstep," I say.

"No, we can't," Claude replies.

I turn to Nate.

"Floor it."

"You got it, boss," Nate smiles as the Peugeot jumps forward.

Darkness is falling fast now and Nate flips on the headlights. Behind us the Citroen has risen to the challenge. Now the question will be, can he catch us?

The suburbs are now far behind us. This stretch of Rte. 175 cuts through forests and farmlands and there are no street lamps. A half-moon hangs high in the sky flirting with dark rain laden clouds. The yellowish cast of the Citroen's halogen headlights seem to be drawing closer. One thing is certain. At the moment, we are the only two cars on the road.

"I've got it flat to the floor, boss," Nate tells me. "I can't out-run him."

"Then outsmart him," I say.

"Right," Nate says.

This section of the road is bordered by tall pines and in the moonlight they whip by noiselessly casting shadows across the macadam. Nate's eyes are searching ahead even as he contin-ues to fight for maximum speed from the Peugeot. A sign looms up on the right with an arrow pointing left. The legend reads 'Cremerie Bouchet'.

"Hang on," Nate says and without slowing, goes into a con-trolled skid that puts us onto a narrow gravel road that promises to lead us deep into the woods. I look back and see the Citroen try to slow for the turn but the driver overshoots it. He is hav-ing to back up. We are gaining time and distance. Our head-lights knife into the gloom. Luckily the road is fairly straight and Nate is not forced to slow down. But then, without warning, we break out of the forest and find ourselves speeding through a pasture. Up ahead several hundred yards away is a farmhouse and behind it, two large barn-like structures.

Suddenly Nate slams on the brakes and we skid forward on the gravel, turned sideways as we hurtle toward a metal gate stretched across the road. As we lurch to a stop, it's apparent that the entire property is fenced.

"What is this place?" I say.

"A small dairy farm," Claude replies as he turns and looks behind us. The lights of the Citroen are barely visible but he's coming in our direction and he's coming fast.

"Make for the farmhouse!" Nate shouts climbing out of the car. We scramble out after him and head for the gate. It's secured by a huge padlock but it's obviously not electrified. Despite his age Nate is up and over in one smooth move. Claude is having trouble with his climb and I give him a boost. He's heavier than I thought but I get him to the top of the gate. But when he tries to ease himself down, he slips and falls heavily on the metal cattle guard on the other side. He cries out in pain as Nate tries to help him to his feet. I make it over the fence and we start off but immediately we know we're in trouble. Claude can't put any weight on his left foot. We look back as the Citroen emerges from the woods and swathes us in the light from its high beams.

Nate leans down and pulls his pistol from its holster. He turns and fires off two shots in the direction of our pursuers. As he does, they cut the Citroen's engine and switch off the headlights. Now, except for the moonlight, it is dark and when the moon is suddenly obscured by a cloud, it becomes inky black. We grope our way up the road toward the farmhouse. Nate and I hold Claude between us as we half-carry, half-pull him forward. Three shots ring out and we can hear the bullets whine past, high above our heads.

We hit the ground.

"What the hell?" Nate says. "I've got a five year old nephew who can shoot better than that." He rises up kneeling and fires twice more in the direction of the gate.

I look toward the farmhouse as the porchlight goes on and a man steps out of the house carrying a rifle. He shouts something in French. Claude yells back at him. I hear a word I know. Surete. I think Claude is telling the farmer to call the cops.

Now we lie very still. We can hear a woman's voice as she shouts at the farmer from inside the house. He shouts back. Behind us, the Citroen's headlights are switched on and then its engine turned over. The car starts to back up and within a minute or two, it is heading back into the forest, it's red taillights receding into the darkness.

We get to our feet and continue to hobble toward the farmhouse. The farmer comes forward to greet us, still carrying his rifle.

It is now 10:15 and we are sitting on hard benches at Surete headquarters, awaiting the arrival of Inspector Villiers. We are not sure he is coming but we are prepared to sit here all night, if necessary. The farmer turned out to be a very gracious gentleman who called the police at our request. The flying bullets had caused no damage that he was aware of. His wife, not so gracious, is sure that in the morning the cows will give curdled milk.

The officers who arrived on the scene could not find that a crime had been committed and after taking our information, were prepared to let us go on our way. We refused, demanding that they escort us to Surete headquarters. If on the odd chance the brothers were lying in wait for another chance at us, the squad car guaranteed us safe passage back to the city.

Claude is feeling better. The police have taped up his ankle and provided him with pain killers. If it's no better tomorrow, he'll have it looked at. Meanwhile we sit and wait. If it were just me and Nate, we would probably sit until doomsday but one does not easily slough off one of the city's leading attorneys. And sure enough, at 10:25 Villiers appears dressed in formal wear sporting a top hat and an opera cape lined in red silk. He glares at the three of us as he places his top hat on top of a filing cabinet and then ushers us into his office. He does not ask us to sit and he does not waste time with the amenities.

"This had better be damned important," he growls as he continues to glare at us. And then his eyes settle on Nate. He frowns.

"Nathaniel?" he says curiously.

"Yes, sir," he says.

"What are you doing with these men?"

"I am employed by Mr. Bernardi, sir. Or rather by his studio."

"You retire after twenty-five years only to end up like this? A common chauffeur?"

"The movie studio was looking for men of a certain background, sir. Besides, they pay very well. I could not resist."

"Another two or three years and you would have been promoted to Inspector."

"Meaning no disrespect, sir, but unlike you, I have no independent outside income. I couldn't live on an inspector's salary. Oh, not even close, sir. My sainted mother continues to eat like a starving alley cat while my sisters spend a fortune on makeup, hair products, lingerie and other female niceties. I am doing my level best to get them married off, sir, but at 53, 55, and 58, do you think maybe I am mired down in a hopeless situation?"

He stares at Villiers deadpan and Villiers stares back. Anyone else would be laughing but Villiers sense of humor is still in the embryonic stage.

"All right, why don't you gentlemen sit down and let's hear what this is all about."

We sit and Claude lays it all out, starting with the Gonsalvo brothers' first threats to Daniel Bruckner weeks ago, then the veiled threats at the church door and finally the chase and shoot out at the dairy farm. Villiers leans back in his chair and tents his fingers thoughtfully as he listens.

"All right," he says. "First, did any of you actually see the Gonsalvo brothers in or near the Citroen this evening?"

We shake our heads. Claude says, "No, it was too dark, but there was no mistaking the car."

"Plate number?" Villiers asks.

We look at one another dumbly.

"Surely one of you must have gotten the plate number."

"As I said, it was dark," Claude replies. "But it was the same car."

"It might have been, M. Le Pen, but you are a lawyer. You know the requirements of the law. Proof, not supposition. New white Citroens? I understand the rental company at the airport has a half dozen of them available. Now here is what I think. You were chased by a white Citroen driven by a man who was sent to prison for ten years because of your inept defense of him and now, having been recently released, he is seeking revenge."

"That's preposterous," Claude sputters.

"Precisely. But it is no more preposterous than your unfounded assertion that one or both of the Gonsalvo brothers was at the wheel of the car that chased you this evening." He looks at the three of us thoughtfully. "Gentlemen, I understand your anger and your frustration and you would love nothing better than to prove that the brothers were M. Bruckner's killer. But it doesn't work quite that easily. Five weeks ago when M. Bruckner came to this office to report death threats to his person by the Gonsalvo brothers, I immediately investigated. The St. Catherine's authorities told me that the brothers were undoubtedly involved in a lot of shady dealings but personally, they hadn't had a run in with the law for over ten years. At their age and with their power, they hire people to do their dirty work."

"Doesn't that amount to the same thing?" I ask.

"It does, Mr. Bernardi, but we lawmen are fussy. We need proof. I checked. At the time your partner was killed, M.Le Pen, the brothers were at the St. Catherines civic center attending a fundraiser for the mayor who was running for re-election. Yes, they could have sent someone here to Quebec but that someone would have to know exactly where M. Bruckner was going to be at that time of night and how to gain entrance into the apartment house without being seen. And although this assassin is professionally a man of violence, I find it hard to believe that he doesn't bring a weapon but counts on finding a letter opener handy on the desk. And then immediately afterwards he has to run around the city looking for Mlle. d'Arcy and her car so that he can plant the incriminating bloody weapon. He does all this without leaving behind a fingerprint or any other piece of evidence to show that he was even in the city, let alone committing a murder. No, no, gentlemen, I have ample evidence to charge and try Mlle. d'Arcy and not one shred to involve the Gonsalvos."

"I know how it looks, Inspector," I say, "but you are wrong. Jeanne d'Arcy didn't kill anyone."

"Then bring me the proof, M. Bernardi. Trust me, I have an open mind but wishing and speculation will not absolve the young lady."

He gets to his feet,

"Gentlemen, you must excuse me. I promised my hostess that I would rejoin her soiree as soon as possible and I shall do so now. I leave you with one word. Proof."

He exits the room. We all look at one another.

"Well, at least we know where we stand," Claude says.

"Right," I say. "In second position behind the champagne and the pate de fois gras."

Outside the headquarters building we climb into the Peugeot. Claude asks to be dropped off at his office. He has people working tonight and they won't leave until he shows up. After we drop him, Nate and I head straight for the Frontenac.

"So, you're an ex-cop," I say to Nate.

He nods.

"I am," he says, "and glad of it. Here's the truth of it, Joe.

The early days were good but toward the end I could see where I was headed. An inspector spends a lot of time at his desk bogged down in paperwork. I saw no future in that so I took my pension, which is substantial, and started my own little chauffeuring service. It pays well enough but the best part is, I don't find myself cooped up in a stuffy office. I get about and meet people. I hire out to those I fancy and recommend my competitors to those I don't. My hours are my own and that's the way I like it."

I smile.

"I could learn to envy you," I say.

"Many a man does," he replies with a wink as he turns into the driveway that leads to the hotel entrance. Before I let him go, I ask Nate for a favor, now that I know he has connections with old friends in the Surete.

"The Gonsalvos are pretty high profile visitors to the city, Nate," I say, "so somebody's got to be keeping an eye on them. Can you find out what hotel they've been staying at and what's more important, what their activities were tonight?"

"I can try, boss," he says.

"If it's an imposition, say so. You didn't sign on to go back to police work."

"That I did not but Villiers made it clear he'll do nothing to help clear the woman which means it'll be up to us. For my part, I don't care one way or another but you care and if you care then I'll try to care."

"Fair enough, Nate. And thanks. I'm going to need you in the morning."

I get out of the car and then lean back in.

"Just not too early in the morning."

"Sleep well, boss. I'll be waiting in the office," Nate says as he gives me a high sign and drives off.

Inside, I check at the desk for messages. There are none. I wander down to the production office. Connie's left for the day but one of the other ladies is filling in. Again, I ask for messages and again there are none. I find this strange so I call Claude at his office. He has not yet closed up. I ask him if received any messages this evening while he was out. He tells me he did not.

Odd, I think to myself. Very odd.

CHAPTER ELEVEN

For once exhaustion swallows me whole. I don't hear room service deliver my breakfast at 7:30, I don't hear the vacuum cleaner in the corridor or the young people screaming and romping on the grass underneath my window. I am not blinded by sunlight streaming in my window and best of all I don't hear the newlyweds in the next room who seem to have no grasp on the time of day, propriety or moderation. I've only seen them once but if I were casting a movie, they would be playing the ring bearer and the flower girl. Are they really that young or at 33, have I become that old?

I stir at 11:45. By noon I have swung my feet into the floor and by 12:20 I have emerged from the bathroom, teeth cleaned and shaved and showered.

I'm about to down some now-cold coffee from the carafe on the room service tray when my phone rings. It's Esther Laval.

"You expressed some interest in visiting Jeanne at the jail," she says.

"I did," I say.

"Come by my office and I'll smuggle you in on the pretext that you are an associate."

"Thanks," I say.

"Were you sleeping with her?"

"Beg pardon."

"You heard me. I know all about these short-lived location romances you Hollywood people indulge in."

"I really don't think it's any of your business, Miss Laval," I say.

"It's Mrs. Laval and it is my business, young man. I'm going to have enough trouble convincing a jury that the lady's affection for Daniel Bruckner was noble and deep-rooted. I don't want to have to explain why she dropped her panties for a man she'd known for only two days."

"Rest easy. We were just colleagues."

"That's what she said. I wish I could believe you. My office, Mr. Bernardi. 2:45 sharp." She hangs up.

I like this lady. I have a feeling Jeanne is in good hands but even good hands can't make pork chops out of pig's feet,

When I finally get downstairs I find Nate sitting at my desk in the production office. He gets up as I approach.

"I hope you haven't been here long," I say.

"A couple of hours but it hasn't been a total waste. I have a date tomorrow night with Constance, the cute blonde at the desk by the door."

"I thought you'd learned your lesson, Nate. Two divorces and all that."

"Divorces, boss. I'm not yet dead."

"Good luck. What have you got for me?"

He takes a sheet of paper from his shirt pocket and unfolds it.

"The Gonsalvos checked out of the Manoir Victoria early this morning to catch an 8:15 Trans Canada flight to St. Catherines. They still had the Citroen and presumably returned it when they got to the airport. They had self-parked the car at the hotel instead of giving it to the valet so no one could be sure where they were last evening or if they'd taken the car or if they had, where they'd gone."

"So Villiers didn't have anyone sitting on them."

"Nope. You heard what he said, boss. He's got his killer. The brothers aren't his concern."

I check my watch.

"Let's take a ride out to the airport."

The Aeroport de Quebec is located in nearby Sainte-Foy and services most of the Canadian Airlines and some U.S. carriers. There are three car rental companies on the premises, Hertz and two Canadian firms, one of which, Les Voitures de Francais, has contracts with French car manufacturers like Renault, Peugeot and Citroen. This is where we're headed.

The girl at the counter speaks halting English. I speak no French. We don't get very far. I ask about the Citroen the Gonsalvos returned that morning. She thinks I want to rent a car. I tell her I am merely looking for information like how many miles did the car travel and were there any gas receipts and where were the stations where the gas was bought. Bewildered she hands me a brochure. Nate jumps in but things don't improve. Finally she gets it. She cannot give out this sort of information except to the police. By now there is a line forming behind us and the young lady, not to mention those in line, are getting impatient. We give up and go outside.

That's when Nate spots the kid washing off a blue Renault 2cv. Off to the side is a white Citroen, wet but drying off. It's just been washed. Nate asks the kid what time the Citroen came in this morning. He says he thinks it was around 7:30. When he washed it was there anything unusual about it? For instance, scratches on the side of the car where it might have been scraped by underbrush or maybe there were traces of gravel in the tires. No, nothing like that, the kid says.

While he's talking to Nate I walk over to the car and start to look it over. As I said it's clean and the kid's done a good job. I get down on my knees and look under the chassis hoping to find a small branch or twig jammed up in there but there is nothing. I look closely at the Michelin tires. No gravel. I stand up and stretch my back. That's when I see it. A small ding on the chassis just beyond the hood and below the windshield off to one side. It's elongated but not very deep, just the sort of dent a bullet might make if it grazed the car.

I call the kid over and ask him about it. He frowns. It's obvious this is the first time he's noticed it. He walks over to a table and rummages around, finally coming up with a sheet of paper. He brings it back to the car and I see it contains black and white outlines of the Citroen, left, right, front and back. In a couple of places on the sheet there are little red circles.

"What is it?" I ask.

The kid points to the ding.

"This is new. It was not on the car when it was taken from the lot."

"Are you sure?"

"Oui, monsieur. Before we send a car out we check for blemishes and dents. This one is new."

I nod and look around. There are a couple of dozen cars parked in numbered spots. Four of them are brand new white Citroen Traction Avants.

"How many of these white Citroens do you have for rent?" I ask him.

"Five," he says. "This is the only one that's been rented in the past few days."

I nod and share a look with Nate. Maybe, just maybe, we might be on to something.

As soon as we return to the hotel I put in a call to Claude Le Pen. On a Saturday morning this is no easy task and I finally catch up with him in the bar of his country club. He's just come off the golf course.

"I hope this is important, Joe," he says. "I make it a rule to forget work as much as I can over the weekends."

"I'll make it short, Claude," I say and proceed to tell him about the Citroen with the ding out at the car rental agency.

"Are you sure it was caused by a bullet? Could have been a stone," he says.

"That's what we need to find out," I say, "and we're not going to get any help from the cops."

"No secret there. I have someone I can call. Ex-Surete turned private. He'll be able to tell. If he says it was a bullet, we'll take it to Villiers."

"Good."

"Anything else?"

"I don't know. You tell me. You're a smart lawyer. You remember when I called you after we returned to the city on Friday night and I asked if you'd had any messages, You said you hadn't."

"That's right."

"I hadn't either."

"What's your point, Joe?"

"My point is, Marie Bruckner was damned anxious to have us drive out to the lake to talk with her but when we don't show up, she doesn't even place a phone call to see where we are. Why not?"

There's a moment's silence while Claude mulls this over.

"Yes, why not indeed? "He hesitates again. "There may be a simple explanation."

"There may be, Claude. When you find out what it is, let me know. I can't wait to hear it." I hang up.

At 2:45 I am sitting in Esther Laval's waiting room. She emerges from her private office carrying a brief case and a lavender umbrella. She has on a navy blue dress with yellow polka dots. Around her neck she wears a gaudy necklace of yellow and pale blue stones. Atop her head is a wide brimmed felt hat decorated with a yellow ribbon that hangs down to the middle of her back.

"Expecting rain?" I ask as I open the door for her.

"Young man, in my profession, we learn to expect rain, snow and the seven plagues of Egypt. I am prepared for the least of these." And with that she swaggers ahead of me to the staircase that leads down the street below.

As we pull away from the curb, Esther says to me, "There's a reason I've asked you to join me at the jail today."

"My chiseled Mediterranean good looks? My uproarious sense of humor?" I ask.

"Not even close, M. Bernardi."

I breathe a mock sigh. Disappointment is written all over my face.

"Mlle. d'Arcy and I have a cordial relationship," she says.

"Good," I say.

"Not good, young man. I do not need friendly and polite from the woman, I need to shatter her reserve and find out what's going on in that attractive head of hers. I suspect that you might be able to mess her up long enough for me to get a peek."

"Aha," I say. "Joe Bernardi, undercover inquisitor."

"As you wish. I know only that I cannot defend a stranger."

"Did she do it?"

"She says she didn't."

"And you believe her?"

"I operate from that premise."

"You didn't answer the question."

"For the moment I have given you the best answer I can," she says.

Now I'm troubled. Esther is sharp and she's been at this for a couple of decades. If she senses Jeanne is hiding something, she's probably right. But what and why? Client-attorney privilege is still alive and well in Canada. She's a fool if she's not telling Esther everything she needs to know.

With Nate driving we reach the jail in record time. He opts to stay in the parking area with the car, probably to avoid having to chat with former colleagues. Esther and I go inside.

Jeanne's not looking all that great. She's managed to comb her hair and apply lipstick but that's about it. She looks drab and acts it. I guess a few days in jail will do that to you. Or maybe the enormity of what she's facing is wearing on her. She gives me a big smile but it comes from her lips and not her eyes. We've been told not to touch and so we don't but I'd love to give her a big encouraging hug. I reach in my pocket and take out a fresh pack of Gitanes and toss them on the table along with a book of matches. Within seconds she has one lit.

We're gathered in a very small interview room. Esther has her briefcase open and her papers spread out. She's asked Jeanne some obligatory questions about her treatment here and she has no complaints. I tell her about the run-in with the Citroen at the dairy farm and couch it in the most inconsequential terms possible. She reacts with real concern when I mention the gunshots and when I finish she shakes her head.

"Joe, I want you to leave this alone. Please. I'm afraid you could get hurt."

"The Gonsalvos have left town," I say.

"And they could come back. I'm in good hands with Esther. Please say you'll back off."

I smile. "Can't do that, Jeannie. You need all the help you can get. Besides they shot at me. I take that very personally."

She nods.

"I can't understand that Inspector. Finding the bloody letter opener in my car. How stupid does he think I am? Does he really believe I would pick up that letter opener, stab Daniel, then take it with me and hide it in my car where anybody could find it? For God's sakes, we have a huge wide river right at the edge of the city. I would have tossed it in the water in a heartbeat."

She's right. Every day in every way Villiers proves he's a mediocrity as a cop, more interested in Quebec's social whirl than doing his job. On the other hand there are the fingerprints and the fact that the killer, like Jeanne, was left handed and the certainty that the killer had a key to open the access door in the garage. Jeanne's had such a key for months, dating back to the days when nothing seemed to matter except Love with a capital L.

"Is it possible Daniel was seeing someone else?" I ask.

"While he was seeing me? Impossible," she says.

"Answer with your head, Jeanne, not your heart," Esther says.

"I would have known," Jeanne says.

"Monday evening, after you dropped me at the hotel, why did you drive over to Bruckner's apartment?"

"I didn't. I went straight home," she says. She avoids my look. I'm getting very edgy. Esther may be right.

"What time?"

"I don't know. Was I supposed to check my watch? I'm a big girl now, Joe. I don't have curfew."

"Did anyone see you?" My tone is getting sharper.

"How the hell should I know?" she replies frostily.

"You might have seen someone. A neighbor, perhaps. Come on, Jeannie. Think!"

"Why are you asking me all these damned questions? I told you I'm innocent. Don't you believe me?"

"I don't know. Should I? Perhaps you were seen by someone walking a dog? Maybe a delivery van?"

"Stop it!" she cries out. "Why are you doing this to me?"

"I want the truth. All of it!"

She looks at me in a rage.

"You think I'm a murderess? You think I killed him? Damn you!"

"Did you kill him, Jeanne? Did you hate him that much?"

"No, no!" she wails as she starts to cry. "Why are you doing this to me? Leave me alone!" she sobs.

"I can't do that," I say.

I fall silent and so does she except for the muffled sobs. I glance over at Esther who is watching Jeanne carefully.

"I didn't kill him," she whispers, her body wracking with sobs.

I pause.

"No, I don't think you did," I say. "But I do think you are a very high strung young woman whose nerves are shattered and if you can't stand up to these questions when I ask them, the Crown Prosecutor is going to mash you into sausage and feed you to the jury, one patty at a time."

She stares at me wide-eyed and then looks away. Esther takes a clean handkerchief from her purse and hands it to her.

"Look, Jeanne," I say, "this is no fun for either of us but it's got to be dealt with. Now sit back. Breathe out. Relax." I push the cigarettes in her direction..

"Light up," I say.

She shakes her head.

"Not right away," she says.

"I know the so-called evidence looks overwhelming but most of it can be explained away," I tell her. "You're left handed. So what? So are a lot of people. You have a key to the door in the parking garage. Maybe the killer didn't even need a key. Maybe he just waited by the door until someone came out and before the door closed he slipped in. A fingerprint on a glass in the kitchen cabinet? It could have been put there months ago and the glass just hasn't been used in a long time. The cigarette butts in the ashtray? Somebody buys a pack of Gitanes, smokes a handful, saves the butts and leaves them behind in the ashtray. The only thing I can't figure is the lighter." I look at Esther. "It's brand new, right? Isn't that what the housekeeper said?"

"Yes, he'd just bought it and put it out on the coffee table the day before," Esther says.

"And so there's no way Jeanne's prints can be on that lighter." I look at her. "Can you explain that?"

She hunches her shoulders, shaking her head.

"So it's impossible," I say. And then I give it more thought. "Unless---"

"Unless what?" Esther asks.

"Unless there was another lighter just like it that Jeanne had handled some time in the past and the killer substituted one for the other and----" I stop. "No, that's too farfetched. It makes no sense."

"A lot of this case makes no sense. M. Bernardi, but there is a logical explanation for everything and in the end truth will out and we will prevail," Esther says.

I look up at the little window that was cut into the door. The guard's not watching so I take Jeanne's hand in mine and squeeze it gently. "Esther's right. Jeannie. Don't get discouraged. We'll figure it out."

She squeezes back and smiles but I see no hope there, merely resignation. Nothing I've said seems to have made a difference. She's as depressed now as she was when Esther and I walked into the room. For once the Bernardi optimism has fallen flat and there's nothing I can do about it.

CHAPTER TWELVE

aturday nights are always special on location and it doesn't matter much if you're in St. George, Utah, or downtown San Francisco. The pairing off starts in late afternoon. The prelude has been going on all week, the flirting, the joking and the probing. Marital status is of no consequence. Neither is the engagement to the young man/woman you left behind in Los Angeles. Only one rule applies to location flings and that rule is, there are no rules. Hundreds of miles away from day to day obligations and societal restraints, libidos are set loose without guilt or shame because everyone who participates knows that when they board that plane that takes them back to Los Angeles, a curtain falls. What was, never was. What happened, never happened. Loving husbands are reunited with loving wives. Protestations abound. Of course I missed you. How could I not? I thought about you constantly and to prove it I've brought you this beautiful pearl necklace. Children are hugged. Dogs are petted. All's right with the world.

I've participated in this ritual several times when I wasn't otherwise spoken for but for me, it gets old fast. I guess I'm not a roll-in-the-hay kind of guy. Call me old fashioned but I like sex to mean something. Maybe not a lot but something. And in the aftermaths I always feel awkward and uncomfortable which is probably why I don't play the game any more.

I'm standing in the middle of the production office scanning the movie times in the newspaper. John Ford's new film, 'The Quiet Man', has just opened at a theater about five blocks away. I've heard nothing but good things about it. There's something a little loser-like about going to the movies by yourself but right now I don't care. I need to drown myself in fantasy for a couple of hours because reality is depressing the hell out of me. I look over to the doorway. Connie is giggling with the young kid who tends bar in the Men's Grill. I suspect they have plans. I know she has plans tomorrow night with Nate. I met her husband once. An accountant. A quiet kind of guy who I hear is terrific with their kids. I wonder if he gets wild and crazy at those C.P.A. conventions in Bakersfield. The world sure has undergone some changes since the boys came marching home in '45.

I look up as Karl Malden walks in the room and looks around. When he sees me he smiles and walks over to me.

"Been looking all over for you, Joe," he says. "You got anything on for tonight?"

"Not really," I say.

"Good. We're organizing a poker game in my room this evening. You interested?"

I am. Jack Ford will have to wait.

"I'm in. Stakes?

"Hundred dollar buy-in, no rebuys."

"Who's playing?"

"You, me, Aherne, Otto from wardrobe. I'm looking for Monty. Have you seen him?"

"No. Have you tried the church?"

"They haven't seen him since breakfast."

"Maybe he's out sight-seeing."

"He was supposed to go out to Montmorency Falls this afternoon with several of the priests but he never showed up."

"And he didn't call?"

"No call," Malden says.

"Odd," I say.

"Not like him," Malden says. "Maybe we should notify the police."

"Bad idea. It'd be all over the city by midnight and in half the U.S. newspapers by morning."

"You're right."

"Get a hold of Anne. Maybe she knows where he is. Meanwhile I'll check Transportation and see if he ordered up a ride earlier today."

"I'm on it," Malden says heading for the door.

I sit on the edge of my desk and check with Transportation. They've had no contact with him. Now I'm starting to worry. Ninety-nine percent of movie fans are average folks who love their movies and love their stars. But there's that small group, that tiny percentage who make up the stalkers and the weirdos and with someone like Monty, as big a star as he is, out there alone in a strange city, anything is possible. The police are a last resort but if he doesn't show up soon, I'm going to have no choice. At that moment Connie gives me two quick buzzes on my intercom and I pick up.

"Mr. Bernardi?"

"Yes."

"This is Cosmo Claxton."

Who? Never heard of him.

"We met the other day when you were asking the crew about that newspaper article in the L.A. Herald Examiner. I'm the lens puller. I work with the camera operator."

Now I picture him. Short, elfin, lots of facial hair.

"What can I do for you, Mr. Claxton?"

"I'm sitting in a booth in a pub called The Bit and Bridle. Mr. Clift is with me."

I come alert.

"How is he?"

"Drunk,sir. God awful drunk," Claxton says. "He's asking for you, sir. He's getting quite insistent."

"I'm on my way," I say. "What's the address?"

"Just tell the cabbie. Everybody knows this place."

I head for the door, telling Connie to let Malden know I won't be joining the game. I opt for a cab instead of bothering Nate. It's Saturday night. He probably has plans. The cabbie looks at me funny when I tell him where I want to go. Once we get there it doesn't take me long to figure out why.

The Bit and Bridle is a falling down hole in the wall in a lousy part of town. The front window is so crowded with neon and decals that you can't see in which is probably just as well because once I step inside the front door, I realize the interior is just as dark and dingy as the exterior. I also notice something else. There's a lot of laughing and hilarity, a dart game in progress, a snooker table at the moment unused and five or six couples doing the Lindy Hop on the postage stamp sized dance floor. At the rear I see a door marked "Gents". I see no door marked "Gals." Probably unnecessary as there isn't a female in sight.

Two or three of the patrons give me a smile and a wink as I press through the crowd looking for either Monty or the little guy with the beard. A big bald guy tries to grab my arm and dance with me. I brush him off gently by telling him I'm going steady with Louis St. Laurent. By the time he figures out that Louis is his Prime Minister, he'll doubtless be in the arms of some other Ginger Rogers wannabe.

I spot Monty in the last booth at the far side of the room and slide in, opposite him.

"Hi, Joe," he smiles. His eyes are glazed. He's blotto.

At that moment Claxton is returning from the bar carrying a steaming mug of hot coffee. He slides in next to me.

"Thanks for coming, sir," Claxton says. "I didn't know what to do with him and he's just getting worse."

"How long has he been here?"

"Hours, the barkeep says. The fellas here know who he is but they've been leaving him alone."

Claxton nudges the coffee mug toward Monty.

"I brought your coffee, Mr. Clift."

Monty doesn't hear him or at least pretends not to.

"Drink up, Monty," I say. "It'll be good for you."

Monty looks at me, ignoring the coffee.

"She's not coming, Joe," he says.

"Who's not coming?"

"Elizabeth. Elizabeth's not coming, Joe. She called me yesterday. She said she can't come."

"I'm sorry to hear that."

"Something about the baby and the airplane. Her doctor said no. I don't think the doctor knows what he's talking about. What do you think, Joe? Do you think the doctor knows what he's talking about?"

"I have no idea."

"Neither does he," Monty says and then giggles. "He has no idea at all."

There's a half-finished drink in front of him and he reaches for it. I slide it out of the way.

"Coffee's better for you, Monty," I say.

"Hate coffee," he says. He slides over to the edge of the booth and looks out over the crowd. He looks back at me. "Queers," he says.

I say nothing.

He slides back into the booth.

"I hate queers," he says. "Disgusting people doing disgusting things." He picks up his coffee mug and takes a sip, then puts it down. "What am I doing here with these disgusting people, Joe?"

Again I don't respond. He takes another sip of the coffee.

"Why don't we go back to the church, Monty? You could get some sleep."

He nods. "Good idea. Did I tell you Elizabeth's not coming?"

"Yes, you did," I say. I take out my wallet and reach into a compartment where I keep a one hundred dollar bill for emergencies. This is an emergency. "Give me a hand with him," I whisper to Claxton.

We slide out of the booth and help each other get Monty on his feet. Between us we half-walk, half-carry him toward the bar. The dancers see us coming and step back out of the way, Claxton is too short to be much help but he tries. When we get to the bar I look around at the patrons who are staring at us.

"Mr. Clift would take it as a personal favor if you all could forget that he was here today," I say.

"No worry on that score, laddie," a voice pipes up from the back and a wave of assent crosses the room.

I smile. "Thanks, boys." I lay the hundred on the bar. "Drinks all around," I say to the barkeep. A murmur of gratitude wells up behind me as I start to take Monty outside. The big bald guy who wanted to be my dance partner blocks our way.

"Cab drivers talk too much," he says. "I'm parked right outside." He grabs Monty's arm and we head for the door.

A minute later we are stuffing Monty into the front of a

pickup truck with "BRUNO MULKEY—Building Contractor" painted on the front door panels. Amazingly, there's room for four across the front seat if we squeeze a little and moments later we are headed for Eglise Saint-Roch.

The priests are delighted to see him and the first one down the steps to help is Father Leo. I hear Monty tell him that Elizabeth is not coming. Fr. Leo is properly sympathetic as he and another priest grab Monty by the arms and help him into the rectory. We get back in the truck. Bruno has volunteered to drive me back to the Frontenac.

We sit in silence for a minute or two and then I look over at Cosmo Claxton.

"What do you hear from Astrid Ankers?" I ask.

He looks at me and then looks away quickly.

"You are the one who fed her the information about the situation on the set." It's a statement, not a question.

He is silent for a moment and then he says, "She threatened to write about me."

"That you were a homosexual."

"That's right. Nobody knows. I don't flaunt it. I don't know how she found out."

"And she threatened to expose you."

"She said she wanted a story. She didn't care what as long as it would stir things up."

"So it was either Hitch and Monty or you."

"That's the way she put it."

"She lied. She never would have gotten it past her editor."

He looks at me confused.

"I didn't know," he said.

"Well, now you do," I say. Bruno has pulled up to the hotel entrance and I get out. Claxton looks at me anxiously.

"Mr. Bernardi, what do I do tomorrow? About work, I mean?"

"You show up," I say, "and if you hear from that woman, you let me know and I'll handle her."

He nods with a grateful smile. I thank Bruno for the ride and hurry inside. It's only ten past eight. Plenty of time to join the game in Malden's room. Then I remember I left my buy-in bill on the bar at The Bit and Bridle. I have seven bucks left in my wallet. No one's in the office so I can't get reimbursed with petty cash and I've missed the 7:25 showing of "The Quiet Man". I decide to go to my room and order room service. I stop by the gift shop to buy a book. Most are in French. I'm intrigued by one published in English entitled "How to Get Rich in Washington" by a guy named Blair Bolles. I already know the answer in two words: Get Elected. I'm curious to see how he is going to expand these words of wisdom into 323 pages.

So off I trudge to my room, book in hand. Just another riotous night on location in the glamorous movie business.

CHAPTER THIRTEEN

Bells, bells, bells.

How could Poe have missed them? He was inspired by Christmas bells and wedding bells and alarm bells and the deep sonorous intoning of funereal bells but not a word about the Sunday church bells that summon the faithful to the altar to worship Him in all His glory.

They started at six o'clock, waking me from a sound sleep. It is now just past eleven in the morning and still they continue. Loud, overlapping, seemingly unceasing. I don't know exactly how many churches there are in Quebec City but I think it's even money it may hold the per capita world record. If God decided to fashion himself a little pied a terre here on Earth, I suspect this is where he'd locate it.

I'm a non-believer. Always have been but even more so after experiencing the horrors of the war in Europe. I'm not proud of it. In fact I envy those blessed with faith in the Almighty and Life Everlasting. I try to live by the Christian ethic but the idea of Divinity escapes me. Maybe some day I will have an epiphany but until then I will just have to muddle along, making the best of my agnostic life and doing my utmost not to bring misery to my fellow man.

I am dressed and ready to face tonight's proceedings which are already starting to fray at the edges. With Jeanne in jail, I'll have to oversee every detail on my own. We also may have a table without a host unless Monty makes a remarkable recovery, physically and emotionally, from yesterday's overindulgence. I can always fill in but who wants to have dinner with a press agent? I know I wouldn't.

Before I go downstairs to the production office, I call Eglise Saint-Roch. Fr. Leo has just returned to the rectory after having celebrated ten o'clock mass. He tells me that Monty went to bed immediately yesterday and is still asleep. I thank him and ask him to call me as soon as Monty is up and about. He says he will.

The production office is nearly deserted. Sherry Shourds is at her desk poring through piles of paperwork. A production supervisor's work is never done and Sunday is just another day on the schedule. Connie's absent. The young girl taking her place at the main desk is maybe 16 and that's stretching it. I smile as I walk in with the Sunday paper under my arm and a container of coffee in my hand. I tell her my name in case someone phones me. Her name is Angelique. I notice a French-language movie magazine on the desk by her half-finished Coke. A sexy John Derek smiles up from the cover. I wonder if Angelique's parents know that she is associating with movie people.

I sit down at my desk, take a sip of coffee and then start to rummage through the morning paper. The front page is heavy on Quebec and light on the rest of the world but I spot two items of interest below the fold. Eisenhower, who is running well ahead in the polls against Stevenson, has just pledged to go to Korea and put an end to this unpopular war that has sapped the strength of the American people. There's also a short squib involving Charlie Chaplin who has been denied re-entry into the United States after vacationing in Europe. The Commie scare hasn't abated. If anything, it's gotten worse. I don't need this aggravation. I go in search of news less depressing.

It takes a while. Finally I spot a major story about the Quebec City Aces, the local hockey team which plays in something called the Quebec Senior Hockey League. Not exactly the Canadiens or the Maple Leafs but Quebecers don't seem to care. At least their sports writers don't. I scour the pages looking for news of the major league pennant races. I finally find yesterday's scores and the standings in a little box at the bottom left column of the third page. Without a magnifying glass, I am tempting serious eyestrain but I do my best, grumbling to myself that these Canadians have no clue as to what constitutes major league sports.

The news is not good. My beloved Cardinals are mired in third place and with two weeks to go, have no chance of overtaking the Brooklyn Dodgers. This means that the National League will be humiliated in the World Series when the Dodgers once again collapse like a punctured balloon at the hands of the New York Yankees. The wag who once said the only sure things in life were death and taxes never heard of the bums from Ebbets Field.

I hear two sharp buzzes coming from the desk next to me which is unoccupied. I look toward the front desk where Angelique, her brow furrowed, is trying to make sense of the phone system. I hear two buzzes from the desk in back of me. Also unoccupied. Angelique looks over at me frantically.

I call it to her. "Is that for me?"

"Oui, monsieur," she calls back.

"I've got it," I say with a wave.

She smiles and nods gratefully as I pick up.

"This is Joe."

"Bonjour. Claude here, Joe."

"Bonjour, Claude," I say.

"I dislike disturbing you on a Sunday, my friend, but I thought you should know. After your call about the rented Citroen and the blemish next to the windshield, I called my friend and asked him to get right on it. He went out to the airport but by the time he got there they'd already sent the car to the body shop for repair. At the body shop he found the blemish already repaired and the fresh paint drying."

"Damn," I mutter quietly,

"I agree," Claude says. "So although we may speculate, Joe, we have no proof that a bullet was fired at that car."

"Do you think they'll be back?" I ask.

"The Gonsalvos? I don't know," Claude says. "If their intent was to intimidate they'll wait to see what I do. When I continue on, which I am going to do, then we shall see what sort of move, if any, they will make."

"Have you told Marchand?" I ask.

"No, it would only terrify him," Claude says.

"But it doesn't terrify you," I say.

"I am concerned, my friend, but I cannot let that stop me from doing my duty. If I did I have no business being an attorney."

"If I were you, Claude, I would have Philippe Bachelet, your private detective, at your side twenty-four hours a day until this trial is over."

"Unnecessary," he says. "And what about you, Joe? What makes you so sure it wasn't you they were after when we were attacked?"

"Me? Why me?"

"If they killed Daniel and have gone to a great deal of trouble to point suspicion at Jeanne d'Arcy, they are certainly not happy with your efforts to prove her innocence. It is possible that you may be in as much danger as I, perhaps even more."

"I have Nate McIver," I say.

"So you do," Claude says. "Let us hope you will never actually need him. A bientot," he says and hangs up. Slowly I follow suit.

I lean back in my chair, discouraged. Jeanne's in jail at the mercy of a closed-minded police inspector who, even though all the evidence points to Jeanne's guilt, refuses to look at the case objectively. What can I do about it? Not much. I am embroiled in a location shoot which threatens to shatter at any time, given Montgomery Clift's personal insecurities, Alfred Hitchcock's notorious lack of patience with actors, and some members of the press like Mackenzie Starr who would like to blow our location shoot to smithereens to enhance their own journalistic careers. So, given all that, I really haven't got the time to devote to helping Jeanne but if I don't, who will? Not Esther Laval who is a lawyer, not an investigator. Not Claude Le Pen who is in the middle of arguing a critical case which may be at the heart of the murder for which Jeanne has been arrested. Not Phillippe Bachelet who is Le Pen's man, not mine, even if I knew enough about him to trust him which I don't. So here I am, the circus seal, trying to balance a beach ball on my nose without falling off my stool. I get up with a sigh. Tonight we party. Tomorrow things may improve. I marvel at my capacity for self-delusion.

It's nearing five-thirty. The press dinner starts at six. I am in the small banquet room checking last minute details. Five tables with eight place settings each have been set. Everything is first class from the china to the silverware to the crystal goblets. An expensive cabernet and a chardonnay have been placed on each table. The open bar is well stocked and we have three bartenders to ensure that no one will have to wait overly long to get a buzz on. Two photographers are on hand to shoot the members of the press shaking hands and chatting with the celebrities. Over in the corner is a table holding forty press kits which will be handed out at the end of the festivities. Each kit contains photos. bios, a copy of the script, and quotes from the principals (some of which are things they actually said). And finally adjacent to the tables is a small platform about eight inches high holding five armchairs. During coffee Hitch and the stars will field questions from our guests.

Except for one minor setback, I am ready. The setback is Monty's disappearance from the rectory around three o'clock. Father Leo called at three thirty, brimming with apologies. He never saw Monty leave. There is no note, no explanation. With trepidation I have phoned The Bit and Bridle but he's not there and they have promised to call if he shows. I've queried the other cast members. They haven't heard from him. Again, I'm concerned, not so much for the dinner because we will make it work no matter what, but for Monty himself. Where is he? What's he doing? Is he safe? All questions I can't answer and I haven't got time to send out a search party.

Karl and Brian are among the first to arrive. They are quick to tell me that I missed a terrific poker game last evening. No, neither of them won. In fact all the money was scooped up by the propmaster, a softspoken Acadian who said little, smiled a great deal and won all of the big pots. I think I'm glad I wasn't there.

The press starts to drift in. The level of chatter increases. By six-thirty we have close to a full house. Hitch is weaving his way through the milling throng, smiling, throwing out bon mots, and generally endearing himself to everyone. Our photographers are grabbing shots of everything and everyone. Anne Baxter, who is here unattached and, it is rumored, about to divorce John Hodiak, is surrounded by four eager males who seem not to have left her side since she first walked in the door. The bar is doing a thriving business but no one has become obnoxious or combative. Canadians seem to be civilized drinkers. Maybe it's all those churches.

And then I look over toward the entrance and see a familiar figure standing in the doorway. Oozing relief from every pore, I hurry over to him.

"Hi, Joe," Monty says. "Sorry I'm late."

"Not a problem," I say. "How are you feeling?"

"Fine," he says. "I spent the afternoon over at the Plains of Abraham at Battlefield Park and lost all track of time."

"Well, everyone's been asking about you. They'll be glad to see you."

"We'll see," he says. Then: "Listen, Joe, thanks for yesterday."

"No thanks needed, Monty," I say.

"No, I made a damned fool of myself. I get to feeling sorry for myself, down a snootful and it happens. Anyway, it won't happen again."

"Good," I say, "but if it does, I'll be there."

He smiles.

"You know, Joe, I'm really lousy at these press things but for you, I'm going to do my best," he says. "See you later." I watch as he walks over to one of our guests who is standing by himself nursing a drink. Monty puts out his hand and they shake and start to chat. Good start, Monty. You're better at this than you think.

I feel someone tapping me on the shoulder and I turn to face

Byrne O'Malley, our head security guy, who's stationed himself in the corridor to keep out the uninvited.

"Mr. Bernardi, I got a guy out here with an invitation but no press credential. What do I do with him?" he asks.

I look past O'Malley's shoulder. Standing in the middle of the hallway is Mackenzie Starr looking in my direction with an icy stare.

"Leave him to me, Byrne," I say as I brush by him and go to confront Starr.

"What are you doing here?" I say gruffly.

"I've got an invitation."

"We sent you that when you still had a job."

"I'm free lancing," Starr says.

"Not here you're not," I reply. "Credentialed reporters only."

"Look, Bernardi, I don't give a fig for your film or your movie stars, I'm here to see you."

"About what?"

"Tell me about Friday evening."

"I don't know what you're talking about."

"Route 175 north of the city, a car chase, gunshots exchanged."

"Really? Where'd you get all that?"

"I have my sources."

"Your sources are nuts."

"I've already talked to the dairy farmer and his wife."

I hesitate for a split second.

"Well, then, I guess you have your story," I say.

"Who was chasing you? Why? What were you and Le Pen doing out in that part of the city at that time of night?"

"You mean you don't know? Well, just make something up. That seems to be your modus operandi."

He shakes his head angrily.

"Don't be a jerk, Bernardi. I've got enough already for a decent story and I'll go with it if I have to. And if I have to make educated guesses I'll do that, too. This is my ticket back onto the payroll at the Chronicle-Telegraph."

"You cut your own throat last Wednesday with that article about Jeanne d'Arcy. Now get out."

"What do the Gonsalvo brothers have to do with Friday night?" he asks, refusing to back down.

I turn and signal to O'Malley. He hurries over.

"Let's take this sack of garbage out to the front door," I say.

He grabs one arm and me the other as Starr struggles.

"Side entrance would be less public, sir," O'Malley says.

"I know," I say. "That's why we're taking him out front."

Starr struggles mightily but we get him out to the main entrance. A dozen or more people waiting for cabs are staring at us in disbelief. I look Starr squarely in the eye.

"If you come back, I call the cops and have you arrested."

I turn and go back inside leaving O'Malley to drag him to his car and make sure he leaves the premises.

Back in the banquet room, dinner is being served. I'm sitting at a table across from Monty who is conversing quietly and thoughtfully about the state of Hollywood, films, the art of acting, and is it true he's been signed to play Prewitt in the upcoming production of 'From Here to Eternity'? (It is.) At times I catch his eye and he actually seems to be enjoying himself.

After dinner I organize the Q&A and I might as well have left the actors out of it. Hitchcock holds sway as only he can with his pixie-ish sense of humor, irreverent outlook on life and encyclopedic memory of every film he has ever directed. One reporter asks him what it was like working with Tallulah

Bankhead. "Interminable." he replies. "Next question." He is asked how long he thinks a movie should be. He takes a moment and then says the length of a film should be directly related to the endurance of the human bladder.

I'm scanning their faces and I can see that we have them exactly where we want them. Throughout the evening our stars have gone to great pains to say what a marvelous working environment we have going for us, or in Hollywood terms, a "happy set". By this time any thought of friction between Hitch and Monty has been forgotten.

By nine-thirty the room has emptied out. I've said my good-byes to the press, thanked my co-workers for all their help,and been thanked in return by both Hitchcock and Alma for organizing such a relatively painless fraternization with the press. Now I am exhausted, adrenalin gone, feet sore from standing and butt sore from sitting. I am lounging on one of the chairs. My shoes are off, my feet are up, my tie is at half mast and I have a half-full brandy snifter in my right hand. The hotel staff is hard at work clearing the tables, dismantling the platform, packing away the unused booze and vacuuming the carpet upon which, happily, no one heaved their cookies.

I've seen the schedule. Eleven more days of location work here in Canada and then we're back to the States to finish up on the sound stages. I think of Jeanne d'Arcy sitting in a tiny cell down at the city jail and wonder what, if anything, I can do for her before I must go. If I am unable to make progress I will feel guilty about leaving even though I have no choice. Tomorrow might be a good time to make a miserable pest of myself because I firmly believe that unless I start poking around this investigation with a sharp stick, Jeanne is going to be railroaded into a life in prison for a murder she did not commit.

"Joe?"

It's a woman's voice. She's right behind me. And almost immediately I know. This isn't just any woman.

I turn in my seat and look up.

Jillian Marx is smiling down at me.

CHAPTER FOURTEEN

've been sleeping with Jillian for the past seven months. This makes me a very lucky guy. It started with a blind date that my ex-wife Lydia was trying to arrange. I managed to beg off but Jillian was having no part of my reticence and bullied me into taking her to lunch the following day. Reluctantly I agreed. Best decision I ever made. In addition to being sexy and sultry with a libido as active as Mt. Kilauea, she is smart and sassy with a sense of humor as sharp as one of King Gillette's blue blades. She writes and illustrates kiddie books and thinks I am a genius just waiting to explode onto the literary scene. It's not every man who gets to sleep with a beautiful woman who is both mistress and acolyte.

I get to my feet, take her in my arms and kiss her. She responds in kind.

"What are you doing here?" I ask when I finally come up for air.

"I missed you," she replies.

"I thought you were on a book tour," I say.

"It starts Wednesday. San Francisco to Portland to Seattle with a lot of stops in between. Then we head east."

"How long?"

"Seven weeks, maybe eight."

"I'll be back in the city a week from Thursday," I say.

"I won't. Can't be helped. A girl's got to make a living."

I take her by the arm and lead her toward the doorway.

"Shall we go upstairs?"

"Not just yet."

"Drink at the bar?"

She shakes her head.

"I've been hanging around the dining room and the bar for the past three hours. I need fresh air," she says.

"Sounds good to me," I say.

It's brisk out. Cool but not cold and so far the fresh air coming up off the water feels good. We walk along the hotel pathways that overlook the St. Lawrence River and look down at the scows and freighters that glide noiselessly in both directions. To the east are the lights of the Old Town. Across the river we can see the glow of activity from Levis, the adjunct city which has yet to retire for the evening.

"Did you leave your luggage with the concierge?" I ask her.

She shakes her head. "I just have one small overnighter. I left it at the hotel at the airport."

I laugh. "That was a silly thing to do," I say.

She shrugs.

"I won't be staying long," she says.

It's the way she says it that causes me to stop. She also stops and turns to face me.

"I have a flight back to Los Angeles first thing in the morning," she says.

Now I'm really puzzled.

"You flew all the way across the continent to spend one evening with me?" I ask.

"Yes. Are you making any progress with Mr. Cockburn?"

she asks me. Cockburn. Damn it. I should have known she'd find out about him. I think I should say something but I don't because I don't know what to say. "I've known for several weeks now, Joe, that you are still trying to find Bunny." she continues.

"I'm worried about her," I say lamely.

"Yes, of course. That's one of the things I admire most about you, Joe. Your loyalty. To her. Perhaps not to me."

"Jill, I---"

"Don't explain. I understand. I've always understood, actually. You're a man without guile, Joe. Easy to read. Do you remember back when we first started seeing each other, I asked you about Bunny. You said she was gone. You said she was out of your life. You said you didn't expect to hear from her. You said it all with the exception of one thing. You failed to tell me you were still in love with her."

I look out over the river.

"God's truth, Jill. I didn't know what I thought."

"Don't quote God to me, Joe. I know you better than that," she says sharply. "There's a staircase ahead on the left. Let's walk down to the street."

I walk alongside her as we descend the long flight of stairs that leads to the Boulevard Champlain below. The temperature is starting to drop and I am starting to feel it. My suit jacket is no match for the increasingly frigid Canadian night air.

"Leaving God out of it, Jill, I meant what I said. As times passes I think I'm in danger of idealizing Bunny to the point where no woman could live up to this flawless portrait I've created. That's not fair to you or to any woman. I know what I thought she was. I don't know what she has become or what she will be in the future and I have to find out."

She smiles. "Elegantly thought out and well articulated," she says.

"I mean it, Jill," I say.

"I'm sure you think you do, Joe. I don't. "

We've reached a landing halfway down to the street and Jillian stops to light a cigarette.

"Your first one tonight," I say.

"I'm trying to quit," she says blowing a cloud of smoke into the air. "I knew after a week that I wanted to marry you, Joe. After two weeks I also knew that you didn't want to marry me."

"Jill, I---"

"Don't deny it, Joe. You're a bad liar."

"I never knew that marriage was part of the equation. You went out of your way to assure me of that."

"Well, I lied!" Jillian says sharply. "All women lie about things like that. If we didn't we'd have run out of people a long time ago." She takes a long drag on the cigarette and then smiles at me. "Would you like to get married, Joe? It's not hard to arrange. I did some research just in case. Tomorrow morning we go to the Municipal Clerk's office and get a license. Tomorrow afternoon we get married and just about anyone can perform the ceremony. The Mayor, a Judge, a Justice of the Peace, a Borough Council member, even a deputy clerk. Oh, and there's no blood test and no waiting. All you need is a driver's license and a passport. So, what do you say, Joe? Are you game? I'll promise to love, honor and obey if you will."

Her eyes are burrowing in on me. I look away.

"I thought as much," she says. She walks over to a nearby bench and sits down. There's a faraway look in her eyes and she's deep in thought. I move to the bench and sit down next to her. I try to take her hand. She pulls it away.

"Jill, I never lied to you. Not knowingly," I say.

"No, I don't suppose you did," she says. "Maybe you should have. Maybe that would make this easier."

For the second time I'm on red alert. What does she mean by 'this'? Is she dumping me? Is that what this is all about? She flies four thousand miles to give me the old heave-ho when a phone call would have done just as well?

"I would have married you in a heartbeat, Joe. Where you went I would have gone. No complaints. No regrets. No second thoughts. At 37 I was running out of options and suddenly I run into the guy I've been looking for all my life. For a few days, maybe a week or two, I think it's mutual until I realize he's a man dealing with demons. Wherever we went, whatever we did, Bunny was there, silent and unseen. I tried to fight it but I couldn't and after a while I didn't try. I decided to take what I could get and let the rest go."

I look at her curiously. Another strange remark. Our eyes meet.

"I'm pregnant, Joe," she says.

I hear her but for a moment it doesn't register and then it settles in on me and I feel an icy cold knot forming in my stomach. The cold starts to spread to the rest of my body as a breeze disturbs the night calm. I shiver.

I try to think of something to say that is intelligent or sympathetic or at the very least comforting and all I can think of is, "Are you sure?"

She smiles gently.

"Yes, Joe," she says, "I'm very sure, which is why I am here, to tell you face to face, because in eight weeks when I return to Los Angeles, my condition won't be much of a secret."

"But I thought, I mean, you said you had that covered," I stammer uncertainly.

"And I did, until near the end."

I frown. Did I hear that right? Did she deliberately stop using preventive measures in the hopes of conceiving a child? It certainly sounds that way. Now fear is giving way to anger.

"I see," I say coldly.

"No, Joe, you don't see," she says. "Look, you're not the only one who hasn't been totally honest. In some ways I have a lot more to answer for than you do."

Nervously she lights another cigarette. This quitting business seems to be losing traction.

"About a year ago I got tired of being an unseen Mommy to all of my thousands of readers. I wanted a child of my own and I knew I was running out of time. I began seeing men, all kinds, almost all of them unacceptable. A lot of the time you don't know if an apple is rotten until you bite into it. I did a lot of biting in those days. I became manic. My doctor had given me two good years, maybe three, before conception became difficult if not impossible."

I shake my head. This is no shake down. This is something else entirely and I don't like it.

"So you were running around looking for an acceptable sperm donor, is that it?"

"Don't put it that way," she says.

"No? How should I put it?" I ask angrily.

"Joe, please. I've lived alone all my life. Yes, you're right. I really wasn't looking for a husband. I liked my life just the way it was, quiet and without complications, but I was willing to take a husband if it came down to that."

"And wouldn't he have been a lucky fellow?" I say sarcastically.

"Not you, Joe. From that first meeting, never you. You were special."

"Thanks."

It's easy to see that I'm hurting her and I don't like myself for it but I'm angry. I've been badly used by this woman who I have liked and admired, a woman I might even have come to love some day, and a woman who is carrying my child that I already know without being told I will have nothing to do with.

"Don't be angry, Joe," she says.

"And how should I be, Jill? Overjoyed? It's not every guy that gets to be treated like a sperm bank. And I wasn't even in on the joke."

I can see her grit her teeth as she looks away.

"Go ahead, Joe. Don't stop now. If the idea is to hurt me, it's working." She faces me. "Go on, whatever you have to say, I've said it to myself a hundred times. I've used you and betrayed you and anything you can think of to say I agree with. I wish I'd had the guts to be honest with you but I didn't and I'm sorry for that, really truly sorry."

I can see her trembling and I think about the courage it must have taken for her to fly out here to tell me this. Not a letter, not a phone call. That would have been easy. She's chosen to do this the hard way.

I hesitate for a long time, trying to let the anger wash away.

"How far along are you?" I ask.

"Four months," she replies. "And as I said I couldn't bring myself to tell you on the phone and with the book tour looming, I couldn't wait."

"Hence the overnight plane trip."

"Yes."

"You're going to give birth to this child whether I like it or not."

"Yes."

"And an offer of marriage is not expected nor even wanted?"

"That's right."

"So I can presume I am to have nothing to do with the child's rearing and support."

"That's correct, Joe."

"I could give you a lot of trouble over this, Jill."

She nods her head. "I know. But you won't."

She's right. I won't.

"Child support?"

She shakes her head in annoyance.

"For God's sake, Joe, I'm rich. This baby is not going to want for anything."

"Not even a father?" I say.

She looks up at me sharply, eyes flaring.

"I'll make it work," she says.

"And if you can't?"

"I'll make it work. I have to."

For the first time since I have known her I see tears forming in her eyes and in a moment little rivulets are streaming down her cheeks. I take her hand. This time she does not pull away. She squeezes my hand hard.

"What can I do?" I ask.

"Nothing," she replies.

"I want to help," I say.

"You can't."

"No, I'm sorry, you can't shut me out completely," I say. "You're not the only one who's wanted to have kids."

"You're not part of the equation, Joe."

"But I am and you know it. Bend a little, Jill. This could get nasty. Neither of us wants that."

She's tapping her foot nervously, trying to sort everything out. She takes a last puff on her cigarette and grinds it out.

"Yes, you're right. If you wish, you can visit two or three

times a year. Kindly, good natured Uncle Joe bearing gifts for his favorite niece or nephew. But that's as far as it goes."

I nod.

"I can live with that."

She smiles. "Good. I think it will be nice if he or she has a kindly Uncle Joe. A lot of kids don't."

"Believe me, I know," I say. Jill is aware I was raised in foster homes. An Uncle Joe would have been a blessing.

She finds a Kleenex and pats her face dry, then smiles.

"We came close to making it, didn't we, Joe?" she says.

"Very close, Jill," I reply.

She stands.

"I'll say goodbye here. There's a taxi stand at the bottom of the stairs."

"I'll walk you down," I say.

"I'd rather you didn't," she says.

She comes to me and puts her arms around me and holds me very tight. Then she turns and walks to the head of the last flight of stairs leading to the street below.

"Jill," I call out. She turns toward me. "Two things. One, I know you're wealthy but money isn't always an answer. If you need anything from me, anything at all, promise you'll let me know."

"Sure, Joe. I promise," she says.

"Second, put my name on the birth certificate as the father."

She starts to shake her head.

"No, I---"

"Yes," I say firmly. "Outside of an estranged father, you have no family. If something were to happen to you, illness, a freak accident, a plane crash, anything, the child would be grabbed by the state and swallowed up in the system."

"I'm not going to die, Joe," she says.

"Everybody dies, Jill, and there's not a lot we can do about it. I'll never use it against you. I'll never abuse your trust. But I want it spelled out, just in case."

She hesitates for what seems a long time. "All right, I'll do it, Joe. Don't make me sorry."

"I won't. Call me when you get back in town."

She gives me one last smile.

"I will," she says. Then, almost sadly: "I hope you find your Bunny, Joe. I hope she comes back to you."

She turns and starts down the staircase. I watch her go and I wonder if a chapter of my life is ending or if a new one is just beginning.

CHAPTER FIFTEEN

t's another sleepless night. This time Bunny is far from my thoughts. I have been agonizing over Jillian and my child who will never be more than an acquaintance to me. I promised Jillian I would stay away and now I wonder if that was a mistake. I am not interested in marriage, I have no enthusiasm for actually raising a child on my own and yet the baby is my flesh and blood and cannot be ignored. If there is an easy answer to this conundrum, I have yet to see it.

My phone rings even before room service arrives with my pot of coffee and rolls and jam. On the line is Father LaCouline, the film's technical advisor. He tells me the two of us are wanted in Hitchcock's suite immediately. The good father is not given to dramatics and that is why I am concerned. His tone is grim. I tell him I will meet him outside Hitch's door in fifteen minutes.

Hitchcock welcomes us into his suite and offers us coffee. He is dressed in his usual dark suit but he is not where he is supposed to be. The company had a six-thirty call and he is supposed to be directing. He gets right to the point.

"I have just returned from Notre Dame de Victoires where we were supposed to film this morning and where we have now been denied access by the Archbishop." He glances at Fr.

LaCouline. "I thought we had resolved those difficulties, Father. I see I was mistaken."

"I know nothing about this, Mr. Hitchcock. No one contacted me."

"Unfortunate," Hitchcock says. "It seems the Archbishop has not only barred the door at Victoires but at every other church we planned to film over the next several days. I have been told that this situation has arisen solely because of the scandal involving the young lady from the film commission. Tell me, Mr. Bernardi, what have you heard?"

"Nothing, sir."

"Well, this will not do, gentlemen," he says. "No, not at all. As experienced as I am, I do not know how to shoot a film about churches without churches to film. I suppose I could rent a large barn and dress it up with a lot of crosses and stained glass but I hardly think the audiences will be hoodwinked by such tom-foolery."

"Doubtful, sir." I say.

"Yes, we seem to be in agreement, Mr. Bernardi, which is why I need you and Father LaCouline to chat with the Archbishop and convince him to reopen the churches as soon as possible. I would do so myself but I know nothing of Miss d'Arcy and her situation. Actual murder is a subject with which I am not familiar so sally forth, Mr. Bernardi, and may angels be at your side in your quest."

I have never met Armand Boudreau, the Archbishop of the Diocese of Quebec. Fr. LaCouline has and he assures me that the old fellow is as starchy as a peck of potatoes. This is an encounter I am not looking forward to.

Notre Dame de Quebec Cathedral where the Archbishop resides is a short walk from Chateau Frontenac but at the front door of the hotel we find our driver waiting with a newly washed Lincoln town car. Someone has decided that we should arrive in style and not skulk up to the front steps like mendicants looking for an apostolic handout.

"Where's Nate?" I ask.

The driver, whose name is Lee, smiles. "He says to tell you, sir, that he's off doing what he does best and he'll be in touch soon."

If I'm supposed to understand what Lee just told me, I don't, so I forget about it and Father LaCouline and I get in the back seat of the car.

In no time we are there and even as I am exiting the car I am impressed by the majesty of this church, the oldest in Canada, a national landmark beloved by the people. No tete-a-tete in a rectory living room or chit-chat over coffee in the kitchen for this Archbishop. He is putting us in our place even before we mount the steps to the massive front doors that tower above us. I'm reminded of Dante's warning at the gates of Hell, "All hopes abandon ye who enter here." I am imagining a similar sign across this entrance: "Enter if you must but here God wins all arguments."

The Archbishop, formerly Armand Boudreau of Chantilly, France, is a tall, spare man of 60 some years with flowing locks of grey and white and deep set piercing green eyes that see into everything and reveal nothing. Although French by birth, his English is perfect and with hardly a trace of accent. Put him in a choir and he sings basso profundo. He is, indeed, imposing made all the more so by his surroundings. His office is lavishly furnished with heavy pieces of upholstered furniture. On the walls are quality prints of famous religiously themed paintings from the Renaissance. The carpeting is plush. All of this has little to do with Father LaCouline and I as we approach the Archbishop's massive mahogany desk which seems to have been raised several inches above floor level. We are directed to sit in two uncomfortable straight back chairs planted in front of the desk and when we sit we find ourselves looking up at the Archbishop while he is simultaneously looking down on us. I'm amused to find that he and Jack Warner seem to have at least one thing in common.

Father LaCouline introduces me and the Archbishop graciously welcomes me to his church. He forgets to offer coffee or perhaps a decent cigar and gets right to the point.

"I understand, Mr. Bernardi," he says, "that Mlle. d'Arcy, the young lady from the film commission, was working with you before her unfortunate and very public arrest. What can you tell me about that?"

I do my best to describe our working relationship and then at his urging, I tell him what I know about Daniel Bruckner's murder.

"It is my feeling, Excellency, that Miss d'Arcy is innocent of these charges. It is a feeling that is shared by many including Claude Le Pen, the celebrated defense attorney, who is currently defending a man named Louis Marchand in Superior Court."

"Yes, I've been following that story in the newspapers." He looks over at a folded newspaper at the side of his desk. "And what exactly leads you to believe that the young lady did not kill M. Bruckner?"

"She protests her innocence, Excellency. And other small things, too trivial to go into here."

"She threatened the man only hours before he was found dead."

"I know it doesn't look good---"

"Good? Young man, it looks terrible. Now listen to me, and you, too, Father LaCouline. This diocese cannot tolerate a scandal and I personally WILL not. Each day the newspapers cover this story and each day it is something new and untoward and they exploit it to the hilt." He picks up the newspaper and waves it in my direction. "Friday night you and M. Le Pen are out driving and someone tries to chase you down and starts shooting at you. This is Quebec, my son, not New York City. We are peaceful people. We need not tolerate this sort of thing."

I am seething inside, Mackenzie Starr, having few or no facts at his disposal, has invented a story and for the second time, his editor let it slip by. I will deal with both of them later. My immediate problem is Archbishop Boudreau.

"I promise you, there will be no more shooting, Excellency. And as for Jeanne d'Arcy, within days she will be released."

The Archbishop looks incredulous.

"Will she now?"

"Yes, without a doubt. Excellency, I have heard that you are a fair man and I know you would not capriciously shut down this movie company if they were blameless in all that is happening. Further you certainly wouldn't convict Miss d'Arcy of a crime without a trial. I implore you, sir, don't make a hasty decision you will later come to regret."

The Archbishop regards me thoughtfully.

"When you say the young woman will be released, does that mean she will be cleared of any wrongdoing?"

"That is what I believe, Excellency," I say.

"But you are not positive."

I hesitate for a moment.

"What is past I know, but what is for to come, I know not."

The Archbishop's eyes narrow curiously.

"The Apocrypha."

I nod.

"Bernardi. That is Italian."

"Yes, Excellency."

"Are you Catholic?"

"No, I am not."

"Protestant?"

"No."

He looks at me disapprovingly.

"There's not much left," he says.

"When I was a young boy, I was raised in a foster home where the only book I had to read was the Bible, Excellency. I read it many times over and found it comforting and informative. I was not, however, blessed with the gift of faith."

"I see," he says leaning back in his chair. "You might have been better served had you glossed over that last part."

"Perhaps so, Excellency, but while I do not have the gift of faith, I do lead a Christian life and I would not dishonor you or humiliate myself by lying to you in these holy surroundings."

The Archbishop regards me thoughtfully and then leans forward.

"Very well, Mr. Bernardi, I will take you at your word. Tell Mr. Hitchcock that he has another 72 hours of access to our churches and to make the most of it. I fervently hope that at the end of that time that Mlle. d'Arcy has been exonerated and released. If so we will all have made the best of an awkward situation."

He gets up and comes around the desk. Fr. LaCouline and I get quickly to our feet.

"Thank you both for coming. May God be with you."

He holds out his right hand, fist-like, to Fr. LaCouline who kneels quickly and kisses the Archbishop's ring. He turns to me, hand outstretched, still in a fist. Then he opens it with a smile and we shake hands.

"You are a most persuasive young man, Mr. Bernardi. I believe you have found your calling and while it may not be the Lord's work, it certainly isn't the devil's. God be with you."

"Thank you, Excellency," I say.

Outside the church we head for the town car where Lee stands ready to return us to the hotel.

"I'm not quite sure what just happened in there, Joe," Father LaCouline says.

"It's simple, Father. I bought us another 72 hours."

"It seems to me he was awfully easily persuaded."

"No, he wasn't, Father," I say. "I gave him the opportunity to do the right thing and he took it."

"And seventy-two hours from now, if Mlle. d'Arcy is still being held in jail?"

"Then Hitch had better start looking around for a barn."

We pile into the car and head back to the hotel. Hitch is delighted by the news and immediately calls Sherry Shourds who sets about ordering the crew back to the church. Warn everyone it will be a late night, he tells her. He's planning to make maximum use of those 72 hours.

I head to the production office were I place a call to the airport hotel, hoping for a last goodbye to Jillian. I'm too late. She's checked out. I hang up. It's probably for the best that I missed her. She seemed adamant about making a clean break. I'll back off and give her space if that's what she wants but I'm still walking around with that empty feeling I had last night when I went to bed. I hope I'm rid of it soon.

Someone has left a copy of this morning's paper on a nearby

desk. I pick it up and scan Mackenzie Starr's account of Friday night's adventure. It reads like an episode of 'Spy Smasher". It's all hyperbole and supposition larded down with misinformation. I should go to the newspaper office and jam the front page down the editor's throat but I haven't the will or the energy. I have only one priority now and that is to free Jeanne. How, I do not know.

I look over at my phone, I'm being buzzed. I give Connie a wave and lift up the receiver.

"Joe Bernardi."

"Esther Laval, Mr Bernardi. Do you have a minute?"

"Of course."

"I've just come from the jail."

"How is she?" I ask.

"I'm not sure," Esther says. "Detached, Disconnected. She's increasingly becoming less and less communicative."

"Doesn't sound good."

"It isn't. She wants to see you."

"All right."

"Not with me. She wants to see you alone. What's going on, Mr. Bernardi? What do you and she know that I don't?"

"Nothing that I know of," I say.

"You are aware of the principle of privilege, Mr. Bernardi. It is the same here in Canada as it is in the United States. Anything said to me as her attorney is confidential."

"I understand, Mrs. Laval, but I repeat. I'm keeping nothing from you."

"I see. Well, in any case, it's impossible. The Crown has made it clear. She sees no one except her attorneys. A private meeting can't be arranged."

"You've told her that?"

"I have."

"And what was her reaction?"

"Silence."

No, this is not good. What's so damned secretive that she can't even share it with her lawyer? The pressure of being cooped up seems to be getting to her.

"I'll talk to her again," Esther is saying. "Maybe I can get through to her. In the meantime, I am meeting with Marie Bruckner this afternoon at my office. Would you like to sit in?"

"I most certainly would," I say.

"Three o'clock sharp. Don't be late," she says and hangs up.

I replace the receiver. I do, indeed, have a question for Marie Bruckner and it's the same one I posed to Claude Le Pen. If she was so damned anxious to talk to us Friday night, why did we not get a phone call wondering where we were or why we weren't coming? I'm looking forward to hearing her answer.

Just then Nate pops into the room. When he sees me he makes a beeline for my desk, a big grin on his face.

"Let's go, boss," he says to me. "Car's outside."

"Go where?"

"To see the Man. You want to solve this case, don't you?"

"Yes, but---"

"Then follow me."

He starts out. Since I am absolutely nowhere with nothing to do, I decide to play along. I also remember that Lee, our driver, said Nate was out doing what Nate does best. I don't think he meant chauffeuring.

As we drive along the streets heading for a residential section of New Quebec, Nate tells me we are going to meet one of his buddies, a cop named JoJo Rathbone, real name Hector. He works for the Service de Police de la Ville de Quebec which is a longwinded name for the city's traffic cops and other low level functions not handled by the Surete. JoJo is married to Nate's cousin Margaret and at a party on Saturday night they started talking about the Friday night adventure in the boondocks. It rang a bell with JoJo and the next thing he knew, Nate was hot on the trail of a lead.

"What lead?" I ask, growing weary of all this cloak and dagger stuff.

"You'll see", Nate says as he pulls to the curb directly behind a police cruiser. A burly cop is leaning against the fender and smoking a cigarette. He has a round ruddy face and sandy hair and his leather belt is losing a battle with his waistline. We get out of the Peugeot and walk over to him. Nate introduces us.

"Is he in?" Nate asks.

"He's in," JoJo says as we walk up to the front door of the left side of a duplex that fronts the quiet little suburban street. JoJo raps on the door. We wait. He raps again. Finally the door opens a crack and a man peers out at us.

"Good morning, Mr. Steinmetz," JoJo says. "Remember me? Officer Rathbone?"

"Oh, sure", he says. "Who are these guys?"

"Friends of mine. Mind if we come in?"

Steinmetz shoots a nervous look back into the house and then says, "Actually, I'd rather you didn't," he says.

JoJo tries to look past him through the narrow crack in the door. "Company?"

Steinmetz nods. "Yeah. Company. It's my day off."

From inside we hear a female voice calling out. "Lionel?"

"Yeah, yeah, in a minute," he calls back.

"Maybe if you could step out for a minute, sir. This won't take long," JoJo says.

"You're not here to bust my chops, are you, 'cause I gotta tell you, I ain't in the mood."

"No, sir. Nothing like that."

Steinmetz hesitates, then steps out into the front stoop closing the door behind him. He's wearing a short cotton bathrobe and probably nothing else.

"Okay, I'm out," he says.

"Will you tell these gentlemen what you told me Friday night."

"Look, why don't we just forget it---"

"Please."

He sighs resignedly. "Sure. Why not?" He looks at me and Nate. "Friday night, somebody steals my car. I gotta go to the grocery store to pick up some gefilte fish and cole slaw for a late supper. I come out, it's supposed to be parked there--" He points, "It's gone. I think, am I crazy? Did I leave it someplace else? I look up and down the street. No car. I look on the next block. No car. It had been locked and I've got the keys in my hand but I don't have a car. I think maybe a buddy has borrowed it so I go in and make a few phone calls. No, that's not it. Maybe some kids took it joyriding which, where I come from, the Bronx, New York, is not so unusual but then I figure I'm not going to get my car back sitting on my fat Yiddish ass so I give up and call the police to report it stolen. They tell me I'm going to have to come down to the station and file a complaint and fill out some papers. It's only a few blocks away so I walk over. This is a great car, brand new and very expensive and I want it back so I'm going to do whatever I have to do. I wait around for about twenty minutes before anybody gets to me, then it's another forty-five minutes with the paperwork before I'm finished and Officer Rathbone here volunteers to drive me home which I find very nice of him.

"Anyway, we're coming down the street and when we get here I look across the street and there---" Here, he points again. "There parked on the opposite side of the street is my car. So now I am saying to myself, what the hell is going on around here? Is this somebody's idea of a big fucking joke because if it is, I ain't laughing. It's almost ten-thirty and I'm hungry and I'm pissed and some asshole has stolen my car and then brought it back with a hole in the windshield."

I look at him sharply.

"What?"

"A hole in the windshield, a big fat hole," he says starting to lose his calm as he relives the experience.

I look at Nate and then at JoJo.

"Let me guess. He owns a brand new white Citroen Traction Avant," I say.

Nate nods with a big grin in his face. He smiles at JoJo. JoJo smiles at me. Lionel Steinmetz from the Bronx, New York, looks at all three of us.

"Am I missing something here?" he says.

CHAPTER SIXTEEN

Inspector Villiers is not impressed.

First of all, it took me thirty minutes to get to his office at Surete headquarters. Then I spent another thirty minutes in the downstairs lobby waiting for him to return from lunch. When he finally showed he gave me a fishy look as he walked past me to the staircase and I waited another twenty minutes while he got "organized". At 2:25 I was ushered into his office and told to sit while he rifled through some papers. I am pretty sure this is standard operating procedure for dealing with unco-operative inquisitive civilians who insist on meddling in police business. Finally he looked up at me and uttered one word.

"What?"

I spent five minutes telling him about Lionel Steinmetz and his Citroen which someone borrowed to chase Claude Le Pen and me all around the north side of the city. Now I sit and await his reaction. It is not slow in coming.

"So it was not the Gonsalvo brothers who chased you and shot at you on Friday evening."

"No, it wasn't," I say.

He shakes his head in mock sympathy, enjoying every moment.

"And a short time ago you were so positive, M. Bernardi. You must be greatly disappointed."

"No, sir," I say. "Intrigued."

"And why is that?"

"Because it opens up your case to a lot of new possibilities and greatly diminishes the notion that Miss d'Arcy is the guilty party."

"Does it?"

"It does. We, that is Claude Le Pen and I, assumed it was the Gonsalvos because they had reason to harm Claude just as they had reason to harm or even kill Daniel Bruckner. Now it's obvious someone else wanted Claude either dead or frightened off, someone else with a vested interest in the outcome of the Marchand trial."

"Someone from the Maggadino crime family perhaps?" Villier asks.

"Why not?" I say.

"Let me get this straight," Villiers says. "Professional assassins are sent from Buffalo in the dead of night to rub out the famous trial lawyer who stands, erect and unafraid, devoted to the cause of justice for his noble, self-sacrificing client. Is that what we're talking about here, Mr. Bernardi?"

I know when I'm being mocked and Villiers is doing a good job of it.

"I wouldn't put it that way exactly, Inspector," I say.

"No? How would you put it?" He leans forward and the humor is gone from his eyes. "Do you know what your trouble is, Mr. Bernardi? You think life is a movie. Things cannot be obvious, straightforward and uncomplicated. In your world you must have a second act and a third. I find it hard to blame you. Your entire being is tied up in fantasy. You are as conditioned as one of Pavlov's dogs. Well, forgive me if I do not allow you to salivate on my carpet, sir. Jeanne d'Arcy went to her ex-lover's apartment to have it out with him and in the process, stabbed him to death. It is no more complicated than that and the evidence supports that conclusion."

"I disagree," I start to say.

"Allow me to continue, M. Bernardi," Villiers says sharply. "The newly purchased cigarette lighter bearing her fingerprints puts her in the apartment at the time of the killing. The blood found at the scene consists of two types: Type A, the victim's, and Type O Positive which is the same blood type as Mlle. d'Arcy. And as for the blood covered letter opener and what you describe as a clumsy attempt to frame an innocent woman, my response to you is this. She took the letter opener with the full intent of getting rid of it later and never got the chance. It is as simple as that. The Crown Prosecutor is totally convinced he will win a guilty verdict and the only question still open is the degree of the charge. First degree and possible hanging or second degree and a lengthy prison sentence."

"What about the white Citroen?"

"What about it?" Villiers eyes flare with anger. "I think you have a brain, monsieur, but at times you give me cause to doubt it. A moment ago you hint that possibly allies of the Gonsalvos from Buffalo are the ones who allegedly attacked you Friday night. If so why would they do so in an automobile which pointed suspicion directly at their cohorts? No, no, you are so anxious to exonerate Mlle. d'Arcy that you trample all over the obvious."

"Someone tried to kill us," I say angrily.

"Possibly so," Villiers replies, "but you have no proof it has anything to do with Mlle. d'Arcy's case and neither do I. Do I think the attempt on your lives was a crime? I do. Am I having the incident investigated? I am. I have put my best man on it and he had already determined that the Gonsalvos were at their hotel and not driving around the city at the time of the incident. I will pass on this new information and it, too, will be investigated but in my opinion, it has no bearing on the murder charge against Mlle. d'Arcy. Now do me the courtesy of behaving like a guest of this country and stay out of matters that do not concern you."

I have been dismissed. I want to say something in my defense but I can't think of anything persuasive. Besides I glance at my watch. 2:50. I have just ten minutes to get to Esther Laval's office for the questioning of Marie Bruckner.

I rise from my chair.

"Thank you for meeting with me, Inspector. I'm grateful. You will hear from me again soon."

He looks up at me, glowering.

"My God, sir, I hope not," he says wearily.

Nate is not all happy about Villiers dismissal of our new found evidence. As we race across the city he carps to me in English and mutters to himself in French. I'm aware Villiers is not high on Nate's list of most admired people but for all his grousing I see no signs of quit in him. In fact I sense that now more than ever Nate is determined to unmask Villiers for what he is, a close-minded and none too bright bureaucrat.

Nate weaves through traffic as I check my watch. He barely slides by an amber light turning red. I check my watch again. He skids around a corner barely missing a man on crutches stepping off the curb. He screeches to a halt in front of the building where Esther maintains her law office. I skip the elevator and race up the stairs. I throw open the door and dash inside. Esther's receptionist gives me a withering look.

Eleven past three. I am late.

When I enter the small conference room, Esther has already begun deposing Marie Bruckner who is sitting on one side of the table next to a man who is almost certainly her attorney. Esther sits opposite her. At the end of the table, a court stenographer is transcribing the meeting.

Marie looks up at me, then at Esther.

"What's he doing here?" she demands to know.

"I asked him to come," Esther replies.

"I don't want him here," Marie says.

"Well, I do," Esther says. She glares at me. "I believe I said three o'clock sharp."

"You did," I say, "but I got hung up in a one-way conversation with Inspector Villiers."

She nods in understanding, obviously having dealt with Villiers herself in days gone by. She introduces me to Marie's lawyer whose name I forget almost immediately. I sit back in my chair determined to keep my mouth shut in the hopes of actually learning something from this woman. Esther is trying to find out who knew what and when and about who in this seedy love triangle that preceded Daniel Bruckner's death. She's getting nowhere. With every other question the lawyer is leaning in and whispering in Marie's ear. I haven't heard so many "Maybes", "Possiblys", and "I don't remembers" since Frank Costello was grilled at the mafia hearings in front of Kefauver's Senate Crime Committee last year in New York. The only thing she hasn't brought up is the Fifth Amendment and then I remember we are in Canada, not Pocatelo, Idaho. Her lawyer is looking increasingly smug with each of her non-answers. If his job is to thwart the judicial process he is good at it. No wonder lawyers are held in such high esteem.

I feel Esther winding down and I reach over and tug gently at her sleeve. I ask if I am allowed to ask a question. Ask away, she tells me.

"Mrs. Bruckner," I say, "do you remember inviting me and Claude Le Pen to your cottage out by Lake Clement last Friday?"

"Yes, I do."

"And could you tell me why you were so anxious to speak to the two of us that evening?"

Her lawyer pipes up immediately.

"I fail to see what that has to do with these proceedings," he says.

"Maybe nothing. Maybe everything," I say. "What I find curious is the fact that when we failed to arrive that you didn't place a phone to either myself or Mr. Le Pen to find out what had happened to us."

I fix her with a hard stare and for a moment I can see she is off balance.

Finally she shrugs.

"I just assumed you weren't coming."

"And why would you assume that, Mrs. Bruckner?"

"I don't know. I just did, that's all."

"And you were home alone in the cottage waiting for us?"

"Yes."

"Can you prove that?"

"How could I? I just told you I was alone." she says peevishly.

"Then you weren't running around the countryside in a white Citroen taking potshots at me and Mr. Le Pen."

The lawyer rises up out of his seat.

"What?" he croaks.

"What?" Marie echoes.

"Outrageous!" he says.

"Slanderous!" she says.

"Did you persuade a friend come after us?" I suggest.

"Of course not," she says angrily. "This is insane."

"I don't know, maybe it's just me but I have this unshakable feeling that Claude Le Pen and I had been lured out to that road."

"You bastard," she says coldly, getting to her feet.

The lawyer is huffing and puffing as he points a finger in the steno's direction.

"Tell that woman to stop writing this down!" he says to Esther.

Marie starts for the door.

"Come on, Oliver," she says. "Let's get out of here."

I'm on my feet, shouting after her.

"Why can't you answer a simple question, Mrs. Bruckner? What are you afraid of?"

She glares at me.

"Well, I'm sure not afraid of you, sonny. You want to know why I invited you to the cottage? To apologize. I had caviar laid out and champagne on ice and I was determined to patch things up. I barged into your meeting, said some stupid and insulting things and generally made an ass of myself. Claude and I have been friends for over fifteen years. I could not leave things the way they were. Are you satisfied, Mr. Bernardi?" Her eyes are blazing. She may be on the cusp of blurting out something really stupid. Esther senses it too. She makes no move to quiet me.

"I really don't know, Mrs. Bruckner. I suppose it's remotely possible you're telling the truth---"

"Why you arrogant bastard", she says. "I come here in a spirit of cooperation and this is what I'm subjected to. This is all nonsense. A charade. Jeanne d'Arcy murdered my husband in cold blood. You know it. I know it. We all know it. She snuck into his apartment house through the basement garage, confronted him and when he refused to play her sick game, she stabbed him. Was she there? Of course she was there. On the coffee table next to the lighter is an ashtray filled with cigarette butts. Gitane butts. Her brand. The letter opener covered with blood is found in her car with her prints all over it. For God's sakes, Mrs. Laval, what else do you need to know? Plead that poor sick creature guilty before she ends up hanging from a rope at Joliette." She looks from Esther to me with a look of contempt and then turns again on her heel and strides out, Oliver in her wake.

I look over at Esther.

"What do you think?" I say.

She shrugs.

"I think she's an angry, frustrated woman. I also think if she worked it right, she could become some psychiatrist's patient for life."

I nod.

"That assistant tennis pro is falling down on the job," I say.

She laughs.

"No, Mr. Bernardi, the young man is blameless. His involvement with Marie Bruckner was over many weeks ago."

"But Claude said---"

"Claude is a lovely man but seldom au courant when it comes to matters of the heart. I hear there is someone new in Madame's boudoir, who it is I do not know."

"Well, whoever he is, he's just as ineffective in keeping her content," I say.

Esther nods.

"Yes. That would seem to be the case but then I wonder, would any man be up to such a monumental task?"

She arches an eyebrow. I'm forced to laugh.

By the time I stomp down the stairs I am in a really foul mood and Nate and I decide to go drinking. Not to get drunk because we have too much to do to waste the rest of the day. Hitchcock has tomorrow and the day after and that's it. By then Jeanne had better be walking around free or I may be writing press releases for some hamburger joint in Hawaiian Gardens. Nate drives us to this place. It's a real hole in the wall in a sloppy neighborhood but inside it's neat, clean, and friendly and best of all, it's owned by his cousin Velma's husband and the booze is on the house.

I'm on my second beer and Nate's just finishing his third scotch and soda when he loosens up.

"What am I doing, Joe? Am I crazy? Two years ago I quit police work. I was fed up with it. So here I am, back at it like I never left and I think I'm either insane or very, very stupid."

"You're not fed up with anything, Nate. It's in your blood, like it or not."

"No, you're wrong," he says. "I can walk away. It's no problem."

"Then do it," I say. "Drive me back to the hotel, hand in the keys to the Peugeot and go home to Momma and the sisters. Tomorrow you're back to being a chauffeur."

He thinks for a moment and then shakes his head. "No. I couldn't abandon you, my friend. As much as it pains me, I will give it another day or two."

"Such self-sacrifice is much appreciated," I say.

"You are my friend," he says. "Friends are loyal. Besides I want to prove that smug bastard Villiers is a fool. How can I do this driving little old ladies to the grocery store?"

"Good point."

"And so I will help and I will start with Madame Bruckner, the angry widow, who I believe to be full of farm fertilizer."

"Really? Why?"

"A policeman's instinct," he says. "It has never failed me. She invites you and Le Pen to her house by the lake and suddenly we are set upon by a crazy person with a gun. Coincidence? I don't think so. She is hiding something from us and I intend to find out what it is."

He sighs and then says, "But for now, we must return to the hotel." He reaches in his pocket and takes out the keys to the Peugeot. He regards them thoughtfully for a moment and then hands them across the table.

"You drive," he says. "I will take a nap. Don't get lost."

I don't get lost and an hour later I am sitting at my desk in the production office, once again reading the police report and the autopsy report. I have already checked with Sherry who tells me the company is moving right along. They expect a ten p.m. wrap so they can turn around for an eight a.m. call tomorrow morning. The schedule is being shuffled around so that all of the interior church work is finished by late Wednesday evening. Both Sherry and Hitchcock seem dubious about my assurance that Jeanne will be exonerated by Thursday morning. So little faith. I feel almost insulted.

My eyes start to droop. I am tired. I need either sleep or food and maybe both. I decide to go to my room and order in and then play it by ear. I take the two reports with me because, even though I have read them through twice, I am bothered by little inconsistencies. Maybe in the quiet of my room with some food in my belly I will think more clearly.

I am going out as Father LaCouline is coming in. His face is grey and immediately I know something is wrong.

"Joe, I was hoping to find you here," he says.

"What is it, Father?" I ask.

"Jeanne d'Arcy," he says grimly. "They've taken her to the hospital. She just tried to kill herself."

CHAPTER SEVENTEEN

'm stunned by what I've just heard. Jeanne d'Arcy may be a lot of things but suicidal is not one of them.

"I don't believe it," I say.

"It's true, Joe. Somehow she got a hold of a china coffee cup. She broke it and tried to slash her wrists with the jagged edge."

"My God," I say quietly trying to make sense of it.

"Apparently she is in no real danger. Her wounds are superficial. They've bandaged her wrists and are keeping her under observation for the night. Meanwhile, Joe, she's been insisting on seeing her confessor."

"You?" I say.

"No. She gave them my name but she really wants to see Father Joseph."

"And who's Father Joseph?" I ask innocently.

"I believe you are," Father LaCouline says to me.

"Me? That's ridiculous."

And of course, even as I say it, I realize it isn't ridiculous at all. Jeanne told Esther she wanted to see me alone. Villiers said no and Jeanne is not only stubborn, she is resourceful. Whatever she has to say to me must be damned important for her to slash away at her wrists. I tell all this to Fr. LaCouline and ask him if there is any penalty for posing as a priest.

"In law, I doubt it," he says, "although in God's eyes it is not something I would chance."

"Well, I'm devil may care, Father, so I'll risk His wrath just this once." I explain to him why I must see Jeanne alone and ask for his help. He nods in understanding and invites me up to his room.

Twenty minutes later I am standing in front of a full length mirror wearing a black cassock and a clerical shirt and collar. Since Fr. LaCouline and I are approximately the same size it's a good fit. He has given me a small black bag which contains a silk stole, sanctified oils, holy water, a Bible, a prayer book, and a rosary. He explains to me how to use them for appearances sake in case a Catholic guard or doctor or nurse is standing nearby.

"Try to be reverent, Joe," Fr. LaCouline implores me. "We're skirting the fringes of blasphemy here You may not care but I do."

I assure him I will be a very model of priestly decorum.

Before I leave, I use the phone to call Nate. He's not at the Transportation office so I call him at home. A woman answers the phone and when I ask for Nate, I sense a cold wave of suspicion coming back at me over the line.

"Nathaniel is not here," she says. "I am his sister Charity. Am I speaking to Mr. Bernardi?"

"You are," I say.

"I thought as much," she says, her vocal temperature dropping a good ten degrees fahrenheit. "He came in a couple of hours ago. He had been drinking." She says it like he had been smoking opium stark naked in the middle of a town square. "With you," she continues. I feel ice forming in my eardrum.

"Yes, we did stop for a----"

"I'm sure you did, Mr Bernardi. My brother can be easily

swayed in that direction, forgetting of course that he has obligations to his mother and his sisters."

I try again.

"I know that Nathaniel is well aware of his---"

"Two years ago he recognized his obligation to his family and resigned from his dangerous position with the Surete. Now you come into his life and not only is he drinking again, he is running around once more behaving like a policeman."

"I'm not sure that is entirely fair---"

"He walks in, takes some fruit from a bowl and a can of soda pop from the refrigerator and tells us he has no time for dinner, that he has work to do. I know what that is, sir. It is work for you and I hold you completely to blame for his recent behavior. He is not acting like himself, Mr. Bernardi. Not at all."

Now I'm getting irked.

"Excuse me, Miss McIver, but did you ever consider that maybe he IS acting like himself, that whatever you have been turning him into the past two years was not himself and that at heart he is a policeman who is good at a job that makes him very happy."

"My brother's happiness is not an issue here," she says.

"Maybe it should be," I say bluntly and hang up on her.

I look over at Fr. LaCouline.

"I just talked to a woman who is in serious need of your counseling, Father, one of those holier-than-thou Christians who really isn't a Christian at all."

"An Easter Catholic," he says. "They are no strangers to me."

I decide against calling Transportation for a ride to the hospital and call for a taxi to meet me at the side entrance. The fewer people who know what I'm up to the better.

The driver's name is Yves and he is a chubby roundfaced man in middle age. I tell him the hospital at Universite Laval in Sainte-Foy. No problem, he says. He knows it. We are barely away from curbside when he starts to tell me about his wife. After fifteen years, the adorable and compliant young princess that he married has turned into a haranguing, argumentative shrew, with all the tenderness of year old mutton, the manners of a hungry cannibal and the vocabulary of an able bodied seaman too long at sea. Weary of it all and obviously desperate, he seeks my counsel. With great trepidation I toss out a few cliches such as 'adversity breeds strength' and 'God is testing you' and 'God will show you the way." By the time we reach the hospital, he has apparently bought into my well-meaning hokum and feels much better. He thanks me profusely and blesses me. All in all, he makes me feel like a first class hypocrite and a disgrace to the human race. If it weren't for Jeanne needing to talk to me so badly, I'd turn around and go back to the hotel.

I introduce myself to the receptionist in the lobby and am directed to the second floor, north wing. When I emerge from the elevator I immediately spot the uniformed officer sitting on a folding chair directly outside one of the rooms. I stride toward him purposefully. As I reach him he stands.

"Bonsoir, mon pere," he says politely.

I smile. "Good evening, my son," I say, even though his graying hair puts him at least twenty years older than me.

I reach for the door to push it open but he stops me.

"One moment, Father," he says, putting out his hand. "Your bag, please. Just a formality. Regulations. I am sorry,"

I hesitate, then hand it over.

"But of course, one cannot be too careful," I say.

He opens it, peers inside, and satisfied, closes it again. He hands it back.

"Thank you for your understanding," he says, apologizing once again.

I make the sign of the cross at him just like Spencer Tracy did to Bobs Watson in 'Boy's Town'. Lightning does not strike me. The ground does not swallow me up. The guard thanks me again and sits down as I go into Jeanne's dimly lit room.

She is lying in bed, eyes closed, pillows propped behind her head. I reach down and touch her hand. I see that both her wrists are bandaged and I wonder what it is that drove her to this desperate act. Her eyes open slowly and she looks up at me. She manages a smile and grips my hand.

"Thanks for coming," she says.

"A lady in distress? How could I refuse?" I say.

I grab a nearby chair and pull it up to her bedside. I dig into my black bag and hand her the rosary. I slip the stole around my neck as I lean toward her.

"For effect, just in case we're interrupted," I say.

She nods.

"Are they mistreating you?" I ask.

"Of course not. But I've been going out of my mind. I see no one. I talk to no one except Esther and she's all business. Joe, I'm scared. So scared. Maybe I'll never get out. Ever." Her voice catches and I see genuine fear in her eyes. I'm looking for fight and I see none. This is not the Jeanne d'Arcy I know.

"Stay calm, Jeannie," I say. "I'm working on it. We'll have you out of here in a couple of days, promise."

"Joe---"

"My driver's an ex-cop named Nate McIver. Sharp as hell. Between the two of us, we'll find out who's trying to pin this on you."

"Joe, don't waste your time. I did it. I killed him."

I'm brought up short. At first I think I didn't hear her right but when I look into her eyes, I see that she is deadly serious. She is trembling and her eyes are flooded with tears. There's a catch in her throat and she can barely get the words out.

"Oh, sweet Jesus, forgive me. I stabbed him with that letter opener. I did it, Joe. I killed him."

She can no longer look at me. She stares at the ceiling. Her sobs become more pronounced.

"It's okay, Jeannie," I say. "It's okay."

She shakes her head violently.

"Twice I almost told Esther the truth but I don't really know her, Joe, and I'm not sure I trust her. But I knew I had to tell someone and I knew that someone was you."

I nod.

"Okay, Jeannie. I'm here. Tell me. All of it," I say quietly as I dab at her tears with my handkerchief.

"It started at the restaurant. At the table and afterwards in the parking lot. You were there. You saw the whole thing though you didn't understand it." She pauses, remembering. "This is a man I had loved, a man I had given my heart and my body to. I believed he was honest when he said he wanted to end his marriage and marry me. Foolish me, eh, Joe? Not a new story at all. And then when he decided to enter politics, divorce was out of the question but he still wanted to continue seeing me. I told him no. I finally realized I had no future with him but he refused to accept my decision. There were notes, phone calls, and finally the scene at the restaurant. He called me things. A two dollar whore was the nicest. I won't repeat the others. I was humiliated and I was furious. I threatened to kill him if he ever came near me again."

"Not a good choice of words," I say.

"No, they weren't. After I dropped you off, I drove over to

his apartment and parked in the underground garage. I was determined to have it out with him. I still had a key to the entry door and went up to his apartment."

"The night doorman didn't see you."

"Of course not. The elevator from the basement bypasses the lobby. At first the arrogant bastard thought I was there to apologize, that I'd changed my mind, that somehow I had come to my senses and realized I couldn't live without him. I tried to reason with him. I tried to convince him to leave me alone but he was still drunk and still drinking and wasn't even listening to me. After about twenty minutes I realized it was hopeless and I got up to go which was when he grabbed me and tried to force me back down onto the sofa. I struggled, kicking and clawing and managed to toss him off of me. I ran to the door but he grabbed me and threw me back into the room. I got to my feet and backed away but he kept coming. Suddenly I was backed up against the desk. I turned, saw the letter opener and grabbed it. I held it in front of me. I warned him to back away but he just laughed and as he did he jumped at me. I could feel the letter opener plunging into his belly as he gasped in pain. He tried to speak but couldn't and then he fell to the floor and laid there, very still."

Her eyes are wide and she's broken into a sweat. My handkerchief is soaked. I pick up a tissue from her bedside table and wipe her forehead.

"It's okay, Jeannie," I say. "It's okay."

"I was so scared, Joe. I thought I was going to pass out. I didn't know what to do. Everything inside of me was screaming, run! For one brief moment I thought about calling the police but I knew I couldn't. A couple of hours ago I'd threatened to kill him. I've sneaked into his apartment house to confront him and now he's lying dead on the floor. Self defense? A two dollar whore and a prominent respected attorney? Who would believe me? No, I couldn't face that and so I ran just as fast and as far as I could. And that's it, Joe. All of it. And I don't know what to do because I know that Villiers wants to hang me."

"I doubt that. Hanging's not his business. Jeannie, when you left the apartment, are you sure he was dead?"

"Yes. I mean, he had to be. He was laying there. He wasn't moving. I couldn't see him breathing."

"But you didn't check closely."

"I tried. I started to lean in close and suddenly I had one of my god awful nose bleeds.'

A nose bleed. Another piece of the puzzle explained.

"And when you left, you say he was lying there on the floor. You didn't remove the letter opener?"

"Good God, no," she says. "And that's what I can't understand. They find it in my car with my bloody fingerprints all over it. Why? How?"

"The why is simple. Somebody found out that you'd stabbed him. They wanted to make sure the police found it out as well. The 'How'? I'm going to have to work on that."

She nods.

"So, Joe, what do I do?"

"I think you tell the truth. You're in a bad place now, Jeannie. It can't get any worse. Villiers may not believe you but he's going to be forced to think about it and maybe we'll be able to sort things out."

"All right," she says.

"As soon as I leave, I'm going to call Esther and get her over here. You tell her what you told me. You can't sit on this a minute longer."

"I understand," she says, taking me hand and squeezing it. "Thanks."

"I haven't done anything," I say.

"Just knowing you're beside me, that's enough," she says with a smile.

I haven't the heart to tell her I'll be leaving for the States in about eight days. She lives alone and as far as I know she has no one. Unless we can conjure up a miracle, she's going to face this crisis by herself. I try to shut down my brain. This is something I can't deal with.

I get to my feet, lean over and kiss her on the forehead.

"Try to get some rest before Esther gets here," I say.

"I will," she says, smiling.

I turn and go to the door and step out into the corridor.

He's standing there, arms folded across his chest regarding me quizzically.

"Good evening, Father Joseph," Inspector Villiers says. "I think that you and I have much to talk about."

CHAPTER EIGHTEEN

Villiers is sitting back in his chair, hands laced behind his head, staring me in the face. Not talking. Just staring. He's tried talking and it hasn't done him any good. I told him when I sat down, I would say nothing until Esther Laval arrives and since then I have said only one word, 'oui', uttered when he offered me a cup of coffee. Now I sit and continue to say nothing as the clock on the wall behind Villiers desk ticks off the minutes. At the moment it is 9:48 and I am passing the time trying to remember the names of all the Charlie Chan movies I've ever seen and who played Charlie, Warner Oland or Sidney Toler. I dismiss the six Chan movies with Roland Winters as inferior and not worth my attention.

When the clock reaches 9:51, Villiers' intercom buzzes. He responds and in a moment, the door to his office opens and Esther Laval enters. I rise politely to greet her. She takes one look at me in my priestly garb and turns to Villiers.

"That is none of my business, Inspector. I know nothing about it," she says emphatically.

Villiers smiles.

"I am quite sure you did not, Mme. Laval. M. Bernardi seems to enjoy operating independently without the counsel of others.

Please sit down." She does so. "Using the guise of a priest, M. Bernardi was able to gain access to Mlle. d'Arcy in her hospital room for a private conversation. When he emerged from the room, alerted by hospital staff, I was waiting for him and asked him the nature of his conversation with the prisoner. He told me he would say nothing until you were present. Hence, our request that you join us here at this late hour for which you have my deepest apologies."

"Unnecessary, Inspector. I understand completely," Esther says.

"Merci beaucoup," Villiers says with a nod of the head. He turns to me. "And now, M. Bernardi, if you please."

I clear my throat and start in. I don't stop until I have told them everything, just as it was told to me by Jeanne. Villiers is taking notes on a lined yellow pad. Esther is listening intently.

"It's a shame that Jeanne d'Arcy was forced to these extreme measures to see me alone," I say to Villiers. "It could have been avoided it you'd let me visit her without Mrs. Laval present. I'm embarrassed by this whole thing. I wish I hadn't been forced into it."

Villiers smiles. "Your remorse is duly noted, M. Bernardi. Now do I understand that this means Mlle. d'Arcy will be asserting her innocence by reason of self-defense? Mrs. Laval?"

"I'll have to speak with her, Inspector."

"I'll arrange it for early tomorrow morning at the hospital," he says.

"Thank you."

"You realize this changes everything, Inspector," I say.

"It changes nothing, M. Bernardi. We now have the young woman placed at the scene by her own admission. Belatedly she claims self-defense. I, for one, am skeptical."

"Why? The scratches on Bruckner's face and his bruising are clearly spelled out in the autopsy."

"Just because they fought does not mean that M. Bruckner initiated it. Mlle. d'Arcy showed up with mayhem on her mind. He was drunk and perhaps in no condition to defend himself."

"But---" I start to stay.

"Enough!" Villiers says sharply. "I have had enough of your 'buts', M. Bernardi. Perhaps if she had told us this fanciful story from the beginning I might have given it some credence but no, after her denials and her attempted coverup, I have no sane reason to believe her. The case will proceed."

He stands up, indicating dismissal.

"Thank you again for coming, Mme. Laval, and for being so gracious about the inconvenience we have caused you."

"De rien, Inspector," she says.

He turns to me. "As for you, M. Bernardi, I am trying very hard to remember that you are a guest in my country. I would appreciate it if you would do the same. Police business is not your business. Stay out of it. I won't tell you again."

"Or else?" I ask lightly.

"Or else," he says coldly and there is nothing light about it.

"Come, Mr. Bernardi, I'll give you a ride back to the Frontenac," she says.

I get to my feet, give Villiers one last withering look, and follow her out the door.

I'm angry and so is she. She drives like it, ignoring the speed limit and barely recognizing the existence of STOP signs and traffic lights.

"I am disappointed, Mr. Bernardi. No, more than that. I am angry that Jeanne was unable to trust me and even angrier at the way she has tied my hands. Do I go into court and say, yes, my client was lying to police for several days but now she is telling the truth and you can take her word for it. Mon dieu."

"I think she IS telling the truth," I say.

Esther shrugs. "She probably is. At least now her story has some relationship to the evidence collected at the crime scene, but after all her lies, who will believe her?" She glances quickly in my direction. "I will tell you something else, monsieur. Your constant meddling in this case is doing your friend no good. Villiers is furious with you and I cannot even begin to have a conversation with him before he brings up your name. I think now that we have the truth from Mlle. d'Arcy, it would be best if you backed off and let the Surete do its job."

I think about that for a moment,

"I tell you what," I say. "I have a question that can't be answered, at least by me. So I will ask you and if you give me a reasonable explanation, I will walk away and no longer interfere in the investigation."

"Bon," she says, almost smiling. "The thought of you minding your own business is too good to resist. Ask your question."

"Do you believe that Jeanne d'Arcy pulled the bloody letter opener from Bruckner's body, took it with her without wiping off the blood and her fingerprints and then 'hid' it under the front seat of her car where no one could possibly find it?"

Her eyes flick toward me momentarily.

"You ask good questions, M. Bernardi," she says.

"Yes, I do. Do you supply good answers, Mrs. Laval?"

"In this case, no."

"Then can we assume that someone else came into the apartment after Jeanne left and before the housekeeper discovered the body?"

"I suppose we can," Esther says. "And who do you think that someone might be, M. Bernardi?"

"I don't know," I say, "but I can tell you this. It was someone who knew that Jeanne had killed Bruckner and wanted to make damned sure that when the police caught up with her, they would have an ironclad case of first degree murder."

Esther turns into the entrance of the Frontenac.

"And who would hate Mlle. d'Arcy enough to do such a thing?" Esther asks.

It was an obvious question and the answer was equally obvious.

"Marie Bruckner," I say.

Esther nods in agreement as her car pulls to a stop.

"If that is the case, and I think it is, Mme. Bruckner has turned self-defense into first degree murder and we can't allow that to stand. Since we both know that Villiers will do nothing to get at the truth, you and Mr. McIver are going to have to dig into this and find something I can use in court. Otherwise Mlle. d'Arcy is almost certainly going to be convicted."

"Nate and I will get on it first thing in the morning," I tell her.

"Bon chance," she says as Fred, the hotel doorman opens my door for me to exit the car.

"Good evening, Father," he says as I get out. Then he looks at me more closely. "I mean,---uh---". He screws up his face. "Mr. Bernardi?"

"And a good evening to you, my son. Vaya con Dios," I say with a smile and then I hurry toward the entrance, desperate for the privacy of my room.

When the elevator door opens on the second floor, I look across the hallway to the small settee in a little alcove where Nate McIver is sitting quietly. He looks me up and down.

"Not a word," I warn him.

"Heaven forbid, Father, but you certainly cut a dashing figure."

I glower at him.

"I assume you've been waiting for me," I say.

"I have."

"Well, come on then, before I run into some kid who wants me to bless his pet turtle."

Once inside my room I eagerly shed the cassock and collar while I explain to Nate what has transpired.

"So she did it."

"Yes."

"Self defense."

"So she says."

"So the case is over."

"Not necessarily," I say. "Someone wants a jury to believe that it was cold blooded premeditated murder."

"That someone being Marie Bruckner." Nate says.

"Maybe. She makes no secret of her hatred for Jeanne."

"Is there another explanation for the frame job?" Nate asks.

"None I can think of, but I'm not a cop. You are. By the way, I talked with your sister Charity. "

"Got an earful, did you, Joe?"

"I did."

"My sisters Agnes and Teresa are a joy, kind and loving, but God put Charity on Earth to test my faith."

"I can see that," I say. I'm slipping into a UCLA sweatshirt and a pair of jeans.

"Well, ignore her. I do. Now about tonight."

I shake my head.

"I've told you everything I know."

"No, no. Now it's my turn. I drove out to the lake and started to poke around the way cops do, Joe. Yeah, yeah, I know. In the movies it's brilliant deduction but in the real world it comes down to shoe leather and knuckles on the front doors. I found six neighbors home who were willing to talk to me. Quite candid they were, Joe. Marie Bruckner wins no popularity prizes in that community."

"Not surprised."

"First, and most important, for the past several months she's spent almost all her time out at the lake cottage and at least four times a week she has a visitor. Late 20s or early 30's, slim, maybe six feet two with wavy blonde hair and a mustache."

"Phillippe Bachelet, the private investigator."

Nate nods.

"Yes, busy investigating Marie Bruckner on a regular basis until the wee hours of the morning. He drives a late model Buick and one of the neighbors got his tag number. I'll confirm in the morning with the motor vehicle office. It's not exactly legal. I really should have a court order but there's a cute number works there in records named Valentina who wants to make an honest man of me."

I smile. I'll bet there is,

"Interesting," I say. "Marie bounces the tennis pro and Phillippe gets rid of the real estate lady and for the last several weeks they play house. Object what? Matrimony? I think I remember that after spending years refusing to give Bruckner a divorce, Marie suddenly wanted one and Bruckner refused to grant it because of his political ambitions."

"You remember correctly. And by the way, Joe, you'll get a kick out of this. Villiers sent an internal memo to all agents of the Surete forbidding them to cooperate in any way with either you or me in connection with the case. Within twelve hours I had six phone calls from former colleagues offering their help. Off the record, of course."

"Nice to know one has friends. You must be one hell of a guy, Nate."

He smiles.

"I am. No matter what my sister thinks."

I nod and walk to my window that overlooks the city below. I'm deep in thought and I barely listen to Nate who rattles on.

"After I check in with Valentina, you and I should drop in on an old pal of mine named Catch-Em-At-It Cashman. He used to be my sergeant ten years ago before he quit to go private. He knows everybody and he knows what they're up to especially when it comes to his competitors. I'm thinking there are things we ought to know about the lovebirds that maybe he can help us with."

He realizes I haven't been listening.

"Joe?"

"Sorry, Nate," I say. "Look, I'm having second thoughts. Maybe you shouldn't get in the middle of all this. A week from Wednesday I'm going to be flying back to Los Angeles. You have to live in this city, especially with Villiers. He can't hurt me but he can sure make life miserable for you."

He smiles.

"Thanks, Joe, but I can handle it. The young lady needs help. Further discussion unnecessary."

"That's decent of you, Nate, but---"

"Joe, I've been dealing with my sister all my life. And you can't seriously believe I'm worried about a stiff necked pencil pusher like Villiers? Don't think so. Any other questions?"

I look at him, all eager and ready to go, back to what he does best and I can only think of one thing to ask him.

"Why do they call him Catch-Em-At-It?"

CHAPTER NINETEEN

'm up early. Nate and I have places to go and people to see but unfortunately I also have a job and I feel obligated to give it at least a sliver of my time. So far everything that needs to be done has been done. I have nothing pressing which demands my attention. Best of all Charlie Berger and Jack Warner are three thousand miles away and not hovering over my shoulder so I don't have to "make work" when none needs "making".

On my desk in the production office I find an envelope filled with clips put there this morning by Sherry Shourds. Clips are newspaper clippings which, in this case, mention the movie, Warners Brothers, and/or any of our stars. A Canadian firm supplies the service and they've been doing an excellent job. I scan the contents of the envelope. We've gotten substantial stories from seventeen of the papers invited to last Sunday's press conference. All seem to be positive. I expect other stories to follow in the next day or two. I take the envelope over to Connie and ask her to fax copies to Charlie Berger back at the studio. I know he'll be delighted. So will Warner. I tell her that if Charlie calls she is to say I am on the set with the company and not expected back until late this evening. I am already covered on the set by the assistant director who will say I just left with a location party to scout a setting for tomorrow's shoot. If Charlie checks with the location people, the location manager will tell him that I have gone off with a very influential member of the press whose name he did not get. I do all this to protect not only myself but also Charlie who doesn't care what I do as long as I get my job done. Jack Warner is a different story. He is a clock watcher and in his eyes those on his payroll are subject to his whims from dawn to dusk seven days a week.

For a fleeting moment I think about calling Jillian but discard the idea immediately. First of all, it's only 5:15 back in California and secondly, she made it very clear that I was to back off, at least for the foreseeable future. I've agreed and I'll stick to it but it's going to be hard. I'll probably keep tabs on her by checking in with my ex-wife Lydia every couple of days.

"Morning, boss," I hear. I turn and there's Nate. "Ready to go?" he asks.

"Let's do it," I say.

A few minutes later we are cruising along the Rue de Claire-Fontaine heading northeast while Nate tells me that his friend Valentina at the motor vehicle office confirmed that the Buick out by the lake was indeed registered to Phillippe Bachelet. He also got Bachelet's address in case we found ourselves in need of it.

"Most interesting, Joe," Nate says.

"What's that?"

"Bachelet has a reputation for being something of a ladies man, a party goer, what's the term? Playboy?"

"It'll do."

"This life style requires money and not the kind of money a self-employed private detective would bring in. On top of that, I know this address where he lives. An upscale apartment house with exorbitant rents. For me this raises all sorts of questions like, does he have a fairy godfather?"

"Or more likely, a fairy godmother?" I suggest.

"Yes, much more likely," Nate says. He points ahead to the right. "There he is. The grey Chevy sedan."

Nate pulls to the curb and we get out. We walk over to the Chevy and Nate raps on the passenger side window. After a moment the window is rolled down and Catch-Em-At-It Cashman is smiling up at us. He has a 35 mm camera with a long lens hanging around his neck.

"Hey, Sarge. How ya doin'? Long time no see."

"Too long, Mel. And it's not Sarge any more, remember?"

"Sure, sure," he says. "Old habit." He shoots a quick glance at the hotel entrance a few doors down the street. Cashman's a lanky guy, 30ish, almost gaunt, with long stringy sand colored hair. He's wearing a tan windbreaker that says "Melville Chapman, Private Investigations" and a Red Wings baseball cap.

"This is my friend, Joe," Nate says.

"Hey, hiya, Joe. Gladda meet you." He sticks his hand out. We shake. I pull my hand away. It's sticky from something sweet and red. That's when I notice the box of jelly donuts on the dashboard.

"Got a couple of minutes. We need to talk."

"Sure, sure. Hop in," he says. Nate gets in front. I slide into the back seat. "I'm waitin' for this two bit shadrool to show his face so I can grab a couple of shots. Hey, you like that place? See the sign? L'Hotel de Roi de Pais. Sounds like a friggin' palace, right? Inside it smells so bad the rats ran away years ago. For this I shoulda stayed in Cleveland."

"Who's the target?" Nate asks.

"Guy named Morganstern. A real scumbag. Teaches poetry at Merici College. The rest of the time he's trying to dip his wick into one of his wide eyed students, most of whom are barely legal. His old lady who is not too swift finally caught on after four years." He shrugs. "It ain't pretty but it's a living."

"Gotta feed the kids," Nate says. "How are they doing?"

"Great. Got another one in the way."

"Congratulations. How many does that make?"

"Six, I think. Maybe seven. I lose count."

He says it with a straight face and then laughs. "Big family, that's the ticket. Twenty years from now the little squirts'll be taking care of me and the missus and I can quit this lousy racket." He cocks his head at Nate. "So, Sarge, what can I do for you? I know this ain't a social call."

"Phillippe Bachelet," Nate says.

"Ahhh," Cashman says with a thoughtful nod of his head.

"Translate ahhh for me, Mel," Nate says.

"A man of many colors," he says. "What's he done?"

"Not sure," Nate says. "What do you know about him?"

"Big cocksman, so I hear."

"You hear right. What else?"

"Spends money like he has it which he doesn't. A few weeks ago he got sideways with Johnny Zucco. Not a good place to be."

Nat looks back at me.

"Loan shark."

I nod.

"He came close to losing a kneecap. Some big money deal he thought was solid turned out to be horse puckey. I heard a lady he was schtupping saved his ass at the last second. Couldn't swear to it."

"The lady got a name?"

"Not one that I know," Cashman says.

Suddenly he sits up straight.

"Hold it!" he says as he aims his camera toward the hotel entrance and adjusts the focus. I look over as a fat little bald man in a brown tweed suit steps out into the sunlight. Whirr, click, whirr, click as Cashman rips off a couple of shots. Just then another figure emerges from the hotel. Five-four, blond pigtails and wearing a plaid jumper, she looks like a refugee from an all girls parochial school. She looks at Baldy and smiles. He looks at 'Heidi' and smiles back and then they head off in different directions. All the while Catch-Em-At-It is recording it for posterity.

"Jesus," Nate says in disbelief.

I shake my head. It's hard to figure.

Cashman is also bewildered.

"You know, if I'da known when I went to McKinley High just how powerful those Portuguese sonnets were, I'da gotten laid a lot more than I did." He shrugs. "Oh, well, that was then, this is now. What else would you like to know about your Casanova?"

"Whatever you've got. Where does he hang out? Who does he hang out with? Name of some old girlfriends. Anything you can tell me," Nate says.

Cashman gives us what he knows. It's not a pretty picture. Bachelet is not only a ladies man, he's something of a con artist, devious and manipulative, always on the lookout for an easy buck and if he has any scruples, he hasn't bothered to show them to anyone. I'm troubled by this. I like Claude Le Pen and admire him. I wonder how he got mixed up with this loser. It doesn't fit.

Catch-Em-At-It says he's through for the morning and

suggests breakfast. We decline. We have a full morning ahead of us. I can sense the circle tightening around Bachelet, but why he would want to frame Jeanne for Murder One I do not know unless, of course, he was doing it for someone else. This seems more likely and even more likely is the idea that he's done it for Marie Bruckner.

We thank him and head back to our car. Nate drives a few blocks in search of a phone booth and when he spots one, he pulls over. JoJo Rathbone had gotten Steinmetz's permission to dust his car for prints. It's a long shot. Bachelet is an ex-cop and no fool but it seemed worth a try. Now Nate is going to call one of his secret helpers in forensics to find out what, if anything, he came up with.

I watch as Nate completes the call and strides back to the car. He's got a Texas-sized grin on his face as he slips behind the wheel.

"Our boy is smart, Joe, but not that smart," he says.

"He found a print?"

Nate nods.

"Bachelet wiped everything clean but he forgot one spot. The inside of the chrome door handle."

"Now what?" I ask.

Nate smiles, relishing what is to come.

"Now we sweat him."

We pull away from the curb. We spitball ideas back and forth on how best to pressure Bachelet. Because of the Friday night attack at the dairy farm, Nate says the Crown can make a solid case against Bachelet for attempted murder and probably obstruction of justice. A conviction could put him away for ten years, maybe longer and that's our edge. An idea comes to me. I bounce it off Nate. He likes it. We'll go with it.

It's a few minutes to ten when we arrive at the courthouse. Today is the big day. Today is the day when Louis Marchand fingers the Gonsalvo brothers for their part in the school food swindle. The street outside the courthouse is jammed with onlookers. There isn't a parking spot to be had at this late hour. We creep along, hoping for the best. Up ahead Nate sees what looks to be a spot but it's next to a fire hydrant. Nate slides in and comes to a stop. He reaches into the glove compartment and takes out an official Surete Parking Permit which he affixes to the driver side sun visor. He sees me looking at him.

"On loan from a friend," he says with a smile. "Let's go."

We push our way through the milling crowd. At the entrance a security guard tries to stop us but Nate flashes an official looking identity card and we are immediately admitted. Another loan from a friend, no doubt. The lobby area is jam packed and there are guards at every door to the courtroom but at the moment it appears that no one has as yet been permitted in. I look around and spot Phillippe Bachelet over in the corner nervously puffing on a cigarette. I tap Nate on the arm. He looks and nods and we shoulder our way through the crowd to Bachelet's side.

"What's going on?" I ask.

"I'm not sure,' Bachelet says.

"Where's Claude?"

"In chambers with the Judge and the Crown Prosecutor. There's some kind of problem."

I frown and as I do, I look across the lobby and in the far corner I spot the Gonsalvo brothers. They are talking to someone whose back is to me. Whoever he is, he is listening intently to what the brothers have to say and he is taking notes on a pad. For a brief second he turns his head to look toward the courtroom doors and I recognize him immediately. Mackenzie

Starr, unemployed reporter, in search of a story. Even for a man like Starr, this is bottom feeding. I wonder if he has any sense of decency.

Just then the side door cracks open and Claude emerges. He spots us and hurries over. His expression is grim.

"Joe. Nate. Glad you're here," he says.

"What's happened?" I ask.

"They went after Louis last night," he says. "Someone dressed as a jailer got into the cell block and warned Louis to keep his mouth shut. He said if he didn't his family would be killed and then he would be killed in prison and there was no way he could prevent it. I don't have to tell you, Louis is terrified."

"Does this mean a mistrial?" Bachelet asks.

Claude shakes his head.

"The judge says no. Too much time and money has already been invested in this trial. It goes ahead. The police are already at his home guarding his family. As for Louis either he testifies or he doesn't, but the trial continues."

"And will he testify?" I ask.

Claude looks at me dolefully. "I don't know, Joe. I just don't know. I'll put him on the stand but after that----" He shrugs helplessly.

I look back toward the Gonsalvos. Starr continues to query them. I wonder what they're saying. They are smiling and relaxed. If they are worried about the outcome of this trial they certainly don't show it.

The crowd begins to stir and I look around. The courtroom doors are being opened and the spectators allowed in.

"Wish us luck," Claude says hopefully as he starts toward one of the doors. Bachelet starts to go with him. I grab him by the arm.

"Nate, you go in with Claude. I need a moment with Phillippe."

Bachelet looks at me curiously as Nate and Claude head into the courtroom. I take Bachelet by the arm and lead him over to the far side of the lobby where we can talk without being disturbed.

When I'm sure we can't be overheard, I speak to him quietly. "I need your help," I say.

He smiles.

"But of course. Any way that I can," he says.

"This is very confidential. Can I rely on your discretion?"

"You may."

"A member of our film company, one of our actors, has been receiving death threats," I say.

"Mon dieu. Which one?"

"For the moment I would rather not say. It may be nothing, just some lunatic with nothing better to do than write notes. But we have to take this seriously."

"Of course."

"We don't wish to bring in the police. Almost certainly there would be a leak and we can't have that. We need around the clock protection that doesn't call attention to itself. I can also tell you that this job will pay exceptionally well. Are you interested?"

"Very much so," Bachelet says.

"Good. There is a restaurant, Fidelio's, in the new city, small and out of the way where we can talk without being observed or overheard. Will three this afternoon be convenient for you?"

"It will, M. Bernardi. I am looking forward to further details."

"Good." I clap him in the shoulder. "Let's go in and see what's going on."

We start in. The guards are still at the door because the courtroom is filled to capacity. The guard on our side door knows Bachelet by sight but he blocks me.

"Mr. Bernardi is with me," Bachelet says.

"I understand, sir," the guard says, "but there are no seats."

"I'll stand at the rear,"I say.

The guard hesitates, then lets me pass by him.

We walk in and Bachelet continues down front to the defense table where Nate is already seated. I find a spot against the wall. As I do, Claude rises to his feet.

"If it please milord, the defense calls Louis Marchand."

Marchand hesitates for a moment, looking up at his attorney. They lock eyes for what seems an eternity and then slowly Marchand gets up and moves to the witness stand where he is sworn in. Slowly he sits down, nervously clasping and unclasping his hands.

For ten minutes perfunctory questions are asked and answered. It is established that Marchand was responsible for overseeing the purchase, delivery and distribution of food stuffs to the public schools in the Quebec City school districts.

Claude hesitates, then turns and walks back the table and leans on it. He looks up and he spots me standing in the back. I nod to him. If he noticed he gives no sign.

"M. Le Pen?" the Judge says.

Claude turns and faces Marchand.

"M. Marchand, in the performance of your duties was there ever a time when you were approached by outside individuals and asked to divert these foodstuffs elsewhere?"

Marchand stares at him silently and then looks down. A hush falls over the courtroom. It's as if every sound has been sucked out of the atmosphere. The Gonsalvos are sitting back relaxed. Everyone else awaits Marchand's answer with great anticipation.

"M. Marchand, did you hear my question?"

"Yes."

"Did you understand it?"

"Yes."

"Do you need it read back to you?"

"No."

Marchand lifts his head and looks out into the gallery, directly at the Gonsalvo brothers. Again, the pause is interminable.

"M. Marchand," Claude says.

"Yes."

"Yes what?" Claude says.

"Yes, I was approached to steal from the school district."

I shoot a look at the brothers. They have shot forward in their seats and they are no longer smiling.

"You were approached by whom, M. Marchand."

"Two men. Brothers."

"And can you tell us their names?"

"I can. Vito and Salvatore Gonsalvo." He looks out toward the gallery, then gets to his feet and points an accusing finger. "That's them! Right there!" He takes a step toward them. "Salopards! Aller en enfer!"

Sal Gonsalvo struggles to push past his brother into the aisle. As he does two security officers run toward him.

"You motherfuckin' son of a bitch!" Sal is screaming even as the guards are trying to take him down.

Mansard is screaming back at him.

"You try to kill me? You threaten my family? I will see you dead, the two of you! Tu son fils de pute!"

Another guard joins the melee and they have Sal Gonsalvo

down on the ground while Vito stares straight ahead, ramrod stiff, staring hard at Marchand. Marchand stares back, just as hard. The Judge is slamming his gavel and calling for order. Marchand turns and looks over at Claude and allows himself a faint smile. Then he turns and quietly resumes his seat in the witness box as the security guards drag Sal Gonsalvo from the courtroom.

Thirty minutes later Nate and I are standing outside the courthouse. The Judge has continued the case until ten the following Monday but the rest is formality. Since Marchand has admitted his guilt from the stand, all that is left is for the Judge to pronounce sentence, taking into account Marchand's help in implicating the Gonsalvo brothers. A short distance away I see the brothers emerge from the side door. They are in handcuffs and being led by the security people to a police van.

I turn as Claude and Bachelet approach. Claude is smiling broadly. I'm the first to congratulate him.

"I knew Louis would come through," Claude says. "He is too good a man to let those bastards walk away."

I point to the police van.

"Seems to me they're not walking anywhere anytime soon."

Claude nods.

"No, they are not, Joe. The Commander of the Ontario Provincial Police was in the gallery this morning. Based on Louis' testimony, he now feels he has enough evidence to arrest the Gonsalvos for theft and conspiracy." He smiles and his expression becomes thoughtful. "We owe it all to Daniel, you know. It was his idea to have Louis accuse them from the witness stand. He'd have been very proud of this moment."

"I'm sure he would have," I say. "What about Marchand? He's still in danger, especially now that the brothers may be joining him in prison. Is there anything you can do for him?"

"The Crown Prosecutor and I have talked to the Judge. We think he's going to be sentenced to three years but we're trying to make a case for having him serve his time in a prison in one of the prairie provinces, maybe even under an assumed name. We'll know something tomorrow morning. We also think his family will be relocated to an unknown destination out west,"

"Good plan, Claude. Daniel would have been proud of that as well."

He nods. "Well, it's back to the office and a load of paperwork. Call me later, Joe. I want to get together with you some evening before you fly back to the States. Good food, good wine and no shop talk."

"I look forward to it," I say.

We shake hands warmly before he starts toward his car. Bachelet starts to follow him. I grab his arm and say quietly, "Three o'clock."

"Three o'clock," Bachelet replies and then hurries after Claude.

CHAPTER TWENTY

idelio's is a small family restaurant in the Petit Champlain neighborhood of old Quebec City. It is two blocks from the lower terminus of the funicular. Owned and operated by Pietro Bataglia, it serves exquisite Northern Italian cuisine and is wildly popular among the locals who frequent it several times a week. The rest of the city's population has never heard of it and that is just fine with Pietro who has refused for a decade to enlarge the premises beyond a small bar to the left of the entrance, six wall booths and eight tables for six or less. Fidelio's is open from eleven to two for lunch and from six to nine for dinner. It is closed from two until six except for special occasions of which today is one. Did I mention that Pietro's brother is Fredo Bataglia, a veteran detective with the Surete?

Fredo and I are in a back room along with Nate and Zekiel Hoey, an engineer from a local radio station, who is a whiz with reel-to-reel tape recording. A small near-invisible microphone has been hidden among the flowers on the table in the rear booth. We have tested reception twice. It is impeccable. I check my watch. Nine minutes to three. I take my place in the booth facing the front door just in case Bachelet is early. Nate, whom Bachelet knows on sight, will remain in the back room with

Zekiel. Fredo will sit at the end of the bar drinking chianti. One of the booths and four of the tables will be occupied. The number of volunteers willing to defy Inspector Villiers has swelled from six to seventeen. A couple is sitting in the front booth. He is a crime scene photographer. She is the assistant dispatcher for the Surete motor pool. Four men who look like day laborers are sitting at a table in the center of the room, enjoying bread and cheese and good wine while they argue the merits and deficiencies of the country's various soccer teams. All four are off-duty detectives. A retired sergeant and his wife sit at another table. At a third are a man and woman squabbling like husband and wife. He's in press relations. She's his secretary. The squabbling is realistic. I think they've been at it many times before.

Finally a man sits alone at a fourth table. His name is Roger Lescroart. He is heavy set with steel grey hair. He is dabbling at a plate of spaghetti even as he pretends to read the morning newspaper through thick reading glasses. He is a retired Inspector of the Surete who was replaced by Luc Villiers. He considers Villiers a political hack and an embarrassment to the force. He is with us as a labor of love.

Pietro has just brought me a cup of cappuccino and a small plate of bruschetta when the front door opens and Bachelet enters. He sees me and heads in my direction smiling. He slides into the booth opposite me, right where I want him, a foot and a half away from the floral display.

I glance at my watch.

"Right on time," I say.

"I believe in promptness," he says.

Pietro approaches the table, pad and pencil in hand.

"What'll you have?" I say.

He looks up at Pietro.

"Chardonnay, sil vous plait," he says.

Pietro shrugs apologetically.

"I am sorry, monsieur. I have an excellent trebbiano or if you prefer, a verdicchio."

"White?"

"But of course."

Bachelet nods.

"Either one. You choose."

"Tres bien, monsieur," Pietro says backing away.

Bachelet turns back to me.

"So, Joe, who's the unlucky target? Clift?"

I put up my hand.

"In a moment. Before we start, a couple of groundrules. First of all, no publicity. Whatever transpires, you don't talk about it, you don't write about it, you don't put it in your memoirs a dozen years from now."

"Of course."

"I'll need that in writing."

"Naturally," Bachelet says. "What else?"

"No additional assignments. We will pay you more than enough to make up the difference but for the duration of the job, you work for us exclusively. No one else. Not even Le Pen."

"It is not a problem," he says. He is about to say more when Roger Lescroart slips into the booth next to him, sealing off any potential escape venue. Roger smiles at him and says nothing as I do the introductions.

"This is Roger, head of security for the movie company. It was he who suggested we get outside help to deal with this problem."

Bachelet smiles.

"Bonjour."

Roger smiles and continues to say nothing. He doesn't want his voice on the tape. Neither do the others. The only voices that will ever be heard will be mine and Bachelet's.

"I was saying, about exclusivity," I continue.

"Yes. No problem," he says again.

"Your arrangement with Claude was non-exclusive," I say.

"That is correct."

Two of the four men at the center table have gotten up and walked over to the booth. One of them slides in next to me. The other grabs a chair from a nearby table and pulls it up to the booth. Bachelet reacts by looking at me, totally puzzled.

"I thought this was to be top secret," he says.

"These men can be trusted," I say. I point them out. "Armand. Nils."

The two newcomers smile but say nothing. These are not their real names.

"Now, as to exclusivity," I say, continuing on. "We can't allow anything like your escapade last Friday evening when you chased me and my friends all over the north end of the city in that white Citroen."

Bachelet's eyes narrow. His first glimmer that something is going wrong here.

"That is ridiculous. I know of the assault, of course, but it certainly wasn't me. I was told it was the Gonsalvo brothers."

"You were told wrong, Phillippe. They were back at their hotel, in for the night and their rented car never moved."

"This I did not know, but to accuse me----"

"You had already bribed someone at motor vehicles to lead you to a white Citroen identical to what the Gonsalvo's were driving. You found it parked on the street and it was a simple matter to jimmy open the door and hot wire the ignition. Child's play for an experienced private investigator."

The squabbling husband and wife have left their table and now they have taken up positions in the adjoining booth. The other two men from the table of four seat themselves at the table next to our booth. Bachelet's eyes are flicking everywhere, trying to figure what's happening.

"You'd learned that Claude and I were going to meet Marie Bruckner at her lake cottage. You followed us and when we tried to outrace you, you sped up and shot at us, supposedly trying to kill one or both of us. When that didn't succeed, you turned and ran. You drove back to the city and returned the car to the street, failing to notice the bullet hole in the windshield."

Bachelet's eyes are blazing with anger.

"You, M. Bernardi, are a damned liar and I am not going to sit here and listen to any more of this. Excuse me."

He tries without success to shove his way past Roger.

"You will stay seated and you will listen, Mr. Bachelet, because Jeanne d'Arcy isn't going to spend one more day in jail awaiting trial for a murder that she did not commit but that you did."

Here is where I hold my breath. I am counting on the fact that he doesn't as yet know about Jeanne's hospital confession. We lock eyes as Fredo steps away from the bar, slips out of his suit jacket, and hangs it neatly on the back of a chair. He walks toward our booth and then stands behind me, leaning against the wall, staring down at Bachelet who can hardly ignore the. 45 automatic tucked into the holster hanging below Fredo's left armpit.

"I killed no one," Bachelet protests. "What are you trying to do? Who are these people?"

I relax a little. He doesn't know.

"You thought you had carefully wiped away any finger-prints before you walked away from the car and you almost succeeded," I tell him. "You wiped away all but one which the forensic people found on the inside of the front door handle so don't insult me with any more of your lies."

He shakes his head. "No, no. You have it all wrong. Why would I do such a thing?"

"To divert suspicion," I say. "Somehow you learned of the vicious fight between Jeanne d'Arcy and Daniel Bruckner at Clarisse's restaurant. It seemed like a perfect opportunity. You sneaked into the apartment house through the garage door. A locked door presented no problem to a man of your experience. You killed Bruckner and set about creating so-called evidence that he was murdered by his enraged ex-mistress who only an hour or two earlier had threatened to kill him."

Bachelet shakes his head.

"This is insane. Why would I kill him? What motive could I have?"

"You did it for your employer. With Bruckner dead, Claude Le Pen inherits Bruckner's half of the business. Men have killed for less."

"You have this all wrong," Bachelet protests. Tiny beads of sweat are starting to form at his hairline. He tries to hide it but his hand is trembling.

"Almost immediately you realize the sloppy frame you've tried to hang on Jeanne d'Arcy won't hold up to scrutiny, at least not by a smarter cop than Luc Villiers. You need something, anything to divert suspicion away from you. Maybe Claude thinks of it first. The Gonsalvos. Why not? There are those who believe they may have killed Daniel. If so, then why not also kill Claude Le Pen for the same reason, to thwart the trial of Louis Marchand. So Claude calls me and Nate and tells us that we have been invited to Marie's cottage by the lake. Of course,

214

she knows nothing of this. You are waiting and give chase in an attempt to frighten us and implicate the brothers. You fire high and wild to make sure you don't hit Le Pen. I remember Nate remarking on your lousy aim as we ducked for cover. What you hadn't counted on was Nate's ability to return fire and when that happened you ran for it."

"No one will believe this," Bachelet protests but there is no conviction in his words. He takes a paper napkin from the table dispenser and dabs at his forehead. He wants to hide but he can't.

"We drive back to town to file a report with the Surete. A funny thing occurs to me. Why did Marie not try to contact us when we didn't show up? Was she not the least bit worried or even curious? And, of course, the answer is obvious. She didn't even know we were coming."

Bachelet suddenly leans forward, his eyes blazing.

"The hell she didn't!" he says sharply.

"What?"

"She knew," Bachelet says. "She knew everything."

I laugh.

"Oh, I see. Now you are going to blame the widow. No, no, my homicidal friend, that won't work. Everything I have laid out is true. It fits together like a jigsaw puzzle."

"You are an idiot, Bernardi. A pompous wannabe detective without a clue." Bachelet says, contempt oozing from every pore.

I shake my head. "No, I am never wrong. I always have my facts straight."

Now I am playing smug and self-assured, almost cocky. I smirk at him. He wants to reach across the table and slug me. Good. I am doing everything I can to reel him in, slowly but surely as he loses his composure.

He looks around.

"These men, they are here for what reason? To beat the truth out of me? That will not be necessary." He snorts derisively. "Claude Le Pen sanctioning murder. Mon dieu, how stupid are you? The man is a living, breathing catechism, a deacon of his church. He would not hurt a rabid dog that was tearing at his leg. No,no. Not Claude Le Pen. But Marie Bruckner, there we have a different story, my addle brained friend. There is a woman who would cut the throat of her first born just for the joy of watching the blood flow."

I try to look aghast.

"That's a wicked and slanderous thing to say. No, you can't lie your way out of this, Bachelet. We have you dead to rights."

He shakes his head in frustration.

"You think so, eh?" He stares into my eyes, a faint smile on his lips. "You think you know everything. You know nothing. Your sweet little playmate, the vivacious Jeanne d'Arcy who no doubt warmed your bed more than once, eh, that young lady is a killer. She is guilty."

"That's not true," I say, feigning uncertainty.

Bachelet pounds the table.

"It is true!" he shouts, "and if you would shut your mouth for a minute, I will tell you how I know."

I laugh softly.

"Fine," I say. "Tell us your fairy tale. We could all use a good laugh."

He nods and pats his shirt pocket in annoyance.

"Someone give me a cigarette," he says.

Fredo steps forward and proffers an open pack. Bachelet takes one and lights it with a pack of matches that has been lying next to the ashtray. He picks up his wine glass and finishes the dregs. His hand continues to tremble. He looks around and then concentrates on me.

"For several months, Marie Bruckner and I have been seeing each other."

"Socially?"

"Socially," he says icily. "Sure. Socially. I've been fucking her, okay? She got tired of talking about tennis with an adolescent and I found myself getting really bored by the price of housing. We met often out by the lake. It posed no danger. Daniel hated the place. The pollen hated Daniel even more."

I nod thoughtfully.

"Was this entirely an affair of the heart or was there a business aspect as well?"

His expression turns to anger.

"Monsieur, you insult me," he says.

"All right, I'll rephrase it. Did Marie give you money to pay off your debt to Johnny Zucco?"

That stops him cold. He realizes that I know a lot more than I am letting on. He has to be careful.

"I accepted a loan, yes. I was temporarily low on funds," he says.

"You've been temporarily low on funds for months now, Bachelet. That's the way I hear it."

"You make our relationship sound tawdry, M. Bernardi. I assure you it was not. We hoped to get married."

"Difficult, considering the lady already had a husband who wasn't about to give her up."

"He would have done so, eventually. He had no chance to be elected, the experts all said that. When that pipe dream was put to bed, he would have let her go gladly."

"And she would have taken a substantial chunk of his assets

with her. Isn't that what it's always been about for you, Bachelet? A rich divorcee. No more money worries. Once again you're a bon vivant, a man about town, courting the girls and leaving a tiresome wife at home."

"We are in love," he says.

"Have you set a date yet?"

"No. We are showing respect."

"Thoughtful of you," I say. "Does this mean you will get married the day before the funeral or the day after?"

"You are quite the cynic, sir," Bachelet tells me.

"No, just a realist. All right, now tell me about the night Daniel Bruckner died."

He looks up at Fredo and pantomimes his need for another cigarette. Without moving from the wall, Fredo tosses the pack onto the table. Bachelet lights up and inhales deeply.

"We were together at the lake cottage when the phone call came. It was around eleven o'clock. I'm not sure who was on the other end of the line. A female friend who was at the restaurant and saw everything and as friends are known to do, she couldn't wait to call and recount every sordid detail of the incident. The moment she hung up Marie grabbed her car keys and headed for the door. She said she was going to have it out with Daniel once and for all. I offered to go with her but she said no, that she wanted to go by herself. She would be back as soon as possible.

"I made something to eat, cracked open a new book and was reading in a chair by the front window when she returned. I looked up at the clock. It was just chiming three a.m. When she walked through the front door carrying that paper bag I knew immediately that something awful had happened. Her face was ashen and drawn. I asked if she was all right. She nodded that she was fine but then she slumped down on a nearby chair and for a long time she said nothing. Then she looked up at me. 'Daniel is dead'. she said, 'and Jeanne d'Arcy killed him." At first I couldn't believe what I had heard but she repeated it.

"I could see she was shivering and I fixed her a drink. She took it eagerly and swallowed deeply. It seemed to calm her. Then she continued. As she was approaching the apartment building she saw Jeanne d'Arcy emerge from the underground parking area and run across the street to her car which she had parked at curbside. As Jeanne drove away, Marie pulled into the garage. She said she knew immediately that something was wrong and her worst fears were confirmed when she entered the apartment and found her husband dead on the floor, the bloody letter opener protruding from his stomach. He'd removed his jacket and tie which were tossed aside on the floor, perhaps thinking that Jeanne was there to reconcile. His white shirt front was soaked with blood."

He falls silent and takes a long drag on his cigarette.

"What then?" I ask.

"She looked around the room and saw the cigarette butts in the ashtray. Jeanne's brand. That should lead the police in her direction but thinks, will it be enough? She isn't sure so at that moment Marie does something incredibly stupid. Very gingerly and using a handkerchief, she removes the letter opener from Daniel's body and puts it into a paper bag. A last look around and then she is on her way back to the cottage.

"By now she's on her second drink. She has calmed down. Calculated reason has now replaced panic. She points to the paper bag. She wants me to place the letter opener in Jeanne's car as soon as possible. Before dawn if I can. If Jeanne has driven to her cottage at the end of Avrom Pinchot's driveway and left her car outside the front door with the top down, as she always does, it will be no problem, but I don't think it's a good idea and I tell her so. I tell her she should have left the letter opener in the body. She screams at me. If I love her I will do as she asks. When I hesitate she begins to cry. Can't you see? she says. It's what we've prayed for. Now we can get married. I sit beside her and put my arms around her. She is right. Providence has brought us to this point. I will do as she asks."

Bachelet lights another cigarette.

"I need a drink," he says quietly.

I signal to Pietro who hurries to the booth.

"Scotch. A double. Neat," Bachelet says.

Pietro nods and hurries over to the bar.

I stare at Bachelet. He looks haggard but in his demeanor I also sense relief. He won't need to be prodded. He is tired of the lies. He wants it out in the open.

Pietro returns with the scotch. Bachelet takes a deep swallow and then exhales. He is calm now.

"That Friday night," I say. "The car chase up by the dairy farm. Your idea or hers?"

"Hers," he says. "On Thursday you'd gone to see her at the lake. She was drunk, probably hoped to seduce you and failed. Finally you succeeded where I had not. You convinced her that the planting of the letter opener was too obvious, too contrived. In a way it almost indicated that Jeanne d'Arcy was not the killer. Marie said we needed a diversion, anything to point the finger away from her involvement. The Gonsalvos were in town. Weeks before they had threatened Daniel. Now they were threatening Claude. They were made to order. So, you ask, whose idea? Hers. Whose plan? Mine."

"I guess that makes you an accessory after the fact," I say.

Bachelet forces a humorless smile.

"Accessory to what, M. Bernardi?" he asks. "Interfering with a police investigation? Tampering with evidence? After Jeanne d'Arcy is tried and convicted of murder, no one will care. If the Crown insists on pursuing the matter, a good lawyer will be able to get the charges reduced to misdemeanors and a very good lawyer will secure a sentence of probation."

"And you and Marie live happily ever after."

He shrugs.

"Why not?"

I smile.

"If I were a generous man, I would say that you and the lady deserve a chance at happiness. But I am not a generous man nor a forgiving one so the best I can say is that you and Marie Bruckner deserve each other." I wave my hand at him. "You're free to go, the quicker the better."

Roger Lescroart slides out of the booth to give Bachelet room to leave. He hurries toward the door and goes without once turning back.

Roger smiles down at me.

"So now we know. Well done, my American friend. You have the soul of a policeman. I am proud to have met you."

He puts out is hand and we shake.

He has no idea how much I wish that he were still Chief Inspector instead of Luc Villiers.

We have won a battle but with Villiers in charge of the case, the war is far from over.

CHAPTER TWENTY ONE

t's raining.

This is the first bad weather day we've had since arriving in Quebec and strangely it was not expected. The weather reports called for temperatures in the high 50's, overcast in the morning turning to sunny skies in the early afternoon. The company was prepared to shoot an exterior street scene outside the home of the murdered lawyer. Monty was to walk to it from his church and while there spot Anne Baxter in the crowd. Now Hitchcock will have to scramble to prepare an indoor "cover" set which was not scheduled until Friday. Either that or he shuts down and waits for a break in the weather or if the rain is light enough, he can shoot the scene in such a way that the rain will not be visible on screen. After agonizing for twenty minutes, he opts to shoot in the rain.

None of this should affect me. Publicists don't stumble about in rain storms getting soaked to the skin. Like screenwriters, publicity folk get to hunker down under warm dry blankets and ignore the jangling of an alarm clock. A star like Monty Clift gets to stand underneath an umbrella held by the DGA trainee assigned to the picture while the trainee, unprotected from the elements, risks everything from the sniffles to pneumonia for his chance at film immortality.

That's the way it's supposed to be but it's not working out that way. This morning I am standing under the inadequate awning of a patisserie with my feet soaked and a rain laden breeze whipping moisture at me in copious amounts. How could this have happened, I keep asking myself, even though I know the answer full well. It all started last night when I got back to the Frontenac from Fidelio's restaurant.

The first thing I did was call Surete headquarters to speak to Inspector Villiers and make an appointment to play him the tape. He wasn't there but was expected back within the hour. I left word with his assistant to have him call me. I emphasized that I needed to speak with him at his first opportunity. I took the police report and the autopsy report from my desk drawer along with the transcript of the Marie Bruckner deposition conducted by Esther at her office. I brought them up to my room and for two hours I studied them intently.

By seven o'clock I hadn't heard from him so I called again and got the same assistant. Yes, the Inspector had returned and yes, he is aware you called and no, he is not here, he has left for dinner. Where? The assistant didn't know. I left word again. The Inspector is to call me immediately no matter the time, after midnight, three a.m. it makes no difference. I hung up and ordered room service. Onion soup, a sandwich and a small pot of coffee. As I ate I continued to pore over the data becoming increasingly aware that several things didn't fit. It was like putting together a jigsaw puzzle of Mt. Everest. I'd seen the box cover. I knew what the finished puzzle was supposed to look like so assembling it was easy. A piece of snowcapped crag here, a sliver of waterfall there, an edge of blue sky, a corner of a snowy valley, and click,

click, click, the pieces go together smoothly. Unfortunately when I get finished I'm not looking at Mt. Everest, I've put together an Alaskan glacier. How could I have gone wrong? What have I missed? I'm reminded of the old chestnut about the six blind folded men who are told to touch an elephant in different parts of its body and then describe what the animal looks like. Each one comes up with a ludicrous description because none has the big picture and I realize that I am a world class elephant toucher. I, too, am missing the big picture.

By midnight I figured I wasn't on Villiers' to-do list. More drastic action was called for. That was when I picked up the afternoon paper and spotted the item. At eight o'clock tomorrow morning the Inspector is scheduled to speak at a breakfast for the Quebec Ladies Auxiliary for Hospitals. Aha, I said to myself. He can run but he can't hide. I called Nate at home and told him he was needed early in the morning. Front entrance. Seven o'clock. No later. I turned in and tried to sleep but that earlier pot of coffee kept getting in the way.

The Brass Kettle is an old established restaurant in "new" Quebec. It reeks of atmosphere and boasts a five star chef. It is "headquarters" to a half- dozen local organizations which hold their monthly meetings there before the doors are opened for the regular trade. Success, however, has bred a problem. The tiny street where the Kettle is located is narrow and when cars are parked curbside on both sides, only a Mini-Cooper is comfortable driving it. Because of the breakfast, all the parking spots are taken, Nate and the Puegeot are blocks away but we cannot take the chance of missing Villiers so I stand, only half protected from the elements, waiting for his appearance. I would like to wait inside the restaurant but Villiers, who has a bloated opinion of his own importance, has stationed a uniformed officer at the doorway and only ladies of the hospitals are being admitted. I would also like to wait inside the patisserie but the sign on the door tells me it is closed for the day due to a death in the family. No other shops nearby are open at this hour except for a druggist who, on learning I was American, unceremoniously ushered me from his store. And here I was beginning to think that the only rude Frenchmen lived in France.

Then as the rain begins to abate I see him coming up the sidewalk, trudging toward the restaurant, flanked by two plainclothes detectives, one of whom is holding an umbrella over Villiers' head. Avoiding potholes and puddles, I jog across the street to intercept him. He scowls when he sees me coming.

"Not now, M. Bernardi," he snaps gruffly.

"I just need a minute, Inspector," I say. "It's important."

"With you, sir, it is always important. I have no time to waste on your fantasies."

He tries to brush past me but I edge in front of him, blocking his way.

"I have solid evidence that bears directly on this case. I need you to listen to it."

Villiers turns his head toward the lackey not holding the umbrella and whispers something in French. A moment later I have been wrestled impolitely from Villiers' path. Furious I scream after him.

"Why, you arrogant blockheaded fool, how in hell did you ever get to be an Inspector? You're not qualified to inspect the lint in your navel!"

He turns back toward me, enraged.

"Another word from you and I'll place you under arrest," he says.

"For what? Telling the truth? Baring the facts? Go ahead. I'm ready and willing to turn you into the laughing stock of Quebec City, Villiers, and I have all I need to make it happen." I walk up to him and hold out my wrists. "Come on, Inspector. Don't be shy. Slap on the cuffs. I'm going to turn this little curbside tiff into something akin to the Dreyfus affair but you have to do your share. Arresting me would be a good start."

"You're a fool," he says.

"Maybe so, but this fool is not as stupid as you think. At four o'clock this afternoon I am holding a press conference at the law offices of Claude Le Pen. I have invited over thirty reporters and editors from all the major newspapers in Quebec Province. I am personally acquainted with each one of these people and each one has promised to show up. I have guaranteed them an explosive story which will tear the lid off the Daniel Bruckner murder investigation and reveal in detail the hidebound incompetence of the inspector in charge of the investigation. You're welcome to attend if you have the balls,"

I step closer, invading his personal space, looking into his eyes unflinchingly. I do not tell him that the thirty reporters are basically gossip columnists whose acquaintance with real journalism is fleeting at best. I also do not tell him that I haven't actually scheduled the press conference though I am prepared to do so. In fact I am prepared to do just about anything to wipe that smug smirk off Villers' face.

Convinced that I have put the fear of God in him, I turn and start to walk away.

"Wait!" he calls out. I turn back to him. "Just exactly what is it you want of me?"

"I want you to sit down and listen to a thirty minute tape recording. If you do so with an open mind, I'll call off the press."

He hesitates for a moment.

"Very well, my office at one o'clock," he says."Be on time."

"No," I say. "Claude Le Pen's office at noon. My tape, my turf, my timetable. Don't be late."

I again turn and walk away, heading up the sidewalk in search of Nate McIvers and his Peugeot. I feel proud of myself and there's a self-satisfied skip in my step. If things work out the way I hope they will, Jeanne will be freed within the next 24 hours.

It is now ten minutes to noon. Zekiel Hoey has set up the reel- to-reel tape deck in Claude's conference room. Claude is in his office tending to a few details regarding Louis Marchand's sentencing and incarceration. Phone calls are been flying back and forth between Claude and the Crown Prosecutor and the Minister of Justice in Ottawa. It appears a deal is in the offing which will send Marchand west to a prison in Manitoba. Claude has promised to drop everything when Villiers arrives. He wants to be in on the skewering.

An out-of-breath Esther Laval has just arrived and is seated at the foot of the table. When I told her there was a chance we might be able to secure Jeanne's freedom she dropped everything and scurried right over. Already seated at the table is Roger Lescroart, Villiers predecessor as Chief Inspector of the Quebec City Surete. He has no standing here, official or otherwise, but I want him on hand as a symbol of what Canadian justice is supposed to be, something Villiers never knew or has conveniently forgotten in the pursuit of a gaudy arrest record. Nate is sprawled in a chair off in the corner reading the morning paper.

At one minute to twelve there is a light rap on the conference room door. The receptionist enters followed by Villiers and the two cohorts who were with him earlier this morning on his walk to the Brass Kettle.

I greet him but he seems not to notice. He doesn't bother to introduce his lackeys who immediately take seats against the wall. His eyes scan the room and narrow perceptibly when they settle on Roger.

"What's he doing here?" Villiers demands to know.

"Observing, Luc,' Roger says. "Merely observing, The Director-General in Montreal and I had a long chat this morning."

Villiers visibly stiffens on hearing this.

"I don't care if you broke bread with the viceroy, you have no business here, Lescroart." he says.

"He's here because I want him here," I say. "If you object, Inspector, feel free to leave. I have thirty reporters sitting by their phones waiting anxiously for my call."

Irritably, Villiers sits heavily in one of the chairs that flank the conference table. His self-assured bravado seems to be melting away. He does not know that the Director-General is Roger's third cousin once removed, and that the morning's entire topic of conversation involved fly fishing.

"If this is another rehash of your preposterous claim that Mlle. d'Arcy acted in self defense you are wasting my time and yours," Villiers says trying to regain control of the situation.

Roger sighs audibly.

"Look, Luc, I know it's difficult for a man of your intellect but just this once why don't you shut up and listen instead of revealing to all of us everything you don't know."

Villiers is about to respond when Claude enters, greets everyone effusively and suggests, since we are all busy people, that we get started immediately. I heartily concur and a few moments later we are all seated at the conference table and Zekiel Hoey has started the tape.

I have heard it from start to finish three times and taken extensive notes so I concentrate on studying those at the table. Nate and Roger were present at the taping. They know what it's all about. Esther and Claude as well as Villiers are hearing it for the first time. When we get to the part where I accuse Bachelet of killing Daniel on orders from Le Pen, Claude looks at me in a panic. Esther is startled and Villiers, as usual, is confused. I hold up my hand to Claude, palm first and shake my head as if to say, don't worry. More to come. When Bachelet triumphantly tells me that it wasn't Claude at all but Marie who was behind everything, Claude realizes what I had been up to and sits back in his chair, the tension draining from his body.

By the time we get to the end of the tape, everyone in the room has a pretty complete picture of what had been occurring over the past several days. Only one of us has not completely caught up.

"Hearsay," Villiers harrumphs.

"What?" I say.

"All that business implicating Marie Bruckner. Hearsay. Inadmissable," Villiers says.

"My God," Roger mutters to no one in particular raising his eyes to the ceiling.

I lean forward as far as I can, staring Villiers down. "This is an investigative report, Inspector. It is not and never was intended for the courtroom."

"Joe is right, Inspector," Claude says. "Review the forensics and reinterview Marie Bruckner. If Bachelet is telling the truth, and I believe he is, Marie is guilty of tampering with evidence, of interfering with a police investigation and her actions certainly lend great credence to Jeanne d'Arcy's claim of self-defense." He looks over at Esther Laval. "Esther, am I not right?"

She nods.

"You are, Claude," she says. "Inspector Villiers, I suggest you immediately rethink the charges you have brought against my client. In the short term I suggest that you persuade the Crown Prosecutor to release Jeanne d'Arcy without bail while your new investigation is ongoing. I further suggest that you immediately arrest Phillippe Bachelet on charges relating to the shooting incident out by the dairy farm Friday evening last. I further suggest that you use this charge as a bargaining chip in getting Bachelet to testify in open court to the facts which you have just heard here. With his testimony under oath they are no longer hearsay. Have I made myself clear?"

"Probably not," Roger mutters under his breath.

Villiers shoots him a dirty look, then turns back to the rest of us. "Look, I know how anxious you all are to free Mlle. d'Arcy but this so-called confession isn't going to do it. First of all, I don't know whether any or all of this was said under duress. And by the way, who are all these people who were sitting around listening? He said he was afraid they were there to beat the truth out of him. How can anything he said be taken seriously?"

"Because the men who were there were merely observers," I say, "and each one of them is an upstanding citizen of the Province"

"Easy enough for you to say, M. Bernardi," Villiers says smugly.

"I say as well, Luc," Roger says, "and you can put my name at the top of the list."

"Then I am ashamed for you, my friend, a man of your stature associating himself with all this hokum." His look is contemptuous as he looks back at me. "And another thing, M. Bernardi, regarding this notion that Marie went to the crime scene and falsified evidence. We have only Bachelet's word for this and not one scintilla of evidence that she was even there."

"That's where you're wrong, Inspector." I say.

He cocks his head disbelievingly.

"You have a witness that places her in the apartment?"

"I do, and the best kind," I say. "The lady herself."

Villiers eyes narrow suspiciously.

"Explain yourself, M. Bernardi."

"Certainly."

I have brought a plain 9 x 12 manila envelope with me to this meeting. It is sitting in front of me. I open it and take out the two official reports and a copy of the deposition of Marie Bruckner that took place in Esther's office on Monday afternoon. I flip a couple of pages of the deposition until I find what I want.

"Daniel Bruckner died between one and two a.m. on Tuesday morning. The police were summoned by the housekeeper who found his body on the living room floor shortly before seven o'clock in the morning." I pick up the police report and double check something.

"The police arrive at 7:18 and Inspector Villiers at 7:55 followed shortly by the forensics team. The apartment is dusted for prints. Possible evidence is bagged and put aside for analysis by the lab people back at headquarters. Included in this is the new Queen Anne cigarette lighter which carries clear and distinct fingerprints all of which later turn out to belong to Jeanne d'Arcy. Mrs. Bruckner is sent for and brought into town from the lakeside cottage. She arrives with police escort a few minutes before eleven. Her husband's body has been taken away as has most of the bagged evidence. The tape outline of the body remains on the carpet as does a very large bloodstain."

"Is there a point to all this?" Villiers growls.

I raise my hand to shut him up.

"Jump ahead to Monday last. Marie Bruckner is being deposed under oath by Esther Laval. I ask her several cogent questions and she loses her composure. In her frenzied attempt to convince us that Jeanne d'Arcy is a murderess, she mentions the ashtray filled with Gitane cigarette butts which was sitting next to the lighter. Since these items were long gone when she arrived how did she know they'd been there, particularly the lighter which was brand new and only put out on the table the day before?" I look Villiers squarely in the eye. "Inspector?"

For a moment he says nothing.

"Shall I explain it to you, Luc?" Roger says helpfully.

"I understand what was said," Villiers says sharply. "Yes, I see your point, M. Bernardi. She probably was there. I see no other explanation."

"Then you will talk to the Crown Prosecutor?" Esther says.

"Yes, and I will, as Mme. Laval suggested, re-interview Mme. Bruckner. Tampering with evidence and interfering with a police investigation are serious crimes," Villiers says.

"So is murder," I say, never taking my eyes from him.

"Murder? Why do you say murder, monsieur?" Villiers asks.

"Because I believe that Marie Bruckner is guilty of killing her husband."

I wait for a collective gasp of surprise There is none. Not even one. I've been watching too many Philo Vance movies.

"You are out of your mind," Villiers says.

"Am I?" I say. "Let's recap Bachelet's version of events. Marie gets a phone call at the cottage. Daniel has made a drunken fool of himself at the restaurant. He tried to bully Jeanne. Jeanne threatened to kill him. Marie grabs her car keys and heads into the city to have it out with him. Divorce now. No more waiting.

What time did she leave the cottage? Phillippe Bachelet says a few minutes past eleven. What time did she return? Bachelet says the clock was chiming 3 a.m." I look over at Nate. '"Nate, how long does it take to drive out to the lake cottage?"

"Forty-five minutes with average traffic."

"Forty five minutes each way. A total of an hour and a half and yet Marie Bruckner was gone for four hours. Two and a half hours are unaccounted for. What was she doing during those two and a half hours? I'll tell you what she was doing. She was watching her husband bleed to death on the living room floor."

Villiers shakes his head.

"This is nonsense," he says.

"Is it?" I say. "Let's see what the autopsy report has to say about that." I pick it up and quickly scan, mumbling as I quickly read through all the preliminary stuff. "Here we are." I read phrases out loud. "Non-fatal wound. Eminently treatable. Missed all vital organs. Actual cause of death, loss of blood." I look at the Inspector. "There you have it, Villiers. He bled to death while his wife sat there and watched."

"Ridiculous."

"According to Bachelet, Marie arrived just as Jeanne was running away. Jeanne was in shock. She was sure Bruckner was dead but she was too afraid to closely examine the body. Up the elevator goes Marie and then into the apartment. No more than five minutes have passed when Marie Bruckner discovers her husband bleeding from a nasty stomach wound. She can hardly believe her good luck. Her husband dying at the hands of a woman she has grown to despise. When he dies she will inherit everything and be free to marry the man she loves. All that is necessary is to make sure that Daniel Bruckner does not survive. No call to the police. No call for an ambulance. Watch and wait for the inevitable."

"He would have cried out," Villiers says.

"Maybe he was too weak. Maybe he tried to call for help, even as he laid there helplessly. If so that would account for the two anomalies."

Roger's head snaps up.

"Anomalies?"

I slide the autopsy report across the table.

"Second page, near the bottom," I say. "An anomaly. Something that doesn't fit, that makes no sense. There are two things you can do. Try to figure out what it means or ignore it. Inspector Villiers chose to ignore both of them."

"What exactly are you talking about, Joe?" Claude asks.

"A tiny fleck of bandage adhesive on Bruckner's cheek near his lips. And his wrists were slightly chafed as if he had been bound up."

"Bound and gagged," Roger says, sliding the autopsy back to me. "Adhesive tape across his mouth so he can't cry out and some sort of binding on his wrists so he can't remove the tape."

"That's how I see it," I say to him. "Maybe Bruckner's silk tie which was laying on the floor. Smooth fabric, mild chafing."

"Makes sense to me," Roger says.

"What about you,Inspector? Does it make sense to you?" I ask.

Villiers stares at me. He desperately needs to save face and he doesn't know how because he realizes that Roger and I are probably right.

"This is all circumstantial," he says. "I can't be sure."

Roger explodes.

"Oh, for Christ's sake, Luc, you're not paid to be sure, you're paid to be a cop. Certainty is for judges and juries. Now do your job."

Villiers hesitates and then gets to his feet. He walks to a

nearby table and picks up the phone.

"This is Inspector Villiers," he says. "Get me my office, please." He falls silent as he waits. I exchange a look with Claude who allows himself a small smile and a nod of the head. Esther,too, looks pleased. Nate is less subtle. He grins and pumps his fist in triumph.

"Henri, listen carefully." Villiers says. "Contact Mme. Bruckner's attorney immediately and have him bring her to my office at four o'clock this afternoon. Four o'clock, Henri, not a minute later. And tell the gentleman that if she does not appear as requested, I will have an arrest warrant issued in her name. Is that clear? Bon." He hangs up and turns to me.

'Are you satisfied, M. Bernardi?" he asks.

"I am, Inspector," I say. "Very much so."

CHAPTER TWENTY TWO

The Chateau Frontenac is a stately old place, imposing in its size, conservative in its demeanor, catering to the rich and powerful from all over the world, a haven from the violence that pervades modern life. So it may have seem a little incongruous when at 1:30 in the dead of night gunshots are heard coming from the plush Grand Ballroom. Most of the guests do not hear them. Those that do ignore them.

I am standing just inside the doorway behind a bank of lights and yards and yards of cable and watching for the fourth time in the past hour as O.E. Hasse gets ready to meet his maker. The Assistant Director calls out, "Quiet on the set!" and a hush falls over the crew who work efficiently and noiselessly. "This is picture!" the A.D. proclaims and a bell sounds. The second assistant director sticks the clacker in front of the camera lens. The sound man announces "Speed!" which means the audio tape is now recording at the proper speed to synch with the picture. The A.D. looks to Hitchcock who nods. "And action!" the A.D. says. The camera starts to track the length of the ballroom focusing on Clift as Father Michael as he strides toward Hasse who is cringing near a wall having just shot his wife. Hasse, who thinks Clift has betrayed him, raises the gun to shoot but before he can, a shot rings and he falls to the floor. Father Michael hurries to his side. Karl Malden as the cop lowers his smoking pistol.

Everyone turns and looks at Hitchcock.

Hitch says to the A.D. "Cut and print" as he hefts himself up from his chair.

"Cut and print!" the A.D. echoes for all to hear and then adds, "That's a wrap!"

Cheers and applause break out. Principal photography in the province of Quebec has been completed. Tomorrow afternoon at 1:20 the Los Angeles contingent will board a plane for home and if I am very lucky I will be in my very own bed in my very own bedroom by midnight.

Everyone is now milling about with Yanks and Canucks showering praise on one another and swearing to absolutely keep in touch. These promises will be broken the moment the plane lifts off the runway. Movie companies are like close knit families while a film is being shot but once completed everyone goes his or her own way. It is the nature of the business and always has been.

I wander around, shake hands, give voice to platitudes and am asked three times if I would like to join the "gang" at a little going away party at the home of one of the local lighting guys. It isn't a wrap party. That'll come in L.A. after we clean up the few scenes remaining to be shot. I beg off their generous invitations. I'm tired and I want some sleep. Hootin' and hollerin' is for twenty-two year olds and we have no shortage of them.

Monty claps me on the shoulder and thanks me for everything and I sense he means it. Hitch is not a shoulder-clapper but he, too, is generous in his praise for what he calls my "dauntless courage in the face of unfettered adversity". I think for a minute he's going to present me with an O.B.E. but no, I get a simple handshake and that is more than enough.

After a few more minutes, I slip unobserved from the hall and take the stairs to my room. There I find my bottle of champagne in an ice filled bucket, delivered by room service at midnight. I need to unwind and nothing does it like an Alfred Gratien Cuvee Paradis Brut, charged to the room, of course.

It has been eight days since that afternoon confrontation with Luc Villiers in Claude Le Pen's conference room. A lot has happened, some good, some not so good. I lean back in my chair and take a sip of the champagne.

Villiers interviewed Marie Bruckner in his office that same afternoon and decided that there was insufficient evidence to pursue a case against her. He decided also that it was not his place to recommend charges be dropped against Jeanne d'Arcy. Once again Villiers, the politician, had trumped Villiers, the investigator. He was not about to risk his reputation as a social lion among the elite of Quebec City for the sake of an ill mannered trollop nor did he have any intention of offending the newly widowed Marie Bruckner whose social connections are as vast as the Yukon Territory.

The following morning I called the Director of the Surete in Montreal. My status as a Warner Brothers "executive" got him on the phone. My incisive narrative about wanton stupidity and the abuse of power kept him there and by the time I had finished he was thanking me profusely for bringing this matter to his attention.

The next morning I learned from Nate that, unknown to all of us, Luc Villiers was suffering from some unspecified malady that was going to prevent him from performing his duties as Chief Inspector of the Quebec City Surete. A statement from the Director at the Montreal office announced that Villiers was being transferred to a non-taxing desk position in the greater

Montreal area. It was implied that this new post would afford him the opportunity to seek out the sort of high quality medical care found routinely in the provincial capitol. The statement also announced that Villiers' predecessor, Roger Lescroart, had agreed to come out of retirement and manage the Quebec City office as Acting Chief Inspector on an interim basis.

On the morning after, Roger Lescroart issued warrants for the arrests of both Marie Bruckner and Phillippe Bachelet. The warrants stipulated 17 different offenses to her Majesty's government. It was Nate's contention that 15 of these were bargaining chips designed to get her to plead to the remaining two. I agreed with him. In addition Roger persuaded the Crown Prosecutor to drop all charges against Jeanne d'Arcy.

And on the following morning, the Director in Montreal announced that the terms "interim" and "acting" would be dropped from Roger Lescroart's job description. I also found out, again from Nate, that Villiers' new position was in the small town of Sainte Sophie, a considerable distance from the bright lights and hurly burly of Montreal proper. Nate confessed he had no idea what the social life was like in Sainte Sophie but he did learn that the Mayor was a pig farmer.

I take another sip of champagne and look over at the bottle. Two thirds empty. I've been drinking this stuff like it was ginger ale. I put down my glass and rest my head against the back of the chair. A few minutes to rest my eyes and then I'll finish the bottle. Just a few minutes, that's all. And as my eyes close my thoughts turn to Jeanne.

Where is she? Eight days ago she walked out of a jail cell and disappeared. She saw no one, called no one and removed all her personal effects from Avrom Pinchot's cottage. Her Austin Healey is also missing so I presume that wherever she has gone she drove there. Each morning I have scoured the newspaper, searching for, and hoping I do not find, an item about a Jane Doe accident victim. I started to call hospitals but there were too many of them. Finally I gave up. If Jeanne had wished to speak with me, she'd have been in touch. After all I went through I feel ill used but that's just the petulant little boy in me. The important thing is that she is not rotting in prison awaiting a rendezvous with the hangman. Bless you, Jeanne d'Arcy, and God speed, wherever you are.

The insistent jangling of the phone arouses me from my torpor. The sun is streaming through the window. My breakfast of coffee, juice and rolls is sitting on a room service trolley and my watch tells me it is ten minutes to nine. I have spent the night sleeping in the chair and every bone in my body is rebelling. I struggle to my feet and stagger unsteadily to the nightstand by my bed where the phone is located. I rotate my head, trying to force blood into my brain. It doesn't work but I do develop a crick in my neck. I flop down on the bed and lift the receiver.

"Hello?"

"Joe?" It's a woman's voice.

"Jeannie?" I say.

"Jillian," she says.

Ooops, what a way to start the day.

"Sorry, Jill, the phone woke me up and I was dreaming of Jeannie."

"Sounds like a song cue," Jill says."Who's the lucky girl?"

"It's not like that," I say. I realize she knows nothing about Jeanne's travails with the law so I fill her in quickly. "I have no idea where she is or if she's well. I can hope but I don't know."

I can hear the smile in her voice.

"Good old Joe. Loyal to a fault. A friend to those in need no matter what. You're a strange and wonderful man, Joe Bernardi, and I wouldn't have you any other way."

"Seems to me you won't have me any way at all, Jill", I say, unable to avoid the dig and immediately sorry I said it.

"Unfair, Joe. I called in peace," she says. "I think maybe we left things on an adversarial note and I don't want that. I'm still going to raise this child on my own but I see no reason why you can't still be a good friend to both of us."

"That's generous of you, Jill," I say.

"Even if we weren't the greatest lovesick pair since Eloise and Abelard, we were always pals who knew how to share a laugh. Let's not lose that."

"We won't."

"When's your plane get in?"

"Late tonight, Around midnight."

"I'm at loose ends tomorrow evening. How about dinner?"

"One must always eat," I say. "Italian?"

"Why not?"

"You're not going to try to seduce me, are you, Jill?"

"I'll restrain myself."

"In that case, I'll call you in the morning."

"I'll be here. Good trip."

"Thanks," I say and hang up.

I feel relieved. I'm going to be a junior partner in the raising of this kid. A very junior partner but I no longer see Jill and I at each others throats. Good for the two of us and especially good for the kid.

I get up and walk over to the room service cart. I slosh down some orange juice and sip some tepid coffee. I look around the room. Shave, shower and pack and then it's au revoir, mes amis, goodbye Quebec, hello California where bowers of flowers bloom in the spring and also in September.

At noon, I step off the elevator carrying my suitcase, hoping that I will find Nate McIver waiting for me, even though he's been off payroll for the past eight hours. I am not disappointed. I find him sitting on a sofa near the main entrance dressed all in black including a black billed chauffeur's cap. He grins and gets to his feet when he sees me coming.

"Need a lift, boss?" he asks.

"You're no longer employed, Nate." I remind him. "And what the hell is that get up all about?"

"Special occasion. My last day wearing this outfit," he says. "Car's out front. Follow me."

We walk out the main door into the sunshine. It's a gorgeous day. Perfect flying weather. I look around for the Peugeot but don't see it.

"Over here," Nate says as he leads me to a cream colored Pierce Arrow sitting at curbside. "Like it?" he asks proudly.

"Wow!" is all I can say. It is a vintage roadster from the 30's in perfect condition.

"The pride of my two car fleet, Joe. Hop in."

He grabs my suitcase and puts it in the trunk as I slide into the passenger seat. He gets in and starts her up. She purrs like a well fed tomcat as we pull away from the curb.

"I bought her five years ago. You should have seen her, Joe. Dirty, dented, parts missing, a real hunk of junk. A lot of bucks and a lot of sweat later and voila!"

"It's fabulous, Nate."

"Well, you probably haven't heard but she's being retired. Like I said, today is it. My last day in the chauffeuring business and you are my last customer."

I shoot him a puzzled look.

"What's going on?" I ask.

"In good time, my man. First of all, I've been offered my old job back at more money. Roger says he could use a dozen like me. A lovely compliment. I was half tempted to accept."

"But you didn't."

"The reason I quit two years ago still applies. Too much politics. Too much team play. Not enough respect for personal initiative. If anything I've gotten even more used to being my own boss. No, another stretch with the Surete is really not appealing, as much as I like Roger."

"So what are you going to do?"

"I'm going private, Joe. Nathaniel McIvers, Discreet Investigations. Has a ring to it, don't you think?"

I shrug.

"Tough way to make a living," I say.

"Not really," he says. "I already have my first client. The newly minted law firm of Le Pen & Laval. They're making the announcement tomorrow morning."

"Claude and Esther. Formidable. Congratulations," I say.

He laughs. "Say, if Phillippe Bachelet could do it, how hard can it be? Roger's pushing through the paperwork for my license."

"Nice man," I say.

"The best," Nate agrees.

"And how is your sister Charity taking all this?"

Nate smiles.

"I told her if she opened her mouth just once I was going to toss her and all her belongings out onto the street and change the locks."

"And?"

"Not a word, not a peep and tonight she's cooking knockwurst and green peppers, my favorite meal."

The turnoff for the airport looms up on the right and Nate takes it. A couple of minutes later he pulls up in front of the terminal. We get out and he gets my suitcase for me. I stick out my hand and he grabs it. We shake and then he reaches forward and puts me into a big bear hug. When we separate he is smiling and I see a little mist in his eyes.

"Goodbye, Joe Bernardi. It has been my honor to know you," he says. Then he turns and quickly slides behind the wheel of the car. In a moment he is driving away. I stand and watch him for a long time. No, Nate, I am thinking, the honor is mine. Then I pick up my suitcase and walk into the terminal.

I wave to a couple of the crew guys who are hanging around the newsstand. The clock on the wall reads 12:45. Thirty five minutes to kill before we take off. I get on one of two lines that are open. I already have my ticket. Just have to check my bag and get a seat assignment. I'm third on line but the guy at the counter is bellyaching about something and the frozen smile on the ticket agent's face tells me she is really steamed. When at last he shuts up and turns away from the counter grumbling to himself, I see that the loud mouthed troublemaker is Mackenzie Starr. He sees me looking at him and strides over to me.

"I suppose I ought to thank you, Bernardi," he says without humor.

"Really? What for?"

"For giving me all that grief. If it hadn't been for you, I might not have found out what a huge prick my editor was. When he tried to suspend me, I quit."

I happen to know he was fired.

"Made a couple of phone calls and an old pal helped me catch on with this terrific newspaper in northern New Brunswick. Got a 1:45 flight to meet the owner. And by the way, I won't be just a reporter, Bernardi. Editor in Chief of the Bathurst Independent Monitor. Editor in Chief. Chew on that," he says.

"Congratulations," I say.

"Yeah," he smiles, a cocky kind of in-your-face grin. "Like I said, if not for you, it wouldn't have happened."

"AS I said," I mutter under my breath correcting his lousy English.

"What's that?" he asks.

"Nothing."

It's my turn at the counter so I start away.

"Good luck," I say over my shoulder. Too late. He's through with me as he wanders over to the soda fountain swaggering like a peacock. While I check in I flirt shamelessly with the ticket girl and pretty soon I have her unfrozen. She wishes me a smooth flight. I wish her the best. Why aren't there more people like me in the world and a lot less like Mackenzie Starr?

Since I'm about to be cooped up in a cramped aircraft for God knows how long, I decide to go outside for some fresh air and wander around, stretching my legs. By the entrance is a large map of Canada showing all the air routes for all the provinces. I check out northern New Brunswick. It takes me a good minute to find Bathurst. That's because it's a flyspeck of a town on Nepoquit Bay. Ah, that devil Mackenzie Starr. He sure knows how to manage a career.

As I step out into the sunshine, I see it immediately, turning off the access road and roaring toward the terminal at a speed just under mach one. Behind the wheel of the British racing green Austin Healey roadster is a familiar figure, her flaming red hair flying in the breeze as she skids to a stop in a loading zone. She hops from the car and runs toward me. When we collide she throws her arms around me, squeezes me tight and then plants a juicy kiss right on my lips. Wherever she's been hiding out doesn't seem to have affected Jeannie adversely in the least.

"I was afraid I'd missed you," she says, slightly out of breath.

I check my watch. "Twenty minutes to spare," I say.

A voice reverberates through a nearby loudspeaker. First call for boarding the Los Angeles flight. The voice says it again in French.

"Where have you been?" I ask.

"Cap au Renard," she says. "Oh, Joe, I'm so sorry. I kept planning to call and something always got in the way. And then when I called the Frontenac this morning and they said you were flying back to the States, I panicked and I have two speeding tickets to prove it."

"Just so you know, I was worried."

"Yes, yes, I know. I am a terrible person," she says contritely.

I put my arm around her shoulders and we start to amble.

"No, not ever," I say.

"You are kind, Joe. Kind but wrong."

"What's Cap au Renard?" I ask.

"My home," she says. "A tiny little fishing village about two hundred and eight miles northeast of here on the river. When I was a kid I hated the place. The smell of fish was everywhere. I longed for the smell of long stemmed roses and the taste of expensive champagne. I was born there but I was damned if I was going to die there. I left when I was nineteen and never looked back."

"An old story," I say. "Small town girl with big city ambitions."

"That was me. Jeanne d'Arcy, party girl, always good for a laugh and even a roll in the hay if you could do something for me. Onward and upward. Come on, Jeannie, put your back into it, I used to say to myself, and that's what I did, more times than I care to remember. And then a funny thing happened. I found myself in a cold and uncomfortable jail cell facing a trial for murder. You know, Joe, when you're sitting in a cell like that, alone with no one to talk to, you're finally forced to come face to face with what you are and what you've done with your life. I hadn't done much. All in all, I'd had a pretty worthless existence and I promised myself that if I ever got myself free of the jam I was in, I was going to start all over again. That's why I ran when I was released, Joe. I ran back home to the only safe place I've ever known. Back home to parents who had always loved me but couldn't help me and back home to a daughter I hardly know."

The voice comes over the loudspeaker, Second call for all passengers on the 1:20 flight to Los Angeles.

"Daughter?" I say.

"Charlotte Marie. She's eleven now and beautiful, Joe, with red hair just like her Mom. Pop and Momma have done a good job with her. She's a great kid."

"No father?"

"Could have been one of three or four guys. Don't know. Don't care. That's all behind me now. Nothing matters now except today and tomorrow and next year. Disappointed in me?"

I smile.

"How could I be?"

She puts her arms around me and holds me very, very close. She doesn't speak because her embrace says it all. I hug back.

The loudspeaker is announcing the final call for the L.A. flight. I look her in the eye.

"Don't be a stranger," I say.

She looks at me curiously.

"It's an expression favored by my Jewish friends at the studio. It means write to me, call me once in a while, let's not lose track of one another."

"I can do that," she smiles.

I give her one more hug and a peck on the forehead and then I start toward the plane where the last stragglers are climbing the rolling stairway to the open cabin door. As I start up the stairs, I look back. She is still standing there. She waves. I wave back.

I enter the cabin, the door shuts behind me and I go in search of my seat. I find it and look out the window. She's walking back to her car. I'm no longer worried about Jeanne d'Arcy. I can tell by the set of her shoulders. Whatever it is she wants she will find. Of that I am positive.

THE END

AUTHOR'S NOTE

"Pray for Us Sinners" is a work of fiction using as its background the filming of "I Confess" in Quebec City in late 1952. The picture was released on March 22, 1953. Scenes in this book involving dialogue with well-known real people have been totally invented although the subject matter in some cases is a matter of public knowledge. Hitchcock and Montgomery Clift approached their work from different poles and their lack of communication has been chronicled in many other places. In 1966 Hitchcock hired Paul Newman to star in "Torn Curtain" and ran into the same problem. The "method" did not sit well with this international icon and in both movies it showed. Entered in competition at the Cannes Film Festival, "I Confess" caused hardly a ripple and was ignored by the judges. Clift's performance, while professional and understated, was overshadowed by his second film of 1953, "From Here to Eternity", a huge box office hit for which he received his third Oscar nomination for Best Actor. Hitchcock had been trying for eight years to get "I Confess" off the ground, hiring at least a dozen different writers to transform a 1902 French stage play into a shootable movie script. George Tabori seemed to have licked the problem but the production code was not in agreement and neither were the priests and bishops in Quebec City where Hitchcock planned to shoot For free, of course. In Tabori's version Clift's priest fathers a child and is eventually executed for the murder he did not commit. The church was aghast. So were the censors. When Tabori refused to rewrite the ending, William Archibald was brought in to make the needed changes. It made no difference in Ireland which banned the picture outright. Anne Baxter was not first choice for the role of Clift's pre-seminary love interest. Hitchcock had his heart set on a Swedish actress named Anita Bjork but when she arrived in Hollywood with her lover and newborn baby, Hitchcock was told by Warner to get somebody else. As always, the author holds the real life people depicted in this work in the highest regard and nothing written here is intended to diminish or demean.

CPSIA information can be obtained at www.ICGtesting.com
Printed in the USA
LVOW06s1642301213

367456LV00001B/260/P